T0381008

Highest Praise for Leo J. Maloney and His Thrillers

Arch Enemy

"Utterly compelling! This novel will grab you from the beginning and simply not let go. And Dan Morgan is one of the best heroes to come along in ages."

—Jeffery Deaver

Twelve Hours

"Fine writing and real insider knowledge make this a must."

—Lee Child

Black Skies

"Smart, savvy, and told with the pace and nuance that only a former spook could bring to the page, *Black Skies* is a tour de force novel of twenty-first-century espionage and a great geopolitical thriller. Maloney is the new master of the modern spy game, and this is first-rate storytelling."

—Mark Sullivan

"*Black Skies* is rough, tough, and entertaining. Leo J. Maloney has written a ripping story."

—Meg Gardiner

Silent Assassin

"Leo Maloney has done it again. Real life often overshadows fiction and *Silent Assassin* is both: a terrifyingly thrilling story of a man on a clandestine mission to save us all from a madman hell bent on murder, written by a man who knows that world all too well."

—Michele McPhee

"From the bloody, ripped-from-the-headlines opening sequence, *Silent Assassin* grabs you and doesn't let go. *Silent Assassin* has everything a thriller reader wants—nasty villains, twists and turns, and a hero—Cobra—who just plain kicks ass."

—Ben Coes

"Dan Morgan, a former black-ops agent, is called out of retirement and back into a secretive world of politics and deceit to stop a madman."

—*The Stoneham Independent*

Termination Orders
"Leo J. Maloney is the new voice to be reckoned with. *Termination Orders* rings with the authenticity that can only come from an insider. This is one outstanding thriller!"

—John Gilstrap

"Taut, tense, and terrifying! You'll cross your fingers it's fiction—in this high-powered, action-packed thriller, Leo Maloney proves he clearly knows his stuff."

—Hank Phillippi Ryan

"A new must-read action thriller that features a double-crossing CIA and Congress, vengeful foreign agents, a corporate drug ring, the Taliban, and narco-terrorists… a you-are-there account of torture, assassination, and double-agents, where 'nothing is as it seems.'"

—Jon Renaud

"Leo J. Maloney is a real-life Jason Bourne."

—Josh Zwylen, *Wicked Local Stoneham*

"A masterly blend of Black Ops intrigue, cleverly interwoven with imaginative sequences of fiction. The reader must guess which accounts are real and which are merely storytelling."

—Chris Treece, *The Chris Treece Show*

"A deep-ops story presented in an epic style that takes fact mixed with a bit of fiction to create a spy thriller that takes the reader deep into secret spy missions."

—**Cy Hilterman,** *Best Sellers World*

"For fans of spy thrillers seeking a bit of realism mixed into their novels, *Termination Orders* will prove to be an excellent and recommended pick."

—*Midwest Book Reviews*

Also by Leo J. Maloney

Enemy Action

A Dan and Alex Morgan Thriller

Leo J. Maloney

LYRICAL UNDERGROUND
Kensington Publishing Corp.
www.kensingtonbooks.com

LYRICAL UNDERGROUND BOOKS are published by
Kensington Publishing Corp.
900 Third Avenue, 26th Floor
New York, NY 10022

Special book excerpts or customized printings can also be created to fit specific needs. For details, write or phone the office of the Kensington Sales Manager: Kensington Publishing Corp., 119 West 40th Street, New York, NY 10018. Attn. Sales Department. Phone: 1-800-221-2647.

Lyrical Underground and Lyrical Underground logo Reg. US Pat. & TM Off

First Electronic Edition: December 2024
eISBN-13: 978-1-5161-1144-2 (ebook)
ISBN-13: 978-1-5161-1145-9 (print)

¹50³66²78

Part 1

Happenstance

"The past is never dead. It's not even past."
—William Faulkner

Chapter 1

Twenty-Seven Years Ago

"Is it me," Peter Conley said, "or is it chilly out?"

Dan Morgan checked the thermometer built into the arm of his parka. It read: -88F. "Must be you."

"You have to factor in the wind chill," Conley said. "That makes it feel colder."

Morgan didn't think it could ever feel colder. After this mission, he resolved never to complain about Boston winters again. Of course, they could have made the trip through the station itself, but Morgan had insisted that they start spending time outside as soon as possible.

If the mission suddenly turned hot (metaphorically, if not literally) and they had to operate outside tactically, he didn't want that to be their first real experience outdoors in the cold. Plus, they could be here a week, or three months, and he figured the sooner they acclimated, the better.

The trade-off was that the time necessary to put on and then take off their parka, gloves, face mask, and goggles was much longer than the three- or four-minute walk through the hallways.

Since it challenged his sense of efficiency, Conley had complained, but not much. Besides getting used to the cold, it was good practice getting in and out of their cold-weather gear.

Entering the south doorway, Morgan and Conley were met by Walter, the young physicist who had been assigned to orient the partners to the base. Though he looked impossibly young to Morgan, at twenty-five or -six, he was a couple of years older than Morgan and Conley themselves.

But as Morgan had learned from his work with cars, it's not the years, it's the mileage. Walter had likely spent very little of his life outside of a lab. Morgan thought that was a good thing. People like himself and Peter did the high-mileage/high-wear-and-tear work so people like Walter could do the kind of research that they were doing in places like Antarctica.

"Have you talked to Dr. Russell yet?" Walter asked.

"No, but we've read up on him," Conley offered.

"So you know that his work made this research possible. In fact, he largely designed our equipment," the young man said, a clear air of respect in his voice.

"I'm looking forward to it," Morgan replied.

As they approached the open door to Russell's office, Morgan could hear movement inside. By the time they entered, Russell was at the door to meet them.

Russell was maybe sixty years old, trim, with salt-and-pepper hair and glasses. "Walter, thank you for bringing our guests," he said, holding out his hand.

Morgan shook first and said, "Dan Morgan." Conley repeated the procedure.

"Good to meet you, and I'm glad to have you here. Come in." The office was spacious and Russell led them to a small round conference table.

"Again, I'm grateful that your . . . employer sent you to us," Russell said, letting that hang in the air for a few seconds. "Even though we've been getting along fine without a pilot or a helicopter, I know we've been lucky in that we haven't had an emergency that required either."

"Then for as long as we're here, you can rest easier," Conley said.

"And though I appreciate having you both here," Russell said to Morgan, "I have to say that we really don't need an electrical systems technician."

"My attitude is that technicians are a lot like flamethrowers; better to have one and not need it than need one and not have it," Morgan said.

Russell laughed heartily.

"We hardly ever need a flamethrower down here, but we do have them, so I take your meaning; and I am truly grateful to your employer for offering your special *security* expertise," Russell said.

"The Agency is happy to help," Morgan said. That was as close as he would come to saying "the CIA," and that was fine in this company.

Russell had a relatively high security clearance, as did Walter—who had done some graduate work with lasers for a Department of Defense project.

"Why do you think the Russians have taken such an interest in you?" Conley said.

"I'm not sure. Our work in neutrino detection is pure theoretical physics. It doesn't have the sort of practical or military applications that seem to drive Russian physics research." Russell said *practical* and *military* with some distaste, but Morgan didn't begrudge the man his feelings given what he was doing out here.

It must have been unnerving to know that the Russian intelligence agencies had been watching your work for months and that the Russian military had just made the largest troop deployment in the history of Antarctica in your neighborhood.

"Do you think they might want to steal your research?" Morgan offered.

"Unlikely. We're looking into fairly esoteric and cosmic questions here. Again, I can't see them actually caring about our work."

"If they were up to something, say, a secret nuclear reactor in Antarctica, could your system detect it?" Conley asked.

Morgan could see that the man respected the question, but Russell shook his head. "There's no need. If you wanted to secretly generate massive amounts of power—presuming you had something you wanted to do with that much power—there are better ways."

"Better than a nuclear reactor?" Conley asked.

"Of course. Mt. Erebus is an active volcano and is one of hundreds under our feet. If you wanted to generate power in secret, you could build a geothermal plant that would give you as much power with less trouble and less chance of being detected."

"For now," Morgan said, "let's just assume the Russians are just being nosy, and the troop deployment is a show of force unrelated to your work. Perhaps they are thinking about renegotiating the treaty that says no single country owns this continent. There is petroleum underneath the ice here. Perhaps they have designs there and just happen to have chosen your neighborhood for their base."

Even as Morgan said it, his gut told him it wasn't true. In his experience, the Russians were strategic thinkers, and with them, unlikely events happening in proximity to one another were never a coincidence.

However, it wouldn't pay to panic the civilians. If something came up, he and Conley would have to handle it. In fact, if something *was* going to happen, Morgan would prefer that it happen sooner rather than later.

He had business of another sort with a Russian back in the States. Natasha Orlov was ready to defect, but she wouldn't do it unless he was there to see to the details personally.

She didn't trust anyone else at the Agency, and the fact was that Morgan *wanted* to be there. He also wanted to make sure she was safe, and she definitely wanted him to be there when she was debriefed.

And when all of that business was finished, they could continue the personal business they had begun at the Russian Embassy in Washington.

"As I said, I'm glad you are here, but there are only two of you. What happens if the Russian troops become aggressive? I have thirty people to worry about here," Russell said.

"I want you to leave that to the both of us. I'm a very good technician, and Mr. Conley is an excellent pilot. And there are barely two hundred of *them*. We'll do our job so you can concentrate on yours," Morgan said.

That seemed to satisfy Russell. It helped that the man wanted to believe him. It helped even more that Morgan meant it. Heisenberg Base was their mission now. He and Conley would do whatever it took to keep it safe.

"While you are here, I hope you will take advantage of our facilities. We do our best to make everyone comfortable. Walter can show you around," Russell said, his tone politely indicating the meeting was over.

"Actually, I wanted to get right to work and visit the Stack," Morgan said.

"You want to see the equipment?" Russell asked.

"Yes, I've seen the specs and I'm not happy with the failure rate of some of the sensors," Morgan said.

"You suspect sabotage?" Russell said.

"Not at all. I have some concerns about the power system," Morgan said.

Russell's mouth hung open, and Walter was looking at Morgan like he had just waltzed into the Vatican and challenged the pope to an arm-wrestling match.

Russell recovered quickly and said, "We have over five hundred individual sensors and less than a 2 percent failure rate. That is well within our design tolerances."

"No," Morgan corrected him. "It was less than 2 percent for the first six months. Now it's over 4 percent. It's been climbing since you added wind power to supplement your diesel generators."

"I supervised that upgrade myself. Again, we're still within tolerances. In addition, you are here for *security*," Russell said.

"True, but we like to make ourselves useful," Morgan replied. "We'll bring Walter along for the survey, and I won't make any repairs unless you approve. However, it will keep us busy and maybe we can get some more of your sensors working."

"It's not really necessary . . ." Russell began, appearing unsure for the first time since the meeting started.

Conley chimed in. "Not necessary for your current work where you are back-tracing neutrinos to their source. However, if we can get your numbers up, you can start looking at neutrino interactions. Your work identifying neutrino origins is merely confirming accepted theory. But if I read your papers correctly, you have bigger ambitions."

For a second, Morgan didn't know what Russell was going to do. Then the man did the last thing Morgan expected: he laughed.

It took Walter an uncomfortable moment to process that his boss wasn't in a rage, and the young man smiled in relief.

"If you can do that, I'll buy you both a drink," Russell said.

A few minutes later, they had loaded the equipment they needed into the helicopter that Morgan and Conley had taken from McMurdo Base to Heisenberg.

Once they were inside the aircraft, Morgan noticed that Walter had put his safety belt on before Morgan was even seated.

"You know, we usually just take a Snowcat out to the detector. It's a short trip," Walter said.

"I want to get some hours on this bird," Conley said.

Morgan understood. Part of Conley's motive was similar to Morgan's own desire to get up to speed on their new environment and equipment, and part of it was the fact that Conley was excited about this particular helicopter.

Conley knew aircraft the way that Morgan knew cars. He had requested the JetRanger 206 for this mission, and the Agency had obliged. All that Morgan knew about it was that it was a Canadian civilian aircraft based on a military design.

Morgan liked that it was relatively spacious inside, with room for four plus a fair amount of cargo. He noticed that Walter did not seem impressed. In fact, he looked downright nervous.

"You okay to fly?" Morgan asked.

"I've never been in a helicopter before," Walter said.

"Just like a plane, but softer on the landing," Morgan said. "Plus, you are in good hands," he added, gesturing to Conley.

Walter watched Conley studying the controls and asked, "How long have you had your license?"

"Years, I got my pilot's license when I was in high school," Conley said as he started up the chopper.

"Helicopter license?" Walter said. Morgan was impressed. The kid was sharp and had good intuition.

"That's just a formality," Conley said, and before Walter could respond, the helicopter rose off the ground. Morgan could see that Conley had made it a soft takeoff, partly to show off and partly to avoid panicking their passenger.

Once they were in the air, Walter silently clutched the armrests of his seat and watched the horizon.

It took them less than five minutes to get to the Stack, and Conley touched down softly. He turned to give Walter a reassuring smile. "See, piece of cake."

To Walter's credit, he grinned back and seemed to relax.

Once they were on the ground outside, Walter gestured to the snow in front of them and said, "What do you think?"

Honestly, it looked like most of the flat snow plains they had seen in Antarctica. The only difference was that there was some sort of waist-high metal box every twenty yards or so.

"You don't have to say it. It doesn't look like much on the outside, but you are looking at the largest sensor system in the world. The Stack has a half-square-mile footprint and goes about a half mile down, making it effectively a twenty-eight-hundred-foot cube. Each of those boxes is the control panel for a string that holds sixty evenly spaced digital optical sensors on a half-mile-long cable, giving us over five thousand individual sensor units. And that's what allows us to see nearly invisible, charge-less, mass-less particles."

Morgan had read the briefing material and knew most of this, but he let the young scientist talk.

"Do you really think you can improve the system, Mr. Morgan?" Walter said.

"First, you can call me Dan, and second, yes I can," Morgan said, heading into the field. The control boxes were numbered, and it didn't take him long to find one that was on the list of strings with bad sensors. "I'm just going to pop it open and check the capacitor," he said.

On Walter's nervous nod, Morgan opened the panel on top of the box and quickly found the capacitor. "Okay if I pull it? I brought a replacement," Morgan said.

After another even more nervous nod from Walter, Morgan pulled a new capacitor from his backpack, installed it, and turned the panel back on. There was a quick reboot procedure and then the sensor string was back online.

Walter studied the numbers on the panel readout and then his eyes went wide. "Five of the eight inoperative sensors are back on. How . . ."

"I won't pretend to understand your equipment but you made two classic mistakes. First, you ran all of your current on a single line. That means that each sensor attaches to the current at only one point. If there's corrosion, you lose a good connection to the sensor. Easy mistake to make. It's still a problem with Chryslers."

"Chryslers?" Walter asked.

"The cars, any mechanic you ask will tell you stories about Chrysler electrical systems. Also, you have too much variation in your amperage and it degrades your capacitors. Even though the current stays within specs, you get too many ups and downs. It's like having a poor performing alternator; it wreaks havoc on electronics. And the more sophisticated the electronics, the more consistent the power needs to be. Based on what they cost, your sensors are pretty sophisticated. Upgrading your capacitors will help there. I brought enough to replace all of them. Get approval from your boss and we can knock the work out in a couple of days."

"I don't know what to say," Walter said. "Cars . . ."

"Are well-engineered combinations of mechanical, electrical, and electronic systems," Morgan said. "Come on, give us the tour."

Walter walked them through the field of control boxes to a junction box of some kind. Next to that was a four-foot satellite dish on a steel post about a dozen feet high.

"The data goes to the junction and then the dish sends it back to us at Heisenberg Base," Walter said.

Morgan could see that Conley was impressed.

"When we have some time, you'll have to explain what neutrinos tell you . . ." Conley said.

Before Conley could finish, Walter became fixated on the satellite dish. "That's odd," he said.

"What is?" Morgan replied, hearing something he didn't like in the young man's voice.

When Walter was less than six feet from the dish, he raised a gloved hand and pointed at the new addition. "That box. It wasn't there before," Walter said. "And no one could have requisitioned new equipment without me seeing it, let alone created a work order. And they definitely couldn't have installed said new equipment."

The rectangular box was green, easily standing out against the white pole and dish. It was attached to the pole just under the dish. When Morgan noticed that the box had a slight curve, alarm bells started going off in his head.

"Down!" he called out, knowing that that would be enough for Conley. Walter, on the other hand, was still apparently hypnotized by the strange device.

Morgan didn't have to take the extra seconds to read the Russian words on the back of the green box to know what it was: a MON-50 mine—a Russian knockoff of the Claymore. It was attached to a small box that Morgan assumed was an electronic trigger.

At that precise instant, Walter took another step forward, and before a plan had formed in his head, Morgan flung himself into the air, tackling the man.

The explosion followed less than a second later, and Morgan felt the pressure wave pass over him as something solid hit him, hard, in the back.

As his hearing started to clear, Morgan heard Conley calling to him. "I'm okay," Morgan called back, rolling off Walter.

"What about you?" Morgan asked, getting into a kneeling position and pulling Walter up. The man was moving, shaking his head to clear it, and Morgan couldn't see any injuries.

"Can you get to your feet?" he asked, as he stood and continued to pull on Walter, who was soon standing himself.

"I'm okay," he said. "What was that?"

"A landmine," Morgan said.

"What? Why?" Walter said.

"I think it's safe to say that Heisenberg Base is now under attack," Conley said.

Morgan heard his partner sputter and say, "Dan, are you sure you are all right?"

Then Conley was pulling at Morgan's backpack. When it was off him, Morgan saw what had caused the thump on his back. A six-inch spike of metal was sticking out of the pack.

A quick swipe of his hand over his back told Morgan that the spike hadn't touched him. "Like I said, good capacitors . . ."

Chapter 2

"Come on, let's get back to Heisenberg," Morgan said. The three men hurried as much as they could.

It was awkward trying to run in the snow but they managed pretty good time to the helicopter, and Conley had them in the air quickly as Morgan got on the radio to Heisenberg. They were halfway back before he had Russell on the line.

"Dr. Russell, this is Dan Morgan. I'd like you to run that lockdown drill we talked about," he said.

"Lockdown drill?" Russell asked.

"Yes, please start the drill now. It's a good time to practice lockdown procedures. We'll be back at the base shortly, and you and I can review the results in detail—there's no point in discussing it now," he said.

To Russell's credit, there was only a brief second of silence before the man said, "I understand. I look forward to our meeting."

"How long, Peter?" he asked.

"We'll be at the base and on the ground in five minutes," Conley said.

"You couldn't tell Dr. Russell what was really going on because you're afraid the Russians are monitoring high-frequency radio channels?" Walter said.

Morgan decided that he liked this bunch of scientists. If you were working with civilians, best if they were smart.

"Actually, I'm sure they are monitoring all radio channels and I wouldn't trust satellite phones either," Morgan said.

"But the base could come under attack at any time," Walter said. It was a statement, not a question.

"Yes, but I don't think it will. This was an attack on your equipment, not a wide-scale attack on personnel, not yet," Morgan said.

Before Walter could ask, Morgan raised his hand and said, "We'll tell you what we think is going on when we get to the base. In the meantime, do you even have a lockdown procedure?"

Walter shook his head. "I don't think so. I'm not even sure the exterior doors have locks. You don't want anyone to get stuck outside."

"If the Russians had waited another day, we would have started our security evaluation," Conley said. "We could have fixed that."

"Why did this have to happen when you were both off the base?" Walter said.

"That is our good luck. I don't think anyone was supposed to survive the explosion," Morgan said.

Even though Morgan was confident the base was safe for now, he was relieved to see that it looked normal on their approach. On the ground, they secured the helicopter and were met at the door by a man wearing a tank on his back that was attached to a pole in the man's hands.

Russell was standing next to him.

"Is that a flamethrower?" Morgan asked.

"In a way. It's a propane torch," Russell said. "We use it for de-icing. We have a few of these. Closest thing we have to a weapon."

"No guns?" Morgan asked.

"No animals bigger than a penguin," Russell replied. "And the nearest base up until now has been the Norwegians. They're surprisingly placid, even when they drink," Russell said.

Morgan couldn't help but be impressed. These scientists had no locks on the doors, no procedures for dealing with a hostile force, but Russell had understood Morgan's message and had deployed a man with an improvised weapon in less than five minutes. In addition, Russell was also manning the main door himself.

Russell led the way to his office and the three men quickly briefed him on the explosion.

"It doesn't make any sense. Why attack our equipment? We're unarmed. Everybody is unarmed out here. Why not just storm the base?" Russell said.

"They don't want to draw attention, and they don't want you to call for help," Conley said. "I suspect they are playing a longer game. What would you do if the satellite link suddenly went down?"

"We'd work on it here for a few hours, try to reboot it, and then if that didn't fix the problem, we'd send a team out," Russell said.

"And if they didn't come back?" Morgan said.

"We'd wait a bit and send another team," Russell said.

"How many times would you do that before you stopped? Two? Three?" Morgan asked. "By then, your staff of twenty would be down by a third, and you would be missing your most physically capable people. After that, the Russians would likely do something else to draw more of you out, and then launch an attack on the survivors. Or stage a fire. I have no doubt they want to get rid of all of you on this base, and probably destroy the facility as well. Whatever the Russians are doing, they don't want your eyes on them out here."

"But why? We're doing research that is the definition of pure science. We're looking behind the curtain at the secrets of the universe, knowledge that will expand everyone's understanding of space-time. And there's no possible military application to any of it, and it's no threat to anyone."

"We have no idea what they have against you or this base," Conley said. "But we've gotten lucky because we now have a pretty good guess about what they intend."

"A pretty good guess?" Russell said.

"This is all guesswork," Morgan said. "Without solid information, we work with what we have."

"And we have some experience in this area," Conley said.

"Experience dealing with a large hostile force with indeterminate motives in an Arctic environment?" Russell countered.

"Not that *exact* scenario," Morgan said.

To his credit, Russell smiled and said, "I suppose we'll find out what they want soon enough. In the meantime, what do you need?"

"We need to get out there and watch the Russians before they realize we know something is up. However, we don't want to leave you undefended. We brought some rifles. Did anyone on the staff serve?"

"Only in the halls of academia. However, my father was a policeman in Brooklyn. He taught us all to shoot. I'll make sure that anyone handling a rifle knows the basics. And we do have our flamethrowers. And we'll see what else the group can cobble together. Give these people a problem, and you sometimes get surprising solutions."

"I'd like to go with you," Walter said. "If that's all right, Doctor."

"Fine. Good luck to you all," Russell said, leading them into the hallway. "I'll assemble everyone in the dining room. We can meet back there in a few minutes."

Morgan and Conley hadn't been there long enough to unpack their weapons and tactical gear, which were all still waiting in the JetRanger. They grabbed four of the M4 carbines, which Morgan had favored since his brief stint in the US military, and two shotguns with extra shells.

Looking through the remaining weapons, Morgan turned to Conley and said, "Should we leave them any grenades?"

"No!" Walter said from behind them.

When Morgan turned around, Walter looked embarrassed and said, "Too many experimental physicists in that group. You don't want to give them something they have never seen and tell them not to use it unless they have to."

"Fair enough," Morgan said. "Rifles and flamethrowers it is. But if we do our job, the base won't have to worry."

"There are two hundred soldiers out there, who—if you're right—are about to launch an attack on twenty scientists. Do you have a plan to stop them?" Walter said.

"Not a plan, exactly," Morgan replied. "But we do have a few things in our favor; we have the element of surprise, plus we have a helicopter, some good weapons, and a positive attitude."

"Let's get in the air," Conley said, opening the door and climbing in.

Before Morgan could follow his partner, Walter tugged on his shoulder and said, "Wait, Mr. Morgan . . . Dan." The young man looked embarrassed again and said, "I wanted to thank you."

Morgan just stared at him blankly for a second, and Walter said, "You saved my life, less than a half hour ago."

"Sorry, in mission-time that's like a week," Morgan said. "But don't worry about it, if I hadn't dragged you out to the site, you never would have been in danger."

For a second, Walter looked almost angry. "Let me thank you. You threw yourself on top of me, and if it wasn't for your backpack, you'd probably be dead."

Morgan held out his hand and Walter shook it. "You're welcome. I'd say we both got lucky today. Let's hope that luck holds out."

"The Russians are waiting!" Conley called out from inside the chopper.

Less than a minute later they were strapped into the JetRanger, and Conley had them in the air. Morgan noticed that Walter moved without hesitation and with no trace of nervousness about flying this time.

Yet there was much more to be scared of on this trip. They weren't making a routine run to check on equipment, they were flying to meet two hundred enemy soldiers who had already fired first on them. But Walter's face showed nothing but concentration and a touch of anticipation.

It looked like the young scientist had found his own version of mission focus.

It took them less than ten minutes in the air to get close to the Russian base. Though the helicopter had been painted white to make it as inconspicuous as possible, it was far from invisible in the sky, so Conley kept them low and put the JetRanger down about a half mile from the Russians.

They hiked the half mile and took a position behind an outcropping of volcanic rock, which gave them a good view of the base. Morgan scanned it with his binoculars. The main base was an L-shaped two-story structure, nothing unusual given what he'd seen at McMurdo Base and at Heisenberg.

There were a few outbuildings. One had big diesel storage tanks just outside, which told Morgan it was the generator. The biggest building had large doors that meant it was the garage for the vehicles.

On the edge of the compound sat two military helicopters.

There were a few Snowcats of different sizes spread throughout the base. Morgan clocked the largest vehicle as a troop carrier that held about twenty men. There was also a single large full-track hauler that he assumed was used for cargo. Of course, that raised the question: In a relatively small compound, why would they need something to move a large amount of cargo a good distance?

"Can I take a look?" Walter asked, and Morgan gave the man his binoculars.

"Peter?" Morgan asked.

"Just what it looks like," Conley said. "The base has everything you'd expect for a small military installation where you could house troops and engage in maneuvers."

That was what Morgan thought as well.

"They also have an attack helicopter," Conley said.

That got Morgan's attention.

"The big beast is a Mi-26. It's the largest heavy-lift machine the Russians have. It's good for cargo or construction supplies, anything heavy. The smaller chopper is a Mi-28. It's an attack helicopter that carries nothing but a pilot and weapons."

"What?" Walter exclaimed. "There are supposed to be no guns here. McMurdo is the biggest station on the ice and they have one shotgun they keep under lock and key."

"The Mi-28 has three .30-caliber guns, plus missiles," Conley said.

"Why would they need that? There's nobody to . . ." Walter's voice trailed off as he understood.

"The guns alone would take apart Heisenberg in less than five minutes," Conley added. "It would take less time if they also used the missiles."

"Then they could burn whatever was left," Morgan added. "The first storm would hide any evidence, if a military investigation was even launched. By the time they got to it, the US Marshall at McMurdo would likely conclude it was a fire."

"Who are these people?" Walter said.

"Bad guys," Morgan replied.

"What do we do?" the scientist asked, clearly still shaken.

"We stop them," Morgan said.

"How? When?" Walter asked.

"I don't like this," Conley said. "The helicopter has missiles loaded. You don't leave rockets loaded onto your chopper until you are ready to use them, especially in an area with weather as unpredictable as here."

Walter looked like he was about to fall down. Morgan took hold of his shoulder. "It's okay. We're going to stop them."

"How?"

"That, we'll have to figure out," Morgan said. "But the *when* is simple. Whatever happens, we end this today."

Chapter 3

The man was struggling, Morgan could see it, but he wanted Walter on his feet. He and Conley needed this young scientist's help if they were going to solve this problem and save Walter's base.

"Everything really will be okay," Morgan said, looking Walter right in the eye. "Do you believe me?"

Walter blinked and said, "Yes."

"Good, everything else is just detail."

Walter stared off at the Russian base, and Morgan thought he might lose the kid again. Before Morgan could move or say anything, Walter spoke.

"It's too small," Walter announced.

"What?" Morgan asked.

"Too small for that many men," Walter replied.

"The Russians aren't known for the accommodations they provide for their troops," Conley said.

"Not here. You can't afford to pack people in. Especially men. Especially men trained to fight. There's nowhere to go and not much to do. One thing bases don't skimp on is space. People get stir-crazy and aggressive—and that's scientists and researchers. You wouldn't take a chance with soldiers."

The young man sounded confident, and it made sense to Morgan.

"And that hauler won't fit in any of those structures," Walter said.

"And there's no hangar for the helicopters," Conley said.

That hit home for Morgan. In a place where you have dozens of days a year of hurricane-level winds, you would need to be able to put any aircraft inside.

"So there's another base," Morgan said.

"And I'm not sure this is even the biggest one," Walter said.

"That explains why the Russians don't want eyes nearby," Conley added. "They may have something there that they don't want people to see."

"Now we just have to find it," Morgan said. The problem was that they didn't have much time, maybe a day or two before the Russians got aggressive.

"We can wait and follow them to the other base," Conley said.

"If they go soon . . . and go by land instead of helicopter, and it's not too far away," Morgan said.

"What if we made them go," Walter said.

That got Morgan's attention. "What do you have in mind?"

"Do you know what people worry about most in any base down here?" Walter asked. Before Morgan could even consider the question, the scientist continued. "Permanent loss of power, which means permanent loss of heat."

"So if we shut off their power, they will have no choice but to pick up and go to their other facility," Morgan said.

"That would put them all in one place," Conley added. "We could size up their force and determine what the hell is going on over there."

"Of course, shutting down their power could be tricky," Walter said.

"Actually, that area is our specialty," Morgan said.

"More of your amateur electrical engineering?" Walter asked.

"Something like that," Morgan said.

"But we'll need you to stay here," Morgan said. For one, Walter was wearing the dark gray parka that was standard at Heisenberg Base, not the white ones he and Conley had brought for just this kind of stealthy activity. And secondly, Morgan's brand of electrical engineering could be dangerous, especially to civilians.

It didn't take Morgan and Conley long to grab what they needed from the helicopter and put it in the remaining backpack—the only one that hadn't been compromised by shrapnel from the dish.

"We won't be long," Morgan said.

They approached the base from behind one of the heavy equipment buildings. Morgan saw that one of the advantages of infiltrating the only military base on the continent was that the Russians didn't take security very seriously. That made sense when you were a bully and the only military power for thousands of miles.

Not surprisingly, Morgan and Conley didn't see anyone outside. It was the same at Heisenberg. No one went outside unless they had to.

The partners worked their way to the diesel tanks and each placed a high-explosive grenade on the ground between the two nearly touching tanks. By their size, Morgan guessed the containers were at least a thousand gallons each.

"Ten minutes," Dan said.

"Got it," Conley replied.

If the diesel caught, it would be quite a show. The problem was that it was much harder than people thought to get diesel to catch fire because it was much lower in octane than gasoline. If you dropped a match into diesel, it would simply go out.

As a result, diesel engines required higher temperatures and much higher pressure to achieve ignition.

And Morgan wanted to be sure that this fuel burned. If nothing else, it would send a message to the Russians who were planning to wipe out an entire base of civilian scientists.

Morgan handed Conley an incendiary grenade and took one for himself. These they placed on the outside of the tanks. The explosion would compromise the tanks and create, at the very least, a large hole in each.

The incendiaries would do the rest.

"Twelve minutes," Morgan called out.

"Affirmative," Conley replied.

That would give the leaking fuel plenty of time to douse the area, and the incendiaries would burn hot enough and long enough to make sure the diesel caught.

"Generator next," Morgan said. "They might have an alternate source of fuel, here or at their other base."

"You take it. I want to make sure that helicopter doesn't get into the air when the party starts," Conley replied.

That made sense. It would also mean he and Conley would be the only air power in this fight. And that was fair enough, given the difference in force size.

"Meet at the entry point," Morgan said. As a rule, the partners had decided early to set rendezvous at the entry point of whatever site or facility they were working in. It eliminated confusion about where to meet and allowed them to connect and make a quick exit, which was usually necessary.

"Will do," Conley said.

Morgan reached the door to the generator building and opened it as slowly and quietly as he could. He slipped inside and shut it carefully behind him. He was now in a small hallway less than six feet long with another door in front of him.

Almost all doors he had seen were double entry. The hallway acted as a sort of airlock, making sure that an interior space was never exposed to the outside weather directly because of a single open door. It helped keep heat inside and the cold out.

For main entrances, there would be a large vestibule with extra cold-weather gear and enough room to change. However, since this was a rear entrance to a utility space, the tiny vestibule was all that was necessary.

It was also perfect for Morgan's purposes. Inside the small hallway, he was able to peer through a glass panel in the inner door and see into the generator room. At least he could see half of the room—the rest was blocked by the large diesel generators themselves. Morgan was amused to see that the Russians were using American-made generators.

He had no choice but to hope the generator room wasn't manned at the moment. There really would be no need to have someone there unless they were performing maintenance.

Opening the door as quietly and slowly as he could, Morgan slipped inside and listened for any sound other than the hum of a generator.

Nothing.

He stayed to the back of the room and scanned the room in front of him, checking the few feet between the two generators and then the open space on the far wall.

Satisfied that he was alone, Morgan took out two of the high-explosive grenades. He didn't have time to get fancy with their placement, and because of the explosive power of the grenades, he didn't have to.

Morgan simply opened the door to the control panel of each generator and placed a grenade inside, setting them both for six minutes, which he calculated would mean they would go off just after the tanks blew and the incendiaries went off.

His work done, Morgan entered the inner door, sped through the short hallway, and was outside in less than thirty seconds. It would take him maybe two minutes to meet up with Conley, and the—

"*Stap!*" Morgan heard from his right.

He didn't know much Russian, though Natasha had promised to teach him once her defection was a done deal and they were settled.

Morgan turned slowly, raising his arms when he saw the soldier with the AK-47 pointed at the center of his chest.

The Russian barked out a string of Russian words that Morgan couldn't begin to follow.

As casually as he could manage, Morgan said, "The front office sent me. I'm from pest control."

The soldier followed with another string of Russian words.

"We got a call that a bunch of rats were planning to give a hard time to a group of scientists that are out here minding their own business."

The soldier obviously didn't understand what Morgan was saying, but he didn't like Morgan's tone. Even angrier now, the soldier shouted more instructions at him. Holding his ground, Morgan spoke slowly and clearly when he said, *"Moë sudno na vozdushnoy podushke polno ugrey."*

That stopped the soldier cold. His anger was gone and was replaced with one of the profoundest looks of confusion Morgan had ever seen.

Morgan had to struggle not to smile. Since he spoke almost no Russian, Morgan took pains to master the few phrases he did know, down to the native-sounding accent. Slowly, as if he were speaking to a child, Morgan repeated, *"Moë sudno na vozdushnoy podushke polno ugrey."*

If possible, the man looked more confused than he had before, and Morgan knew that this was his chance. The barrel of the Russian's rifle was a good six feet away and Morgan figured he could make it in two strides.

His odds weren't great, but he knew he couldn't wait. The minuscule advantage he had just given himself would last for only a couple of seconds. Rearing back, Morgan tensed and prepared to move, but before he could launch himself, there was a flash of movement behind the soldier, who stood up straight for a second, his eyes wide before he fell face-first into the snow.

"Were you on a break?" Morgan asked as Peter Conley let the small section of pipe fall from his hand.

"A break? You're lucky that I came back for you. Now if you don't mind, we have less than four minutes before the fireworks start," Conley said, already turning and heading toward the entrance.

Morgan caught up with him, and Conley said, "Now explain to me why you told that guard your hovercraft was full of eels."

"I wanted to confuse him," Morgan said.

"It worked, and not just on him," Conley said, finally letting out a laugh.

"I've decided to learn that phrase in as many languages as I can," Morgan said.

"It does seem effective," Conley admitted as they simply walked out of the camp and headed for the patch of volcanic rocks where they had left Walter.

As soon as they were close, the scientist ran out to meet them. "Everything okay?" he asked.

"Sure," Morgan said. "But let's get behind cover." He led Walter back to the rocks and all three men took positions that shielded everything but their eyes and the tops of their heads from view.

"Did you shut off their power?" Walter said.

"Not yet. We used a time delay," Morgan said. Then, before Walter could speak again, Morgan said, "Just watch."

Morgan estimated that it would be just a few more seconds . . .

A few more . . .

There was a dull boom, a brief flash, and a plume of smoke. There was the inevitable silence that followed as the soldiers at the base tried to process what had just happened.

Then there was the sound of voices, followed by the sound of shouting, but before Morgan could see movement, there was a bright flash and then another as the incendiaries went off.

As expected, the diesel caught fire quickly and within seconds there was a large funnel of flame in the air. That burned for maybe half a minute as pressure built up in the compromised fuel tanks, and then there was a double explosion that was so large, bright, and loud that Morgan had to look away.

He kept his head down and waited until the pressure wave passed them by and then looked in time to see a fairly large mushroom cloud of smoke with fire running into its center.

The cloud died down fairly quickly and what was left was still a fairly large fire that consumed the area. When the explosives in the generator building went off, it was almost an anti-climax. There was a thud, some windows blew out in the building, and smoke billowed out the openings.

The noise started, more shouting, and then Morgan saw movement, all of which stopped dead when the helicopters exploded.

If not for the big show with the fuel tanks, the helicopter blast would have been impressive. There was even a small shockwave that passed by them, followed by an even larger blast, which Morgan assumed was the rockets on the attack helicopter going off.

"That's why you don't load your rockets until that last possible moment," Conley said.

Now there were two fires burning in the base, though the helicopters' flames were much smaller. Even so, those choppers would never fly again, and by the time the fire burned out, they wouldn't even be good for parts.

This time, there was no sign of life from the camp for a good five minutes. Then, as if the Russians were satisfied that there would be no more explosions, the base burst into a frenzy of movement.

Soldiers ran back and forth carrying weapons. Morgan heard loud shouting and then saw three groups of Russians form up as others started scanning the base, looking for enemies, or explosives, or both.

"Wow," Walter said.

"They look pretty mad," Conley said.

"To be fair, they started it," Morgan replied.

"They won't be able to stay now," Conley said. "The only heat they will have will be from the fires."

"How long will that last?" Walter said.

"Doesn't matter. Looks like they are planning to evacuate, so we follow them," Morgan said.

If possible, the flames from the fires seemed to be getting larger and the smell of burning diesel was strong. That, in itself, was remarkable. Morgan had been surprised to learn that in Antarctica there was mostly an absence of smells, at least outdoors.

One of the reasons was that there was no dirt on the continent. All the rock formations were volcanic, so there was literally no soil here.

"Can we report in to Dr. Russell?" Walter asked.

Morgan shook his head. "No. We can't take a chance that the Russians are monitoring your communications. For now, we just follow them and see where they go. If it's a base, we evaluate and plan our next move."

"We still don't know why they were here in the first place," Conley added. "And why they wanted your group out of the way. Until we do, Heisenberg Base won't be safe. And we are here to keep you safe."

Walter took a deep breath and said, "This is just a lot for one day. Mostly we check equipment and compile data. So far today I had a satellite dish blow up in my face—which would be plenty on a normal day. Then I saw you take out a military base full of trained soldiers. Now we're going to follow them to what could be an even bigger base."

"I'm sorry, Walter, we have to see this through," Morgan said. "We can't run you back to the base and still follow the Russians."

Shaking his head, Walter said, "That's not it. You're doing this for me and my people. I want to help if I can." He hesitated and looked embarrassed for a few seconds, then he added, "It's just a lot."

Morgan smiled. "It feels like a lot to us too sometimes, but you get used to it. Mostly it's a lot of waiting around and then days like today."

"Look," Conley said. "They are starting to head out."

The first few troop carriers were full and moving out, holding about twenty soldiers each. The three men watched them head out, and after a few minutes, Conley turned to Walter. "Based on their direction, can you speculate on their destination?" Conley said.

Shaking his head, Walter said, "There's nothing out there. No bases. Literally nothing."

"So I'm betting on a secret base," Morgan said. "What about the landscape out there?"

"Just a few dormant volcanoes," Walter said. His eyes went wide as he thought of something. "That could mean there might be caverns. There have been a few recent expeditions to explore volcanic ice caverns. There are interesting forms of life in them."

"And open space?" Morgan asked.

Walter nodded.

"Okay, we'll follow them, but I want to do it in the JetRanger. Our handheld radios won't reach Heisenberg Base if we go any farther. And I wouldn't want to depend on our satellite phones," Conley said.

Morgan agreed with that. The satphones' signal was weak and they didn't work at least half the time. "We'll need the helicopter's radio. Plus, I don't know about you guys but I'm feeling a chill."

The other men smiled, but Morgan would be glad to be back inside the heated JetRanger.

Chapter 4

The cold seemed to make everything take longer. The trip back to the helicopter was less than five minutes but seemed endless.

"Can you follow without them seeing us?" Walter asked.

"We won't be following them exactly," Conley said. "It's safe to assume they will be moving in a straight line, and we'll also assume their base, or whatever it is, is in the volcanic caves you mentioned. I say we get there first. How far away would you say the site is?"

"Maybe ten miles," Walter said.

"And how long would you say it would take in those vehicles?"

Walter thought about that for a minute. "Half hour to forty-five minutes."

"More than we need," Morgan said.

That seemed to surprise Walter, and Morgan explained, "They are already on alert because of what just happened. And however many soldiers are there, we'd rather not face another two hundred. There will never be a better time for us to pay them a visit."

They finally reached the helicopter. Conley started it up, and within two minutes they were warm and in the air.

"Walter, we can't afford to stash you this time," Morgan said. "We're going to need you right there to help us evaluate the base. And we're going to have to move quickly because, whatever happens, we need to be out before their friends arrive."

"I understand. Whatever you need from me," Walter said.

Even making a long arc around the Russians on the ground, they covered the distance in less than five minutes. Morgan could see the mountain up ahead. It wasn't very big by the standards of what he had seen so far in Antarctica. It had a small, rocky platform that was about 20 percent of its height. On top of that was a snow-covered hill.

"Are you sure it's dormant?" Conley asked.

"Pretty sure. I'm not a geologist, but I understand that all of the volcanoes for fifty miles around us are supposed to be dormant," Walter said.

From a distance, Morgan could see a few buildings near the base of the mountain in front of what he thought might be the opening to a cavern.

Conley landed the helicopter near the base of the mountain, closer to the Russian facility than Morgan would have liked but with enough of the mountain rock between them that he was reasonably confident that they wouldn't be seen.

Both he and Conley took a rifle, Morgan packed their remaining grenades into the backpack, and the three men set out. The mountain's stone base gave them good cover and they were soon less than a hundred yards from the buildings, of which there were only two.

One was two stories and was what Morgan assumed was living space. The other was a large garage, with doors big enough for trucks and construction equipment. A third looked like a hangar big enough for the helicopters.

"How many people would you say live there?" Morgan asked, handing Walter the binoculars.

"Fifty, maybe seventy-five. It's going to get tight when the others arrive," Walter said.

"Unless they have more space in the caverns," Conley said.

"Wait . . ." Walter said, still looking through the binoculars. "I can make something out on the side of the two trucks. Radiation. I can't read Russian but the symbol for radiation is universal."

Morgan took the binoculars as Conley looked with his own. There it was, on the side of both visible trucks and on one of the side doors to the garage. Three triangles with a circle in the center.

"Why would you have radioactive anything down here?" Morgan asked.

"Maybe if you were building a reactor, but I can't think of a good reason to do that. Besides violating ten different international treaties, it would be overkill just to power a base."

"So let's get a look inside," Morgan said.

For the first time since they got on the helicopter, Walter looked nervous.

"Not through the front door," Morgan said.

"We've seen underground facilities before," Conley added. "You typically need multiple exits in case you need to evacuate."

"So we find a back or side door and hope it's not guarded," Morgan said.

Hugging the side of the mountain, it didn't take long to find a door. It was a single, standard-sized steel door . . . and it was locked.

Old habits, Morgan thought. In his experience, Russians were not trusting, even of their own people. *Especially* of their own people.

"I've got it," Morgan said, pulling out his lockpick kit.

He had the door open in under a minute.

"Lucky you had that," Walter said.

"I always do," Morgan said.

The door led to a narrow hallway that had been cut out of the volcanic rock. Morgan took the lead and they moved slowly. It was much warmer inside than it was outside, Morgan guessed it was maybe fifty degrees.

But it was warm enough that he could take off his gloves and draw his pistol, the Walther feeling good—if a little cool—in his hand.

After a hundred yards, the tunnel ended in what looked like an open chamber.

Morgan got there first and was amazed at the size of the space. It was like the biggest aircraft hangar he'd even seen and stretched deep into the mountain.

"Damn," Morgan said.

"What?" Conley asked as he joined Morgan at the small landing at the top of two flights of stairs that led to the floor of the facility.

"Well, this explains where they are planning to put their guests," Conley said.

"They'll have room to spare," Morgan said.

Walter leaned against the railing and said, "This also explains what they are doing here."

There was row after row of fifty-five-gallon drums, each with a radiation symbol on it.

"They are storing their nuclear waste," Walter said.

Morgan knew that the Russians weren't exactly scrupulous in their waste-disposal methods—and that included nuclear waste. He guessed they had decided it was better to dump it out here than dispose of it properly at home.

"I guess they don't want eyes on them," Conley said.

"Too late on that," Morgan said. "Do we have enough explosives in the helicopter to take this down, or at least seal it up?" Morgan asked.

Conley thought about it for a minute and said, "Probably, the RPGs should do it, if we hit them at the front entrance."

"Wait, can't you just call it in or something? This looks like a job for the military," Walter said.

"They call us because they want to avoid a military confrontation," Morgan said. "Once diplomats and soldiers get involved, this could turn into a major international problem."

"What about the people inside?" Walter said. "A place like this wouldn't be run by soldiers. It would be a few scientists with soldiers as guards."

"I understand, but look at what they are doing. And it's not like we can ask them to leave," Morgan said.

They saw the first signs of people on the floor of the cavern. Four men in civilian clothes walked across the floor and headed in the direction of the large open space that acted as the front door.

"The thing they fear most in a facility that houses nuclear material is fire. If you set one, this place will clear out pretty quick," Walter said.

Morgan was sure Walter was right. It would give the people inside a chance to get out. That would give him and Conley more Russians to deal with, but if Walter was right, they were civilians.

"Then you wouldn't have to hide what you did on this mission from Natasha," he said. Turning to Walter, Conley added, "He has a Russian girlfriend."

Girlfriend was a small word for what Natasha was to him, but Morgan let it go.

"Okay, stay here. We'll be right back," Morgan said.

As they headed for the stairs, he handed Conley two incendiaries and kept two in his hands.

On the floor, they split up, with Conley headed to the rear of the chamber and Morgan headed to the center, in between racks of nuclear waste. He knew that this brief exposure to the material wasn't dangerous, but he would be glad when he got out of there.

Setting the timer for five minutes, he put one incendiary under a rack of barrels and then the second one about fifty yards farther in.

Turning around, he headed for the stairs at a jog and met Conley at the bottom. They were up the two flights quickly and saw that Walter wasn't alone. He was against the wall with a soldier holding one hand against his chest and the other pointing a pistol at his head.

Damn, Morgan thought.

Walter looked both scared and embarrassed. His eyes darted from Conley to Morgan and he said, "Sorry."

The soldier shouted instructions and Morgan didn't need fluent Russian to know that he was ordering Morgan and Conley to drop their weapons.

"What's the move?" Conley asked.

"We can't, you know that," Morgan replied.

Walter's eyes went wide and he said, "He's going to shoot me. I think he's going to shoot me."

"I know he is," Morgan said, raising his gun to point it at both the soldier's and Walter's heads.

The soldier gave one last, nearly hysterical instruction as Walter cried out, "No."

Morgan squeezed the trigger and there was an explosion of blood and brain matter. Then there was a terrible moment when the two men in front of Morgan seemed frozen. Then the soldier fell to the ground, leaving Walter standing with a stunned expression on his face.

Before the man could fall, Morgan and Conley each grabbed an arm.

"You're okay," Morgan said.

"I thought you were going to shoot both of us . . . to shoot me," Walter said.

Morgan smiled. "Shooting a hostage looks bad for our side. The other agents would never let me live it down."

Walter actually grinned, and Morgan knew the scientist would be okay. Morgan had hit the Russian soldier on top of the skull, near the temple, to try to keep the amount of blood and tissue that landed on Walter to a minimum.

Since Walter was a civilian and Morgan just plain liked him, he didn't want to give the man any more nightmares than were absolutely necessary. In addition, things would go a lot smoother if Walter stayed functional until they made it back to Heisenberg Base.

"We've got to get back to the chopper," Conley said, checking his watch.

Morgan would have liked to hide the soldier's body, but in a few minutes the incendiaries would go off and the Russians would know they were under some sort of attack.

If they found the soldier before that, then they would be just that much more on edge when the fireworks started.

The JetRanger was right where they left it and Conley got them in the air to line them up with the front of the cavern and put a little more distance between them and the base. When he landed again, Dan and Conley took out their binoculars to watch the first incendiary flare from inside the mountain.

Morgan was pleased that the incendiary was bright enough that it was impressive even from this distance.

The flare was followed by another, and then another. The last one was closest to the doors and Morgan had to look away because the flash was so bright.

There was no time to waste now. He handed the binoculars to Walter and started to pull what he needed out of the helicopter's cargo space.

"They are evacuating the nuclear waste area," Conley said.

"In a hurry," Walter added.

"Turns out they don't want to be around flaming nuclear waste," Conley said.

"Whenever you are ready, Dan," Conley said.

Morgan grabbed the three rocket launchers and headed back to the other two men. He handed two to Conley and extended the stock on his, nearly doubling the length of the tube and converting it from carry mode to firing mode.

Morgan liked the M141. Because it was single use, it was lighter than the standard, reusable anti-tank weapons. It was also optimized for use against bunkers and other fortified positions, which made it more useful in his and Conley's line of work.

"Any suggestions?" Morgan asked.

"I'm not sure. I've never started an avalanche," Walter said. "But I would aim for the top of the mountain."

It was as good a place as any. Morgan picked a spot just under the mountain's rounded peak, called out "Rocket," and let it fly.

He felt the familiar jolt of the weapon. It wasn't the kickback you felt from firing a gun of any size. There was a very quick recoil, but that was almost immediately offset by the backblast of the high-speed gasses that propelled the rocket through the firing chamber.

Morgan watched as the RPG flew toward the target, its tail flaring.

In just a few seconds it hit the mountain in an impressive display of light, exploding in the snow and making a dull *BOOM* sound.

Nothing happened for several seconds.

Then several more.

Morgan could see the frenzy of movement in the base increase but that was it.

"One more," Morgan said and Conley handed Morgan the second launcher, which he'd already extended into firing mode.

"I'll try to hit closer to the center," Morgan said. That might destabilize the snow both above and below the blast site.

As soon as his partner was clear, Morgan called out "Rocket" and let the projectile fly. It made a similarly impressive display in the center of the volcano, but again, nothing happened.

"I was afraid of this," Conley said. "I think you're going to have to put the last one right into the entrance of the cavern."

Morgan knew his partner was right. He would prefer not to fire a high-explosive round into a nuclear waste site—even if it was underground—but it looked like he didn't have a choice.

As Conley was holding out the third M141, Morgan heard a low rumble.

"What's that?" he asked Walter.

The young scientist just shrugged. Morgan looked at the mountain. It seemed to blur near the top and at the center, and Morgan realized he was seeing movement.

The snow was moving, sliding down, and now kicking up what looked like a white cloud.

So that's what an avalanche looks like, Morgan thought.

As the moving snow picked up speed, the dull roar turned into an actual roar.

By now, the distant figures at the base saw the same thing and started racing away from the mountain and the mouth of the waste site.

It didn't take long for a huge amount of snow to cover the mouth of the mountain, as well as the side entrance they had used.

For a few seconds, Morgan thought the avalanche would reach the main buildings of the base but it stopped after covering about half the open space between the mountain and the Russians.

The rumble died down, as did the shaking of the ground beneath Morgan's feet.

"I don't think they will be using that site again, unless they brought a lot of shovels," Morgan said.

"Let's get out of here before their friends arrive," Conley said.

Morgan realized that his partner was right. The Russians from the other base would be here in less than ten minutes.

When Morgan reached for the door of the JetRanger, he realized that the ground was shaking again.

Looking toward the mountain, Morgan didn't see signs of another avalanche. Maybe it was on the other side of the mountain. . . .

"The ice is shifting," Walter said, real alarm in his voice.

Morgan realized that was correct. The shaking had stopped; now he could feel the ground moving.

He felt himself tilting backward.

Even more worrying, he saw the helicopter's tail dip a few degrees toward the ground.

"We're getting out of here," Conley said, throwing the door open and practically leaping into the cockpit.

Morgan had the side door open and grabbed Walter by the shoulder, pushing him inside. As he stepped onto the helicopter's pontoon, he felt it move beneath his feet.

Pulling himself inside, he called out, "Get us in the air."

As soon as the last word left his mouth, they heard the engine catch, then roar into life . . . just as the helicopter tilted backward sharply, maybe a full twenty degrees.

"Peter . . ." Morgan said.

"Working on it," his partner said, pulling on the controls.

But they didn't start moving.

No, that wasn't exactly right. The helicopter straightened out a bit and then seemed to drop at least three feet . . . which was an interesting trick since it was on the ground.

"Dan . . ." Walter cried out.

Morgan recalled the survival portion of the mission briefing. A crevasse could form at any time in Antarctica, or be waiting beneath your feet in the snow.

And it could be ten feet deep, or a hundred, or a thousand.

He wondered if they would do better outside the helicopter. Less weight. They might be able to get away from the danger and onto solid ice.

Before Morgan could act on that thought, he heard the engine whirring as Conley pushed the machine as hard as he could.

But it was as if the ground had physically taken hold of them and wouldn't let go—which was pretty much what had happened. He knew that if he looked outside and down he would see the JetRanger's pontoons at least partially covered in snow, or ice, or both.

Conley stomped his foot while pulling on the stick. There was the whine of an engine pushed to its limits, and then it felt like the same ground that had held them tightly a second ago was throwing them into the air.

They rocketed upward for a few seconds, and then Morgan felt a second of weightlessness before the chopper started falling.

Before Morgan could brace himself for impact, he felt the JetRanger level off. He looked outside and saw that they were maybe five feet from the ground—or at least from where the ground was when they landed.

He watched the ice fall away as a hole formed, racing from the spot they had just left into a large arc that didn't stop until it was at least fifty yards out.

Conley raised the helicopter and made a turn that gave Morgan a good view into a new hole in the ground that had almost swallowed them and the JetRanger.

He didn't think it was a thousand feet down, but it was more than a hundred, probably more than two.

"I see something," Walter said, pointing into the distance.

Morgan saw movement on the ice. Vehicles. Men. It was the convoy from the other site.

That was followed by a metallic ping on the outside of the JetRanger.

"They've seen us," Morgan said. Clearly, someone from the waste site saw them in the air and put two and two together, and now the Russians were shooting at them.

Fair enough, he thought, but he didn't want to hang around while they got payback.

Conley was already on it, though. Giving them altitude and putting them into a wide arc kept them out of weapons range and put them behind the mountain.

"Let them wonder where we came from," he said.

Conley put the JetRanger into an even wider arc that would take them back to Heisenberg Base.

There was no doubt that the mission was a success. They had routed the Russians from their primary base, uncovered the secret nuclear waste site, and then rendered that site useless.

The Russians would have to find somewhere else to dump their nuclear waste.

Morgan and Conley had also ensured that Heisenberg Base would remain safe since the Russians no longer had a secret to keep. Morgan had done the math. Based on the number of Russian soldiers and personnel, the nearest base that could accommodate them even temporarily was the Norwegian outpost that was nearly twenty miles away. It would be a difficult trip, even with the vehicles they had, but the Russians would survive. Morgan found he was glad about that.

He would not have looked forward to explaining to Natasha that he had buried dozens of them in a mountain of radioactive ice. Of course, he would not have had to tell her. In many ways, secrecy was par for the course in their business.

However, she had given up a lot to be with him and to defect to the American side of the decades-long struggle between the two nations. Morgan didn't want to begin their life together with a lie or by withholding the truth.

The fact was that because of Morgan's work, the truth was even more important to him in his personal life. If he and Natasha were going to have a future, it would have to be based on the truth and on trust.

As they flew back to Heisenberg Base, Morgan found that he was looking forward to that future.

Chapter 5

The Present

Diana Bloch's screen flashed "No Signal" for the fifth time, and she muttered a curse under her breath, something that no one who worked at Zeta had ever heard her do.

She didn't like to miss her weekly calls with her nephew, and she rarely did. Even after he'd been posted to a base in Antarctica, they had rarely missed a call. And all of those times had been due to weather, usually the frequent storms that plagued the windiest continent on Earth.

Because the extreme cold isn't bad enough, Bloch thought.

Right now, Jeffrey's base was in the middle of a category 5 storm. In Boston, 150-mile-an-hour winds would be devastating and the event of the year. In Antarctica, it was much more common but she tracked each one and never fully relaxed until she heard from Jeffrey after the storm passed.

She had too many people at Zeta that she had to keep safe. Was it too much to ask that the only family she had left choose a nice, safe job somewhere?

Of course, Bloch's sister had a nice safe job and that had not protected her.

Cursing herself for wasting time worrying about things she could not control, Bloch decided to do something that might actually be productive.

She hit the intercom button on her phone and said, "Send him in."

Lincoln Shepard entered her office wearing his trademark jeans, T-shirt, and hoodie. His walk was unusually purposeful and Bloch could tell from the young man's face that she wasn't going to like what he had come to tell her.

"Director," he said as he took a seat in one of the two chairs on the other side of her desk. Though there were no formal titles at Zeta Division, Shepard and the rest of her people insisted on calling her Director and she had given up discouraging them.

It more or less described her role in the organization, and in any case, it was what they needed her to be, so she allowed it.

She could see that Shepard was not just concerned but worried. That told her something about what was coming.

"We have a situation in the Caribbean," he said.

"What is it?"

"How much do you know about Prince Fahad bin Nasef?"

"Saudi prince, but not an important one. Playboy. He runs around on yachts with models," Bloch said. "I understand he's a bit of an embarrassment to the royal family."

"Yes, he's also a treasure hunter. For the last two years, he's funded and personally overseen searches for famous undersea wrecks. He's had some success there. However, our analysis shows that each of his recovery operations or search areas also corresponds with nuclear weapons that were lost at sea."

"Lost at sea?" Bloch said.

"There were three US nuclear bombs that went down in bombers that were lost in the ocean," Shepard said.

"When I was in the navy, there were stories about a nuke lost near Spain," Bloch said.

"The Palmores incident in 1966," Shepard said. "There was a midair collision and a nuke that was never found. Of the thirty-two 'Broken Arrow' incidents we've had in which a nuclear bomb was jettisoned during an emergency or lost in a crash, all but three have been found. It's remarkable that there weren't more. Throughout the sixties, both the US and the Soviet Union always had nuclear bombers in the air."

"So I presume Russia lost some as well?" Bloch said.

"And England, France . . . almost all of the major nuclear powers. And we only know about a portion of them. But someone else has access to that information. Now, a Saudi prince has been running around using his treasure hunting as a cover to search for nuclear warheads."

"I presume that O'Neal's threat-assessment system made the connection?" Bloch asked.

That system was one of Zeta's secret weapons; it was based on a search algorithm that used patterns in metadata to identify threats with uncanny accuracy. Bloch wouldn't pretend to understand how it worked, but there was no question that it did work.

"No," Shepard said. "This isn't a threat, yet. At this point, it's someone just looking for weapons-grade uranium."

Just looking for weapons-grade uranium, Bloch thought. She would have liked to chide Shepard for minimizing something so horrendous, but given the kind of active threats they had faced lately, this one truly wasn't critical . . . at least not yet.

"How did you identify the situation?" Bloch asked.

Shepard looked uncomfortable and said, "I programmed our system to look for anyone nosing around near potential sites of fallen nukes. This was one of the operations we mapped out when I was in college and a member of Friends of Feynman."

That explained everything, even the fact that Shepard looked both embarrassed and anxious. As an undergraduate, he had been a founding member of a small group that performed thought experiments that were turned into full-fledged plans for everything from breaking into bank vaults to hacking national banks to repurposing satellites.

None of these operations got out of the planning stage and Shepard himself had disbanded the group when he didn't like how seriously some members were taking their work.

"Shepard, that was a long time ago, and you've now spent years putting your mind to stopping those kinds of threats. It was a game, and you were very young," Bloch said.

Well, even younger, Bloch thought. Shepard was not even thirty now.

"It's not that, Director. I just don't like the coincidence. We determined that the easiest way for someone to get their hands on weapons-grade material was to find a ready source that no one was even looking for," he said.

"It is clever," Bloch acknowledged. "Someone else could have thought of it."

"No doubt," Shepard said. "But I don't like the timing. We've seen too many situations recently that remind me of some of our projects."

"You think someone from the group is making use of the plans?" Bloch said.

"It would explain more than a few things, but I don't think so. I keep track of all the surviving members," Shepard said.

"Surviving?" Bloch asked.

"There was one suicide and one death in a traffic accident," Shepard said.

"Who else would have had access to your plans?"

"The FBI confiscated everything," Shepard said.

Bloch decided to be the one to say it. "I assume you are thinking that Ares might have access to the group's plans. If it is Ares, then I don't think we can rule out that they might have gotten into FBI archives. Can I assume you still have access to the FBI network?"

Shepard looked mildly offended to even be asked. "Of course. I will check any access to our work. With your approval, I'll also go deeper on the surviving members. Up until now I've limited myself to public records."

Bloch almost smiled at that request. Zeta had no legal standing to peek at either the FBI computers or any private citizen's records. At best, Zeta was merely tolerated by the US government and other intelligence agencies. Yet Shepard was so earnest that even though he had the power to penetrate almost any computer system on Earth, he was reluctant to use it.

"This is important. Do whatever you have to do to find your answers," Bloch said. "If Ares has access to any of your group's plans, then we need to know it, and start preparing for all worst-case scenarios. In the meantime, send me the details on our prince's recovery operation and I'll get someone out there."

Shepard nodded and got up to leave. He had the look of someone glad to have a job to do, but he also looked very, very worried. Bloch decided that she would need a briefing about exactly what was in those other plans.

Once Shepard had his answers, Bloch would insist on that briefing, but she was sure that she wouldn't like what she heard.

Bloch hit the button activating the intercom to her assistant. "What is the status of Alex Morgan's current operation?" Bloch asked.

* * * *

Alex had to admit that her father was right.

If you are infiltrating a supply chain, Dan Morgan maintained, the origin point is the place to start; security is always weakest there.

Alex and Lily Randall watched their approach to the rail station from a video feed on their phones, while they sat in a hidden compartment of the box truck behind the truck's cab. The space was less than two feet wide, so Alex and Lily had to sit facing each other as the truck bounced on the rough asphalt of the road leading to the rail yard.

The video gave them the feed from the truck's dash cam and four other cameras hidden on the vehicle's exterior.

Outside, it was flat and gray. There was a single guard shack at the entrance to the rail station. There was one man inside. As they pulled up to the shack, Alex could hear their driver exchanging words with the guard. Alex didn't speak Albanian, and neither did Lily.

However, Valery Dobrynin did. The ex-KGB agent and one-time nemesis of her father now freelanced for Zeta Division and—even more surprisingly—worked at her father's business, Morgan Classic Cars.

When she'd asked her father about that, he'd simply shrugged and said, "He's a hell of a negotiator."

Like many things that Alex didn't understand about her father, Alex was sure there was more to it, but she also knew that was all she would get on the subject.

Alex had heard Dobrynin negotiate and he was certainly a *loud* negotiator. He had also taught Alex to speak excellent Russian with a Leningrad accent.

And he had not only arranged much of Alex and Lily's current operation, but he was driving the truck. After a few minutes of driving around the warehouses at the yard, the truck came to a stop.

On her phone, Alex toggled through the cameras on the outside of the vehicle, which pulled up to the front door of one of the buildings. She watched Dobrynin get out and talk to someone who came out of the warehouse.

The Russian handed the man an envelope. As soon as the counting was done, four men appeared from inside the warehouse. They opened the back of the truck and started unloading the crates of weapons that were their official cargo.

Of course, those weapons would be tracked by Zeta, and the recipients would get a surprise shortly after they accepted delivery.

Alex and Lily were the truck's unofficial cargo and remained hidden behind the cab, with a thin false wall between them and the cargo area of the truck. Alex could hear and feel the men walking around inside the truck and picking up the crates that had been piled against the false wall.

Holding her breath, Alex reached into the pocket of her coveralls and grabbed her Smith & Wesson Shield 9mm. However, the men completed their work quickly and within a minute had left and closed up the back of the truck.

When the last crate was inside, Dobrynin reached back into the cab. Alex watched him head back to the warehouse, carrying another envelope and two more bottles. One was the Tsarskaya vodka that she knew was Dobrynin's favorite. The other was a fancy bottle of raki, a type of brandy favored by Albanians.

Dobrynin was greeted enthusiastically by the man Alex now thought of as the warehouse manager and the two men led the others inside to drink.

As soon as the warehouse door closed, Lily was sliding the panel that formed a narrow door to the truck's cab. She slipped into the cab, and Alex was right behind her, sliding the panel back into place as soon as she was clear. The two women checked the area around them through the truck's windshield and windows, as well as through the feed on their phones.

Lily gave Alex a brief nod, opened the passenger side door, and jumped outside. Alex followed, and the two women were now between the truck and the side of the warehouse.

Both Lily and Alex had memorized the layout of the rows of warehouses and headed for the building that was their target. It was lunchtime, and as the women made their way to their destination, they didn't see anyone outside.

That suited Alex just fine. Their disguises consisted of the type of light flannel jackets worn by the yard workers. The disguises would hold up at a distance but not close up.

Fortunately, they made their way easily to the back of the warehouse that was their target. Pulling her lockpick set out of a compartment in her jacket, Alex had the door open in less than a minute.

Alex took some pride in the fact that she was better and faster at defeating locks than Lily Randall, who was several years older than Alex and had had a storied career in British Intelligence before she joined Zeta. Of course, Lily excelled at nearly everything, so Alex was happy to take what she could get.

They slipped inside and Alex quickly pulled the door shut behind her, careful to lock it again. They were in the back of the warehouse, hidden by a maze of crates. Alex removed her flannel jacket as Lily did the same. Underneath, they were wearing identical light-blue overalls.

Carefully, they made their way to the front of the warehouse. Near the large front door, there was a mostly open space with crates placed haphazardly on the floor. Sitting on those crates were about forty figures wearing the same light-blue overalls that Lily and Alex wore.

Most of the women had their backs to Alex but she could see a few in profile. They were awake but far from alert. They looked listless, and Alex assumed they had been drugged.

They were young, and with all of them wearing the same clothing, they looked interchangeable—more like the identical crates in the warehouse than women, more like products than people.

That made sense; to the men guarding them they were a product.

Those four men were sitting at a table and eating lunch. They all had rifles strapped to their backs.

At the moment, the men paid the women they were guarding no mind. Instead, they were focused on the food in front of them. It was some form of *byreck,* a local dish that was a sort of a pie with meat, vegetable, and cheese fillings surrounded by a flaky crust.

It was the Albanian equivalent of comfort food.

By all accounts, the men were enjoying their lunch, talking and laughing as if they were simply men who worked together sharing food.

Of course, to them, that was all that they were doing. They happened to be guarding live young women, but as far as they were concerned, they could have been guarding machine parts.

Alex felt a ball of rage forming in her stomach and start rising up toward her throat.

A soft touch from Lily shook Alex out of it and she realized that she was once again clutching the gun in one of the large front pockets of her overalls.

Alex forced herself to relax and stay focused on her mission. Taking out the four clowns having lunch would make her feel better, but it wouldn't achieve their primary objective.

Moving slowly and carefully, Alex and Lily split up and approached the women sitting on crates. Lily took a spot at the outer edge of the group and sat, while Alex did the same.

A young woman who was maybe eighteen looked up as Alex took a seat. All Alex saw on the woman's face was the acknowledgment that Alex was there, along with a look of dull fear.

The women had been drugged, Alex was sure, but even the drugs couldn't mask all of the fear that they were feeling.

The young woman's eyes dropped and Alex did her best to imitate the posture and expressions of the women around them.

Less then a half hour later, Alex heard activity up front. The men put away their lunch and opened the large door.

There were another four men outside. Then the entire group approached the women and started shouting in Albanian. Alex didn't have to understand the language to know they were being told to stand, and then they were led out the door in single file.

Alex matched the slow, awkward gait of the women in front of her and saw Lily doing the same several feet ahead. They headed toward a waiting cargo train. There was a ramp that led to a platform big enough to hold a fair amount of cargo . . . or about forty women.

There was no delay. As soon as the first of the women got to the platform, they were led inside the car. In just a few minutes, they were almost all loaded inside and then it was Alex's turn to enter.

She was expecting an open space but was surprised to see benches on each side of the car and two more in the center. Each one would hold ten to twelve women.

As she took her seat, two things occurred to Alex. The car was cleaner than she expected, and the bench she sat on was worn—as if dozens if not hundreds of women had taken this ride.

Without Lily's calming hand, Alex had to force her anger down on her own. Whatever happened, this would be the last trip of this kind that anyone took in this train car.

The last few women were ushered inside and there was a bit of a commotion. Alex had heard the men counting off each prisoner as they entered the train. This was necessary to make sure none of the women had escaped or had been diverted by one of the guards.

This was the first time, Alex guessed, that there had been any *extra* women in the car. The men seemed equal parts angry and confused.

This was one of the most dangerous parts of the operation, Alex knew. If the men started to look too closely at each woman—or interrogate them—Alex and Lily would have to start the fight early.

Part of her wanted that to happen, and she relished the image of these men coming face-to-face with women who weren't drugged and docile but *armed and angry*.

However, Alex knew it was better for the mission if it played out as planned, and far more women than this single group would be helped if they succeeded.

In the end, the commotion was short-lived, and human nature won out. These guards were no doubt the lowest paid and least important people in this chain, and they were happy to close the door and send the train on its way—making the accounting discrepancy their superiors' problem.

With very little delay, Alex felt the train start to move.

She forced herself to relax; it would be a few hours before they reached their destination. Then the hard part would begin.

Chapter 6

Shepard was glad to have something to do. He knew that agents in the field had what Dan Morgan called "mission focus." They leveled up their physical and mental performance in a number of important ways.

Situational awareness was increased. Reflexes were sharpened. Reaction times were shortened. Even physical strength could get a bump.

In his own work, he found the same thing often happened, especially when one of the Zeta agents were depending on him to keep them safe.

Through a patchwork of hacked security cameras, Shepard and his people had been able to keep a pretty good eye on Lily Randall and Alex Morgan. However, as often was the case, Shepard could only track the agents and watch what happened to them. There was little he could do to actively assist them.

He didn't care for that part.

Karen O'Neal, his partner both in Zeta and in life, had been on a single field mission with Alex Morgan. It was a simple undercover infiltration and intelligence-gathering operation in a university setting.

Karen had to pose as a graduate student and the risk was so low as to be negligible. And yet the mission had ended with Shepard nearly losing her in a desert lab at the hands of Chechen terrorists.

And there was nothing low risk about this operation. Alex and Lily were walking into a highly sophisticated and very dangerous operation that traded in human beings. It was also the last stop for more young women than Shepard wanted to think about.

While he was watching Alex and Lily in the warehouse and in the train yard, he was busy, but he had felt useless. And now that they were on the train and would be for several hours, he didn't even have that constant activity to keep him occupied.

"You're concerned about Lily and Alex," Karen said, from her position next to him in their joint workstation.

Together, they ran the computer and engineering department at Zeta. When they weren't together at work, they were together in their apartment or in their specially designed living space in "the basement," the lower levels of Zeta Division.

And Shepard wouldn't have it any other way.

"Yes, I'm worried," Shepard replied.

"But that's not all that's bothering you," Karen said. It wasn't a question.

Sometimes Karen had trouble reading people, but not him. He'd learned long ago that he could not keep anything from her.

"Something happened in your meeting with Bloch," Karen said. Again, not a question.

"Yeah. I'm . . . uncomfortable with some of the patterns I've been seeing in the Ares operations. There are too many coincidences, too many things that remind me of the ideas we toyed around with in college," Shepard said.

"Your Friends of Feynman," Karen replied. "What do you think is happening? Do you think Ares has somehow gotten hold of your thought experiments?"

"I do think that might have happened, but there's . . ."

He didn't quite know how to phrase the next part. The expectant look on her face made it even harder.

"I'm embarrassed," he said. "I'm embarrassed that I was ever part of that. And I'm more than just embarrassed that people might have been and might still be hurt by what I did."

Karen shook her head and said, "You didn't do anything wrong. You are not responsible for anything Ares or any other terrorist group does. And even if they did somehow get hold of your group's plans, you would not be responsible for what they did with those plans."

She watched his face, clearly hoping to see that she had gotten through. He understood what she was saying, intellectually, but inside . . .

"It makes me feel like a criminal," he said. It was the simplest way to explain how he felt.

Karen's grin surprised him. "Lincoln, you are forgetting who you are talking to. Of the two of us, I am the only one who has been arrested and spent any time in federal custody."

He responded without even thinking, "But you didn't do anything wrong."

Karen grinned again. "The Securities and Exchange Commission saw it differently."

They did, Shepard knew, but she still hadn't done anything wrong, or even unethical.

"The algorithm you developed was too good at predicting stock movements," he said. "There wasn't even anything illegal about it, not really."

"I certainly thought so at the time and made a fair amount of money using that algorithm system. Yet the United States government saw that my work was a threat to the system. And to be fair to the authorities, legal or not, it was," she said.

"Yes, but your work on that algorithm is now the basis of our threat-identification system. I don't think we could even count the number of lives it has saved," he said.

"And what about your work in college? The skills you developed and the plans you made at the time have helped you save more lives than we could count," Karen said.

"That's different," he said.

"How?" she asked, that same expectant look on her face.

For a few seconds, he didn't actually have a response.

"You were young," she continued, "and experimenting with everything from safe cracking to designing nuclear devices. You never hurt anyone, and you shut down the group when you thought it might get dangerous. And it was the FBI investigation into your activities that put you on Diana Bloch's radar and got you here."

Shepard sat with that for a minute.

"Okay, but the question is, what now?" he said finally.

"Who in the government might have had access to your file and whatever computers or hard drives were confiscated by your group?" Karen asked.

"The FBI, definitely, also the NSA and possibly even the CIA," he said.

"And we have access to all of their systems," she said.

"Of course," he said. There were few places that his and Karen's system could not see. Their access to US government networks was nearly total, and *definitely* illegal. However, Bloch and the people who ran Zeta approved of Shepard and O'Neal's hacking—especially since it had helped Zeta *save more lives than they could count.*

"Let's start with the FBI and see where the chain of evidence takes us," Karen said. "And maybe it's time that you told me about all of the plans you made with your group. We can program them into the threat-detection system."

They had a few hours before Alex and Lily would arrive at the port in Montenegro. There was no reason they couldn't start now. It would keep him and Karen busy, and it might do some good.

* * * *

The train crossed the border from Albania to Montenegro in the first hour of the trip. Though Alex didn't have a watch, she estimated that it had been at least five hours since then.

The ride was smoother than she had expected. The Belgrade-Bar rail line was the only international rail link to Montenegro. Originating in Belgrade, Serbia, the line was cargo only. Recently it had been extended to lead right into the largest port in Montenegro, Port of Bar.

It was the end of the line for the train, but the port was supposed to be just a transit point for the women in the train car. The trafficking ring that ran this operation had plans to ship the women to several points in the Middle East and North Africa.

If Alex and Lily had anything to say about it, those plans would change.

And Alex intended to have plenty to say about it.

Three hours or so into the trip, women in the car had become incrementally more alert and restless. None of them spoke or seemed fully aware of where they were, but they were fidgeting and moving about in their seats in very small ways. That told Alex that whatever sedative their captors were using was slowly wearing off.

This was a dangerous point in the operation. If the guards intended to readminister the sedative by injection, Alex and Lily would have to start active operation early. They could not allow themselves to be sedated. There was too great a risk they would wake up in some godforsaken hellhole with the women they had failed to help.

If it came to a fight, they would have the element of surprise, and Alex was confident that they could quickly overtake the four armed guards.

However, she didn't relish a close-quarters gunfight in a train car with forty densely packed prisoners.

Even if she and Lily won, there would no doubt be casualties.

Alex watched with her peripheral vision when the two guards at one end of the train stood up from their seats. Without looking, she could hear the two guards on the other side doing the same.

The guards then opened a locker, took out a few bottles of water, and started giving each of the women seated in the car a drink. The guards held the bottles and only gave small sips.

That told Alex that the sedative was in the water and the guards were carefully managing the dose . . . so as not to damage their cargo.

When the guard approached Alex, she listlessly raised her head as she had seen the other women do and accepted the drink. Of course, she didn't allow anything but a few drops in her mouth and faked swallowed the drug-laced water. Fortunately, the guard was easily fooled and quickly moved on.

Because she didn't hear any commotion, she assumed that Lily had done the same.

Of course, Alex knew that she had taken a few drops of the water in her mouth, but she was confident that it wouldn't affect her performance when they reached their destination.

Within a few minutes, the other women had settled down, presumably because the drugged water had taken effect. Alex tried a couple of slow movements to confirm that she hadn't been affected by the small amount she'd ingested. She assumed that Lily was also ready for the next phase of the operation.

That phase will come soon now, Alex thought. Though she knew that on the outside she had the same dazed look as the other women. Inside, her body was getting tenser by degrees.

She was craving movement. And she felt herself getting angry, and she had to fight not to show it.

Soon enough, she thought.

* * * *

Bloch didn't like the look on Shepard's face when she entered the War Room, which was the name of the room the staff had given to the conference room that had a few computer terminals, a single large screen, and several other monitors around it.

This was the place where Bloch liked to monitor the final phases of active missions. Because of the prevalence of CCTV cameras, more often than not Bloch was able to watch a patchwork of real-time video feeds of her agents at work, especially when they were operating in cities or public spaces.

Right now, Bloch could see the feed from security cameras at the port in Montenegro. It was near the end of the working day, and it was quiet, though to be fair, from what she knew, it was always relatively quiet even in the middle of the day there—at least compared to a Western port.

Like a lot of the Balkan countries, Montenegro was still struggling to recover and modernize decades after their affiliation with the Soviet Union and Montenegro's own communist government. A rush of investment in the 1990s had given Montenegro a large, relatively modern port that was still running nowhere near capacity.

That meant there would be tactical challenges for Zeta's agents. An all-out firefight was more likely in an empty or nearly empty port. On the other hand, if the port were busier, it wouldn't work as well to move human cargo, so the traffickers would have chosen someplace else.

"Director, we have a problem," Shepard said.

Before Bloch could ask, he looked up from his computer and said, "The tactical team is still in the air."

"What?" Bloch said.

"They were scheduled for landing at Podgorica airport twenty minutes ago but the airport is backed up. We've redirected to the other international airport in Tivat, and they will be on the ground in ten minutes . . . then there's the drive to the airport."

"How long will that be?" Bloch asked.

"It's not much farther to the port than Podgorica." Then Shepard paled. "Ground transport will be waiting, but the travel time will depend on traffic."

So her agents' lives would depend on traffic out of the airport?

It was impossible, outrageous, and completely unacceptable, but it was no one's fault. In an ideal—or even a normal—world, Bloch would have insisted on two separate tactical teams, one in Albania for the warehouse and train yard, and one positioned near the port in Montenegro.

But Ares had kept Zeta and most Western intelligence agencies very busy, fighting both real threats and fake operations that Zeta was still struggling to differentiate.

Originally, Bloch had reservations about using Valery Dobrynin, the former KGB agent recruited as a part-time operative by Dan Morgan. The man had proved capable and reliable, though Bloch still felt uneasy about a former KGB agent on her staff. But if Dan Morgan trusted the man (which was remarkable given their history) Bloch decided to do the same. Plus, it didn't hurt that Bloch knew that the KGB very much wanted to get their hands on Dobrynin.

Instead of two teams, Bloch had been forced to settle for a single team that was supposed to fly from Albania to Montenegro ahead of the train. They had taken every precaution and were using a private Renard Tech plane so they weren't dependent on a commercial Albanian airline.

Plus, Zeta had local assets in most countries that could deliver *honorariums* to airport management that would ensure that their plane would be given priority when it was needed.

That planning could compensate for almost all normal delays, but it couldn't overcome a poorly run airport.

"Will the tactical team make it to the port before Alex and Lily arrive?" Bloch asked, keeping her voice even.

"It's hard to say," Shepard said. "Traffic cams and monitoring are spotty at best, and large parts of the system seem to be down."

"So there's a fair chance that Alex and Lily will soon be facing twenty-some heavily armed human traffickers while our agents are armed only with hand weapons?"

Shepard didn't reply. There really was nothing to say.

"How is the camera coverage at the port?" Bloch said.

"It was fair, but the system has been disabled, presumably by the traffickers in their effort to hide the transfer," Shepard said.

Of course, Bloch thought.

So, not only was there a good chance that Alex and Lily would be facing very long odds, but Zeta would be blind while it happened.

Chapter 7

The train started slowing and then made a turn—presumably into the cargo-loading area of the port. When the train was moving straight again, it moved even more slowly than it did when it was turning.

Alex knew that meant they were in one of the rail spurs that led to the docks themselves. It would not be long now, Alex knew. No more than a few minutes.

Alex was glad that their TACH team was led by Spartan herself. The people running this operation were most likely ex-military. And though the trafficking was not a direct Ares operation, it was almost certainly planned and overseen by Ares, so security would be tight.

Besides the satisfaction of taking out these vile men, the operation was important because it would disrupt Ares and cut off one of their sources of funding.

Zeta didn't have many opportunities to hit Ares directly in that way, so it was impossible to pass up, even though there were risks.

The traffickers' security would be ready for an assault from law enforcement, one of the intelligence services, or a direct military strike.

There would be lookouts and guards hidden behind cover, all of which would make a direct assault on the operation somewhere between dangerous and potentially catastrophic for the attackers.

But Zeta had one advantage these men could not have planned for.

Actually, two.

What the traffickers had created here was a reverse of the prison security paradox. In a prison, all of the security and armed guards were directed toward keeping prisoners from escaping. However, getting into a prison from the outside was relatively easy for a determined person.

Here, security was focused on external threats. However, when the traffickers faced a trained and armed attack from two of the previously placid women under their thumbs while they were *also* facing a dedicated external attack, there would be chaos.

That chaos was the edge that Zeta would need.

The train stopped, and the guards stood up, quickly scanning the seated women.

Alex waited for the TACH team signal. It would not be long before they heard the three beeps from the horn of one of the team's vans. In fact, it should have come as soon as the train stopped, to tell Lily and Alex that the other Zeta agents were in place.

Alex waited a few seconds.

And then a few more.

She turned her head to look at Lily, who stared back at her. There were no answers on the other woman's face.

Alex ignored her rising concern. She wouldn't let a delay or other problem with the rest of the team change anything. She and Lily still had a mission, and unless they carried it out, they—and the other forty women in the train car—would be lost.

The door opened and two new men stepped into the car. The body language of the original guards told Alex that these two men represented the senior partners in this arrangement.

One of the guards handed one of the new players a piece of paper.

An inventory sheet? Alex wondered. *Maybe a shipping manifest or a bill of lading.*

The anger rose up again, and this time Alex didn't try as hard to hide it. She would need it very soon.

To Alex's surprise, the new men spoke in clipped Russian, which—thanks to Dobrynin—Alex understood.

The original guards tried to explain the fact that there were two extra women in the "shipment." The new guards were annoyed, and Alex realized that the word for *idiot* was nearly the same in English and Russian.

The old guards were dismissed with a wave. One of the new guards said to the other to start on the far side of the car. She also heard the word *sedation*.

Alex looked for water bottles, but instead, the guard on her side took off a backpack and removed a small case. That was good. It meant his hands were occupied and would not be able to reach for his holstered weapon easily.

The man opened the case as he approached the first woman in Alex's row. Reaching inside the case, he took out a syringe and quickly applied it to the woman's arm.

He tossed the syringe on the floor and moved to the next woman, who was less than four feet away from Alex.

This wasn't water that Alex and Lily could pretend to drink. There would be no faking this. If Alex allowed the man to inject her, the mission would be over, at least from her point of view—if not completely.

Alex waited until he had the syringe out and was right in front of her. Then she spoke in a clear, firm voice. "Behind you," she said in Russian.

The man was serious, highly trained, and almost certainly a killer, but reflexes were reflexes. His head swiveled back to the door, and Alex stood up and grabbed the syringe from his hand.

Before he could register her movements, she had the syringe at his neck, and while his head was swinging back to her, she had injected him just above his shoulder.

Still, training was training, and he was fast. Rather than sort out what had just happened, he simply reached for his gun. It wasn't a completely stupid move.

Unfortunately for him, Alex was at least as fast as he was and delivered a solid punch directly to his throat before he even had his hand on the butt of his weapon.

Alex's father liked to joke that, "No one ever forgets the first time they are punched in the throat."

The man's hands went to his throat as he dropped to the floor. By the time he hit the ground, Alex had her hands on another syringe. While he flailed and gasped for air, she plunged another needle into the base of his neck.

Within just a few seconds, the combination of the two doses of sedative and the blow to his throat did their work and he fell unconscious.

Alex had been so focused on the man that she hadn't been able to spare a thought for her partner. She was not surprised to see that Lily was at the very end stages of choking out the other guard.

That must have been tricky. The man would have been several steps away from Lily when the ruckus with Alex had started. Lily's guard went still, and she relieved him of the pistol that was still in his holster.

Alex did the same with her guard.

"No signal from Spartan," Lily said.

"No. What do you think that means?" Alex asked.

"Nothing good," Lily replied. "We need a plan."

The women scanned the room. Alex saw a small hatch on the roof at the rear of the train car. She pointed.

"There," Alex said.

"Yes," Lily replied. "I'll lock the door. That will give us a little time to sort this out."

By the time Lily got to Alex in the back of the car, Alex had climbed the ladder on the back wall and turned the lock on the small hatch.

Slowly and quietly, Alex opened the door. She peeked out to confirm that no one had seen her, and then she didn't hesitate. She climbed onto the roof of the train car, hugging the surface to minimize how much of her would be visible to the people on the ground.

For this to work, the two women would need a bit of luck and have no one looking in their direction as they climbed out.

Hugging the roof of the car, Alex moved quickly, making room for Lily, who gently closed the hatch when she was out.

"The good news is that they haven't seen us and don't know anything has happened," Alex said.

"The bad?" Lily asked.

"There's a lot of them and no sign of the TACH team," Alex said.

"So we're on our own?" Lily asked.

"Looks like," Alex replied.

Chapter 8

If you included this call, Valery Dobrynin could count the number of times Bloch had called him directly on one finger.

"Mr. Dobrynin," Bloch said.

He understood that the "Mr." was calculated. It didn't have the familiarity of the first name she used with some of the people at Zeta. And it didn't have the professional respect of simply using his last name.

This address was designed to tell him that she would suffer his presence at Zeta and, occasionally, on Zeta missions like this one, but she would never fully trust him. The attitude would offend an American, but it made Dobrynin smile.

Dobrynin had grown up under the Soviets and then dedicated his life and gave up many friends and much of his own blood for their cause. Only someone like him would understand what it was like when your own motherland merely suffered your presence and would never trust you.

That was, of course, before that same motherland decided you had outlived your purpose and had marked you for death.

No, Bloch's mistrust didn't bother him. At least, in her case, she had cause.

"I've been speaking with Spartan. There's a problem. The Albanians will not let you and the TACH teams off the plane."

"Have you made the payments I detailed?" he said.

"I paid all bribes in advance. I even allowed them to inflate the price exactly as much as you suggested, but no more," Bloch said.

Dobrynin had never heard this tone in Bloch's voice before. It was somewhere between furious and frustrated.

"I think they are toying with us. Making us wait just to make us wait," she said.

He understood. They were doing it because they could. Unfortunately, the people running the airport and collecting Zeta's tribute could not be trusted to know why Zeta was there.

The Albanians had lived under the Soviet umbrella long enough to know what it was like to have no power over your own life. And people who had no real power often exercised what they did have in small, petty ways—especially if they had learned from small-minded masters.

Bloch shouted something to someone in her office, and the phone went briefly silent. When she came back on, she said, "They will let you all deplane but they won't release the vehicles."

That was a problem. They were twenty minutes from the port, and even if they could get there without the Zeta SUVs, they would need the armored vehicles when they arrived.

"Can you talk to them?" Bloch said.

"That will not help," Dobrynin said.

"But they were under Soviet control," she said.

"It will not help *because* they were under Soviet control," he replied.

"Oh . . ." she said.

"Albania was among the poorest Soviet satellites. They have . . . *resentments* and are not fond of Russians."

He heard Bloch mutter something angrily under her breath. "Mr. Dobrynin, Alex Morgan is there, and we're running out of time. I know that you and Dan Morgan—"

"Director Bloch," he said, stopping her. "I would do this for Dan Morgan, but I like Alex Morgan better and will do this for her."

It was true. She had been his student in Russian language and culture. And she was kinder to him than anyone had been since he had made America his home.

Dobrynin had never had children (another sacrifice for the motherland), but he had often thought that if he did have a daughter, he would like her to be like Alex.

"Do you have something in mind?" Bloch said.

"I do," he replied. "I will need to confer with Spartan."

"Whatever it takes, but I need you to get that team to the docks. What do you need?" she said.

"I need you to understand that when this is finished, the Albanians may not be very fond of Americans either."

* * * *

Alex counted the four Albanian guards and at least twelve of the new Russian guards. Plus, there were four large vans.

That was significant. It meant that the women would be broken up into four groups, likely heading to four different ships.

It also meant at least two more armed men per vehicle. That gave Alex and Lily a minimum of twenty-four armed enemies on the dock. And that didn't count any other guards hiding under cover nearby.

As if reading her mind, Lily whispered, "Twenty-four."

Alex nodded and replied in her own whisper, "I think this will go even better if the TACH team doesn't show."

Lily didn't even try to hide her surprise. "Really?"

"No, not even close," Alex said. "And if they don't get here soon, we are really screwed."

It was true. Originally, the frontal assault would have drawn the enemy away from the dock and toward the entrance of the compound. Then Spartan would have flanking teams hit the traffickers from each side while they were struggling with the head-on assault.

Meanwhile, Alex and Lily were supposed to hit them from behind, boxing them in and taking out any hidden enemy operatives who were firing at the TACH team.

It was a cliché that no battle plan survived actual contact with the enemy. However, this one had fallen apart before the fight had even begun.

"Let's get down," Lily said. "They may spend a few extra minutes bickering about who gets the two 'extra' women, but they are going to start wondering what happened to the guards inside the train car."

Alex knew Lily was right. They didn't have much time. Once the guards started thinking that something had gone wrong, they would be on edge. And once they found the train car door locked, they would be on high alert.

The women crawled forward, staying low until they reached the gap between this car and the next one. Lily was the first down the ladder between the cars, and Alex followed.

They got to the ground without being seen, and Alex was glad to have the train car between the two women and the traffickers for now.

"We have to assume the TACH team isn't coming. The smart move would be to slip deep into the yard here, get away, and report back," Lily said.

"Are you serious?" Alex said.

"You know it's what Bloch would tell us to do if she were here. We can come back and crush them later," Lily said.

"That's far from certain. For all we know, they change up transport procedure every few weeks. This could be the last time they use this place," Alex said. "Plus, those forty women . . ."

"It's the smart move, Alex. You should consider it," Lily said.

"*I* should consider it? Meaning that you've already rejected it, but you think I'd leave you *and* them?"

"Not for a second, but I had to at least give you a chance to come to your senses," Lily said. The older woman grinned, and Alex understood why Scott Renard was so smitten with her. "Alex, if we're going to walk away from this, we'll need a pretty great plan."

"How about a thrown-together-in-the-last-thirty-seconds plan?" Alex said.

"What are you thinking?" Lily asked.

Alex told Lily, and to Alex's surprise, her friend didn't have anything better, so they moved quickly.

Crouching down, Alex slid under the train car and settled in behind the cover of the rear wheels. She took a second to check the weapon she'd taken from the guard. Not surprisingly, it was a Russian Makarov, depressingly standard issue. It held a factory eight-round magazine, and the guard hadn't even bothered to load an extra round in the chamber.

The least he could have done was get his hands on a ten-round mag, or better yet, use the Makarov variation that took the larger twelve-round cartridges.

The man also hadn't kept an extra eight-round magazine on him, which made Alex shake her head in disgust.

She stuck the weapon into her pocket and pulled out her Smith & Wesson Shield. She always used the fifteen-round magazine and kept an extra round in the chamber when she was on a mission. Plus, she had two extra magazines in her pockets.

Alex agreed with her father on this point: too much ammunition was not enough. She never wanted to embarrass Zeta, her family, and her ancestors by running out of ammunition in a firefight.

And today, with luck and reasonably good aim, she'd run out of bad guys before she ran out of bullets.

From experience, she knew that Lily and her Walther pistol were similarly prepared. Right then, Lily was under the next train car, taking her cover behind the car's large front wheels. That position put the women thirty-some yards apart. That was perfect for Alex's plan.

Though she knew *plan* was a kind word for what the women were going to try to do. After the first stage began, it would all be improvisation.

Alex picked her first two targets from the men in front of her. She was tempted to take aim at one of the first batch of guards, the Albanians, since they weren't wearing any body armor. However, she judged that they were far less of a threat than the new Russian batch who wore ballistic vests and carried AK-47s.

Alex pointed her gun at the first target, aiming for his pelvis and upper thighs—the largest critical area of his body not protected by his armor. She would have preferred a headshot, but even though Alex and Lily were among the top marksmen at Zeta, at fifty to seventy yards, that was far from certain.

Lily let out a whistle, letting Alex know she was ready. Then Alex counted down from three and fired her first round. As soon as she pulled the trigger, she took aim at her second target and fired.

Both bullets were direct hits, and because she'd fired from under the train car, that area acted as a resonating chamber, flattening the sound and making it louder.

On open ground, it was difficult to tell the direction of gunfire directed at you from less than three hundred yards away, and very difficult at ranges of less than one hundred yards.

The echo from the area under the train would make it even harder. On the other hand, it made her ears ring something fierce.

As Alex backed out from under the train, she saw the Russian guards bring up their AKs to a firing position.

However, though they scanned the area in front of them, they had no idea where the shots had come from.

There was a flurry of other movement, which Alex couldn't quite make out, and then Alex was out from under the train. She backed up to make sure her legs would be out of the sight line of the gunmen and then ran to the front wheels of the car.

As she crawled back underneath the train, she saw the Russians— weapons ready—backing toward the nearest cover, which were the vans that were closest to the waterline.

Perfect, Alex thought as she took position. Alex took aim at the nearest van, putting a quick two rounds into the vehicles at driver height.

Then she took aim at the retreating group and emptied her magazine, picking a target and quickly moving to the next one as Lily did the same. She put her last two rounds into another one of the vans and then waited.

Lily and Alex's first volley had the intended effect. Though it put the remaining men on alert, they also moved closer to one another as they headed for cover.

When they heard Alex and Lily's first shots hit the vans, they stopped moving, making themselves excellent targets. Alex watched men go down, falling to her and Lily's fire, one after the other.

When the shooting was over, there were six men left standing, several lying still on the ground, and several more moaning in pain where they lay.

Two of the van doors opened, but Alex didn't track that motion carefully. Instead, she was focused on the remaining standing men, all of whom appeared to be the Russian guards. As Alex put another magazine into her gun, she watched the men spread out, keeping their rifles in firing position and pointed in the direction of the train.

Just as Alex locked in her mag, the men opened fire. Six AK-47s firing at full auto would have been impressive if they hadn't been pointed in Alex's direction. The men were well trained; they staggered their fire so that although each weapon could only fire for one minute or so at full auto, they wouldn't run out all at once and could reload their extended ninety-round magazines while still keeping up a steady rate of fire.

Though the Russians couldn't tell where Alex and Lily's shots had come from, they compensated by strafing underneath and above the train cars.

In the five minutes of sustained fire, Alex heard round after round strike the steel wheels protecting her, as well as the roof of the train.

The gunmen seemed to take care not to fire directly into the side of the car. Protecting their cargo, no doubt.

When the hail of bullets stopped, Alex chanced a look and saw that while the men were firing, they were also backing up toward the vans.

That made Alex's job easy, she realized.

"Lily, you there?" she called out.

"Yes, I'm okay. You?"

"I am, target the gas tanks," Alex said. Before she finished, she started emptying the rest of her magazine into the rough location of one of the van's gas tank.

Five rounds later, the van blew up in an impressive display. As it went up, one of the two nearest gunmen made an attempt to aim his weapon and fire toward the train, but he was swallowed up by the explosion—as was the man next to him.

Alex watched another man who was close by blasted to the ground as a second van went up, presumably because of Lily's fire. That took out another two men, and then a single shot from Lily's weapon brought an additional man down.

It was quiet for a second and then one of the remaining two vans started lurching forward, one of them with a flat front tire.

Alex put the last four rounds in her magazine into the driver's compartment. The van kept moving for several feet but turned into a cargo container and came to a stop.

"Still in one piece, Alex?" Lily called out.

Alex was both pleased and surprised that she was. "Yes, you?"

"I am, but let's keep an eye out for movement," Lily said, her voice getting closer.

Alex backed out and met Lily at the point where the two train cars connected.

"Not a scratch on either of us," Lily said. "That Morgan luck must have rubbed off on me."

"Let's hope the luck holds out. We have to get these women as far from this spot as we can and hope the TACH team is out there somewhere ready to extract us."

The instant the words were out of Alex's mouth, she heard the sound of an engine, one that she didn't immediately recognize.

Then she saw why. It was two Russian Tigrs—the equivalent of an American Hummer. They were painted in camo, which told Alex that they weren't Zeta.

Each also had a manned gun turret on the roof. A .30 caliber, Alex guessed. Better than a .50 cal from her and Lily's point of view, but not by much.

Alex saw that she was out of ammunition for her Smith & Wesson. All she had left was the Makarov and its eight rounds. She looked up and saw that Lily was in the same position.

Clicking back the weapon's safety, she said, "See, that is just not fair."

Chapter 9

"Any thoughts?" Alex said to Lily.

"Looks like it might rain later," Lily replied.

For a moment, Alex didn't know what to say and then she just looked up. It was getting cloudy, and the sky was turning gray.

"Maybe humidity is their weakness," Alex said.

"Let's hope so," Lily said. "Honestly, Alex. I don't think we have much choice now. We can split up and hope that one of us makes it out of the yard to make a report."

That was it, Alex realized. No more bravado. They weren't walking out of here, certainly not both of them. Even one of them escaping was a long shot. And the women in the train car were going to be lost either way.

"We made them pay, Alex," Lily said.

Alex checked her Makarov as Lily did the same. "I'm not done making them pay," Alex said. Lily nodded. It was decided.

Alex knew they shouldn't wait much longer to get moving. The closer the vehicles came, the easier targets Alex and Lily would be. Of course, with a .30 cal on full auto, you didn't need to be a great, or even a good, shot to hit your target.

The biggest challenge the shooters would have was coping with the noise. Though a .30 cal wouldn't turn a person into a pink mist like a .50 cal, people hit by a .30 cal above the shoulders would not qualify for an open casket.

"Alex, I don't suppose you can call up one last bit of that luck?" Lily said.

"I'm working on it," Alex said, but before the words were out of her mouth, Alex heard the sound of scraping metal.

Turning her head, she saw a truck of some kind barrel through the gates leading into the port. The tall chain-link fence practically exploded inward.

"You're kidding me," Lily said.

"You asked," Alex replied.

"What is that?" Lily said.

Alex realized it wasn't a truck but a bus of some kind. And not just one. There were three more behind it. A convoy of buses. No, not quite buses, at least not passenger buses.

They were fairly large airport shuttles, the kind that ferried travelers and luggage.

The first two shuttles raced toward the Russian Tigrs. After covering about half the distance to the enemy vehicles, the lead two buses turned sharply toward one another, skidding so they were now perpendicular to the oncoming Tigrs, forming a line between the Russians and the two other shuttles, which came to a stop about fifty yards behind the first two. The Tigrs stopped, not knowing what to make of the sudden appearance of civilian vehicles in the middle of their firefight.

The side doors of the first two shuttles opened, and two figures dressed in dark, Zeta-issued body armor ran out to join the other shuttles.

The Russians were clearly surprised, but they recovered quickly. Tentatively, they inched closer to the buses in their vehicles. There was a flurry of movement from the Zeta side as three people climbed out of the remaining shuttles with rifles and equipment. Figures went in and out of the shuttle, ferrying equipment, and in less than a minute the eight-person Zeta TACH team had split into four pairs that were crouched behind portable armored stations that were about four foot in height and always reminded Alex of the walls of the plastic playhouse castle she had had as a girl.

A single figure stood up from behind one of the stations and shouted into a bullhorn.

"Comrades!" the voice said, and Alex recognized Valery Dobrynin's voice. "Comrades! You have new orders!"

The two Tigrs stopped their slow advance.

"And these come from the highest authorities," Dobrynin said.

Alex watched as he put down the bullhorn and picked up a weapon. It looked like a cartoon version of an old-style tommy gun. It had a large barrel and an oversized disc-shaped cylinder.

It was a Russian grenade launcher of some kind, one that Peter Conley talked about fondly.

"Who are you?" a voice replied in Russian from one of the Tigrs.

"It doesn't matter who I am. It's the orders that are important," Dobrynin said. "Now listen carefully: *Idi na hui.*"

Alex knew that expressions, particularly insults, didn't always translate well, but this one was particularly perplexing. How could you go to a body part? Particularly that one?

Dobrynin aimed his grenade launcher over the buses that formed their defensive line and fired. There was a flare as the first grenade leapt out of the weapon and barely cleared the top of the now empty buses that sat between Zeta and the Tigrs. Three more grenades followed, and as the last one left the launcher, the first was exploding in front of one of the Tigrs.

Of the four, only one made direct contact with one of the Russian vehicles, exploding as it hit a Tigr on the side.

Unfortunately, the enemy's vehicles were armored, and even if the Tigr wouldn't drive any longer, the machine gun looked intact.

As if to prove the point, a figure popped up from inside the vehicle and manned the .30 cal just as another figure did the same in the other Tigr.

Alex heard multiple pops on the Zeta side as the explosive bolts that would secure the ballistic cover to the asphalt were engaged.

As the .30 cals came alive, the Zeta team hunkered down behind their cover. Though Alex knew the machine gun would be devastating to a person, it was nearly as devastating to the buses now standing between Zeta and the attackers.

Hundreds of rounds tore through the buses and the luggage inside, turning the vehicles' upper halves into confetti.

The barrage lasted for maybe a minute and then Alex heard a shout from the Zeta side. Now it was the TACH team's turn to return fire. There were suddenly six assault rifles on full automatic, firing through the smoking ruins of the airport shuttles.

Dobrynin and one other figure with a grenade launcher stood up and let fly. Each weapon fired six of the impressive explosive rounds and then all at once the fire stopped.

The explosions were, again, impressive, and then for two full minutes there was silence, which was only broken by the crackling of the fire that was consuming one of the Tigrs. The other vehicle wasn't burning, but that was because there wasn't much left of it to burn.

It was over, Alex realized. The last of the Russians were neutralized and it looked like there were no casualties on the Zeta side.

"Lily? Alex? Are you here?" a voice called out. It was Spartan.

"We're here," Lily replied.

She and Alex stepped out from the train and headed to meet the TACH team.

"Interesting transportation," Alex said as they approached Spartan and Dobrynin, who were each still holding their grenade launchers.

"There was a delay with getting our vehicles out of customs, so the Mad Russian here borrowed some alternatives," Spartan said.

Dobrynin shrugged. "We were already running late, which is something I cannot stand," the Russian said.

He was joking, of course, but she knew Dobrynin actually hated to be late, or to wait on others who were. It was something he and Dan Morgan shared.

"We were grateful for your timely arrival," Lily said. "And for the assist with our hosts."

Spartan smiled, a rare and impressive event. "Glad to help."

"Do we have a plan to get out of here? Your borrowed buses aren't very durable," Lily said.

Spartan checked her watch. "As a matter of fact, our rides should be along shortly." Looking up, she turned her head to the gate and the road beyond.

Alex could see a caravan of Zeta vehicles, SUVs and three black personnel transports the size of church buses.

"Do we have somewhere safe to bring the women in there," Alex said, pointing to the train car.

"There's a local facility where they will receive care. After that, Director Bloch will see that they have options," Spartan said.

"We'll help you lead them onto the buses. We'll need to move quickly. Eventually, the authorities will wonder what happened here."

"Yes, but you can't be part of that. The director wants you in the Caribbean immediately," Spartan said. "One of the cars has a change of clothes and a passport. The driver will take you to the airport."

Alex understood, but she had wanted to see this through. She especially wanted to see the women safely somewhere else . . . anywhere else.

After saying her goodbyes to Lily, Alex stopped Dobrynin and said, "Thank you, Valery."

He smiled.

Alex was the only person at Zeta who ever used his first name. In fact, until today, everyone at Zeta either called him by his last name or Mr. Dobrynin. That had changed when Spartan called him the Mad Russian, which Alex suspected pleased the man. She also suspected it would stick.

"My pleasure, Alex. These *svolotchi* were a cancer. If I failed you, I would have to answer to your father, and your mother," he said.

"So we both avoided terrible consequences today. I'll see you soon," Alex said and headed for the car that was waiting for her.

* * * *

Bloch watched much of the final confrontation in Albania on the large monitor in the War Room courtesy of Zeta drones brought by Dobrynin and Spartan and body cams worn by the TACH team.

Actually, though very destructive to the docks and to the enemy, the whole operation had gone well and without a single Zeta casualty. Spartan had made a point of reporting that much of that success had been due to Mr. Dobrynin's last-minute actions to secure transportation.

Bloch's phone beeped and she saw that Alex Morgan had boarded her plane and would be in the Caribbean by that evening.

After the near disaster of today's operation, Bloch was glad that something else was going right. She'd feel better when Alex was in place, looking into that other situation.

For once, they might be on track to stop something before it became a regional or global threat. And keeping a Saudi prince from obtaining nuclear material fit neatly into the category of prevention.

Bloch decided that today's success was a sign Zeta was turning back the tide on Ares operations and related threats. Zeta had dealt out some serious setbacks to Ares; now was the time to dish out a few more.

While Shepard was closing down the feeds, Karen O'Neal entered the room and said, "Excuse me, Director."

It was often hard to read the expression on the young woman's face, but that wasn't a problem now. "What's wrong?" she asked.

"We've gotten quite a few hits from our threat-assessment system, and a number of them have a high degree of correlation to Scott Renard's public schedule."

That was a surprise, and Bloch saw that it piqued Shepard's interest as well.

"Five threat alerts that roughly correspond to times and places he is set to visit in the next month," the young woman said.

That wasn't exactly a surprise. Renard had been the target of an assassination attempt that had almost taken out Lily Randall and Alex Morgan when one of his jets had blown up in its hangar.

Security protocols set up by Zeta and Renard Tech security (which had been chosen by Lily Randall herself) had saved Renard and Zeta's two agents.

Ares might have been the culprit, in addition to half a dozen bad actors around the world from China for economic reasons to more than one petty tyrant who didn't like Renard and his company's tech tools undermining their brand of oppression.

The good news here was that Zeta was getting advanced warning and would be able to take additional steps to make sure that Renard was safe. But five potential attempts on Renard's life was still bad news. Zeta and Renard's people had to maintain a 100 percent success rate at keeping him safe.

The bad guys only had to get lucky once.

If Renard were taken out, it would be a massive blow to Zeta as an organization and an even bigger blow to Lily Randall and a number of others for whom Scott Renard was important on a personal level.

Bloch decided that it wasn't enough to simply stop the endless cycle of attacks. Zeta needed to do more of what they had achieved in Montenegro; Zeta needed to crush the organization and eliminate their ability to do their work in the future.

With that thought, Bloch realized that Shepard and O'Neal were looking at her, waiting for instructions.

"Please relay the threat assessments to Renard security, and let Lily Randall know as well. I'm sure she will want to be personally involved in security preparations. Make sure Renard knows that we will give him any help or resources he needs."

Bloch would be glad to do it. She'd lost count of the times when Renard had given Zeta what *they* needed, exactly when they needed it. She made a mental note to call Renard herself later and realized that she was one of the people for whom the loss of Scott Renard would be a personal blow.

However, before she did anything else, Bloch had one task, this one of a very personal nature. She called her contact at Naval Intelligence.

"Hello, Diana," a voice said on the other side. "I'm afraid we still don't know anything."

"No contact at all with the base?" Bloch said.

"No, but given the extreme weather, that is not a surprise. Equipment failure is routine in this scenario," he said.

"Is there anything you can do?" she asked.

"We're already offering assistance for all search and rescue operations in the region of Antarctica affected by the storms. Because of the sensitive and classified nature of your nephew's work, we can't show any more interest in his situation."

"I understand," she said, and she did. That was the nature of intelligence work. You did what you did in secret, often without the open support of the organization you worked for.

And those organizations had to worry about international relations and the complex political and economic ties between nations—as well as interagency politics.

Zeta's operations were immune from most of those concerns. In that respect, the organization operated more like a family, which was why people like Dan Morgan, who had permanently cut ties to the CIA, were content to work with Zeta. He even had trusted his daughter to the organization.

And Jeffrey was Bloch's family. She'd been Bloch's responsibility since her sister's death more than two decades before. Bloch was determined that she would not fail him now, even though she had exhausted her options in her own government.

There were still a few more contacts she could try. Otherwise, all she could do was wait and hope.

Part 2

Coincidence

"A good plan violently executed now is better than a perfect plan next week."
—General George S. Patton

Chapter 10

Though they drove his longtime partner, Dan Morgan, crazy, Peter Conley liked shopping malls. He liked the energy and the bustle of them. Plus, he had quite a few fond teenage memories (many of which involved girls) from his hours spent in malls.

Now, there was only one woman that interested him, and she absolutely loved shopping malls. Growing up in China, Danhong Guo had little experience with them. Malls existed in China, though they were relatively rare and only for the very wealthy.

Her family was not in that group, even before the Chinese government took her parents away and ultimately murdered them. After that, Dani was focused on school and her career in the Chinese government, which had consumed her time until she had been able to defect to the US with Conley's help.

Conley took her through the main entrance of the mall and her eyes brightened when she saw where they were. The mall was five stories of colorful and brightly lit unadulterated consumerism surrounding an open center. Looking up, there was a large, vaulted glass ceiling. And below, there was an ice-skating rink, making it—as far as Conley knew—the only mall like it in the country.

Though somewhat upscale, the Galleria was definitely a suburban mall, and he knew that was part of the appeal for Dani. She loved the idea that regular people—not wealthy friends of the party—could shop in a place like this.

"It's amazing," Dani said.

"Maybe when the work is done, we can explore. Do you ice-skate?" Conley asked.

"Very much. My parents loved Follow the Dragon Tail and Shoot."

"What is that?" he asked.

"It's a combination of ice-skating and archery," she said.

Like a lot of the cultural quirks Dani told him about China, that sounded very cool to Conley.

"Then it's a date. We'll have to see if the sporting goods store has archery supplies. But first," Conley said, pointing to the escalator.

Their objective was on the top level. Since they had entered on the second floor, that meant going up three levels on a very open escalator.

Normally, Conley would have hated the trip because it left him and Dani vulnerable. However, the open and very public nature of the escalator gave both of them a good view of everyone around them.

Dani, he knew, could more than handle herself, and he felt the comforting weight of the Glock in the shoulder holster under his sport jacket.

There was nothing unusual and no one out of place on the third and fourth levels, at least near the escalator. Though outwardly he appeared relaxed, Conley was on high alert. Dani was as well, though to anyone else she would seem like a wide-eyed tourist.

When they stepped onto the fifth level, Conley still saw nothing unusual.

"Looks clear to me," Conley said.

"Me too," Dani replied.

Conley hoped this would be a simple retrieval. Certainly, the stupid kid they were going to see was not a threat, but Conley would not let his guard down until the package was secured off-site.

They kept their speed to a shopper's stroll, both of them making stops to look inside the windows of the stores they passed—and to scrutinize their surroundings.

When they reached the Game Station store, Conley was pleased to see that it wasn't busy. That was not exactly an accident. He and Dani had chosen this time because it was before lunch and most of the store's clientele were in school.

The twenty-year-old behind the counter was helping the only customer in the store, a harried-seeming woman who also seemed to be in a rush.

The clerk didn't look good. He was nervous, as if he was anxious for her to leave as well. That made sense to Conley, given what this kid had gotten himself involved in.

As soon as the woman left with her purchase, Conley stepped up to the counter. He saw the name GREG on the young man's tag, but Conley already knew his name. The tag also said ASSISTANT MANAGER.

Before Conley could speak, Greg said, "I'm sorry but we have to close for about an hour."

Conley saw that the kid was sweating. He wondered if he should have let Dani make the initial contact.

"You can close after we're done talking," Conley said.

Greg's eyes went wide and he said, "I don't have to talk to you."

"As a matter of fact, you do," Conley said. He pulled out a small leather wallet and opened it for Greg to see.

"National Security Agency," Conley said. He had found that it was better than claiming FBI. Few people knew much about what the NSA did, let alone what their IDs looked like. Conley had Shepard make up an ID and a gold badge.

"I want a lawyer. I don't have to talk to you," Greg said.

"This isn't that kind of visit," Conley replied. "I don't care what you have to say. We're just here for the device."

"I don't know what you're talking about," Greg said.

"I'm talking about the in-flight computer for fully autonomous drones. You know, the prototype with all of the hardwired ports which will make it very easy for bad guys to reverse-engineer the technology."

Greg was doing his best to keep his face blank, though he was now sweating profusely.

"To refresh your memory further," Conley said, "it's also the device that your idiot brother smuggled out of Dallas Aerospace last week," Conley said.

"I can't . . ." Greg said, his voice sounding desperate.

"You can and you will. I'm just here for the computer. You give it to me and my partner, and we leave. You may hear from the FBI, you may not; I don't know, and I don't care. But technically, you and your brother have committed treason and the people you are doing business with are not competitors to Dallas Aerospace, they are international bad guys. Because of that, whatever happens, I can't let you complete your transaction."

Greg seemed stricken, and Conley realized that he wasn't just scared now, he was terrified.

He was also twitching and looking around in a way that didn't quite make sense. It was almost as if he was trying to look over his shoulder. . . .

"Peter!" Dani called out and he could see with his peripheral vision that she had already drawn her weapon. She pointed it behind Greg toward the door to what Conley assumed was a back room.

They're here, Conley realized as he reached for his Glock. Even as he did it, he knew he was going to be too slow. The door was opening already. His only hope was that Dani would fire before the door was fully open. She did.

The first man through the door fell as soon as it opened. The second man took aim in Conley's direction. As Conley lifted his gun, he knew it was going to be a race . . . a race that Conley knew he would lose.

He heard the shot and knew the man was too close to miss. However, Greg was standing between them, and though the gunman was aiming right at Conley, Greg was in the way and took the bullet in the back.

Conley fired but knew he didn't have a shot lined up. However, he hoped it would buy him a second to take proper aim.

By now, Greg realized that he'd been hit and started to fall. Conley suspected that the kid would not be getting up again.

Conley's second shot hit the man center mass, knocking him backward. However, another man pushed past the falling man and sprayed the shop with bullets. Conley and Dani had no choice but to dive out of the way.

As the man scrambled over the counter, Conley saw that he was carrying a medium-sized duffel bag, which Conley assumed had the computer inside.

Conley had a second to line up this shot, and before the man could get out of the store, Conley fired.

Direct hit on the man's left shoulder but, remarkably, he didn't go down.

The gunman almost reached the threshold to the mall's hallway when Conley called out, "Body armor." As the words left his lips, the top of the man's head exploded and Conley knew that Dani had drawn the same conclusion.

As the man hit the ground, Conley got to his feet and Dani did the same. Then, from behind, he felt someone hurl himself between them.

Conley staggered but managed to keep his feet, and he saw Dani go down. From behind, Conley could see it was the first man who had come through the door, the one Conley had hit in the chest. But he'd been wearing body armor as well.

The man flew out the door at a dead run and Conley fired. He would have liked to take time setting up a head shot, but he just aimed from the ground, once again going for center mass, and hoped for the best.

The bullet hit, tossing the man forward, as a shot from Dani did the same. The result was surprising. The man had been running at full tilt when the bullets slammed him forward, right toward the railing that separated the hallway from the large open space in the center of the mall . . . and a five-story drop.

At the last second, the man had the sense to drop the duffel bag and reach for the railing. It was much too little and far too late. His fingers barely brushed the railing before he went sailing over it and disappeared from view.

A quick scan told Conley that Dani was okay, and he holstered his weapon and calmly walked outside, where shocked shoppers were looking down at the ice-skating rink.

Casually, Conley picked up the duffel and glanced down. He could see the man had landed on the ice. Conley was relieved to see that he hadn't landed on one of the skaters.

That was something.

Turning back inside, Conley saw Dani come up from behind the counter and Greg's body. She shook her head. Conley felt a rush of regret for the idiot kid who had somehow gotten involved with Iranian arms traffickers.

He saw that Dani seemed a little pale and he felt a flash of panic.

"You okay? Were you hit?" he asked, struggling to keep his voice calm.

"Fine, I'm fine," she said as he scanned her to make sure there were no visible injuries.

"My stomach. I think maybe our breakfast burritos," she said with a slight grimace.

Conley grinned. Dani had really embraced Mexican and southwestern food, as well as a number of other cuisines.

When they had talked about it, she said, "Before I came here, it was Chinese food every day."

"Come on," Conley said. He led her to one of the department stores as a crowd started to form around the video game shop. Disappearing into the larger store, he and Dani took the interior escalator down to the second floor and headed for the exit.

Once outside, he and Dani had to do some walking to get to their car, hearing sirens the entire way. He was very glad they had avoided parking in the multilevel lot. It was difficult to get out of those in a hurry, and it might be impossible soon if the police closed off the lot.

In fact, the local authorities might well be locking down the mall now since they would not know if there was still an active shooter inside.

Conley and Dani reached their SUV. Because he had parked near the edge of the parking lot, it was easy to pull out, and in less than a minute they were on 635 West and heading to the airport. Originally, they would have simply handed off the device to a Zeta contact who would handle it from there.

Now, however, after the incident at the mall, things had gotten a bit more complicated. They were no doubt on multiple security cameras and their images would soon be making the rounds to local Dallas and Texas state police.

Dani was on the phone with Bloch as Conley drove. From what he could gather from Dani's side of the conversation, they wouldn't be handing off the device, they would be getting on board the Renard Tech jet that was waiting for the prototype.

When Dani hung up the phone, he said, "We're being followed."

Chapter 11

Lily Randall checked her watch again.

Scott was late.

That almost never happened when it came to business meetings, and it *absolutely* never happened when it came to plans with her. At least it had never happened until now.

She might not have worried at all if not for the first serious attempt on Scott's life a few months ago, when someone tried to get to Scott by blowing up the corporate jet he was supposed to be flying on.

At that time, the security protocols that saved his life had been put into place by Lily herself. As safety measures, last-minute changes in travel plans were simple, time-honored and—thankfully in this case—successful.

There had been two attempts since and both had been foiled before he came under any serious risk. However, Lily had the growing sense that the party after him wasn't just one of the oppressive regimes he had pissed off—and there was no shortage of those—but Ares.

There was no question that Ares was nearly a match for Zeta. The problem was that even if Zeta managed to best that shadowy organization most of the time, Ares only had to succeed once to eliminate Scott Renard, whose company, Renard Tech, had been an essential ally to Zeta and other friendly intelligence organizations. Zeta and those groups would take some time to recover from his loss.

For herself, Lily Randall knew she would never recover from it.

Adding to her concerns was her knowledge that Scott was up to something. He'd arranged to meet her in Paris after she had finished her last mission. He had also checked them into "their" hotel. The Hotel Marignan Champs-Elysees was where they had taken their relationship from security consultant and subject to whatever it was that they were now.

His excitement had come through very clearly on their phone call yesterday. He'd had a lot to be excited about; while she was on her last mission, he had successfully mined an asteroid. At least, the remote probe that Renard Aerospace had sent to the asteroid belt had returned with a small batch of ore taken from the asteroid.

For the last month they had been together, Scott had been like a boy waiting for Christmas. From a technological point of view, Lily knew that it was a major achievement. And Scott maintained that once Renard Tech was able to scale up the process, it would literally change the world, driving technology in all areas but particularly in clean energy, which depended on minerals that were difficult to mine on Earth, at least cleanly.

Recently, he had been exploring deep-sea mining, though he maintained that it was only a stopgap until his asteroid mining system was fully up and running. However, realistically, that would take years.

Lily was sad that she hadn't been there when the rocket returned with its booty but she was prepared to make it up to him. In fact, she looked forward to making it up to him. And she definitely appreciated that his boyish enthusiasm for his work always turned into enthusiasm for her.

And the fact was that she needed him. She needed to be with him because she loved him and because she needed to wash off the stink of the last mission in Albania and Montenegro.

In her work, she often saw things that stayed with her longer than she would have liked. Since her days at MI6, she had understood that that was the price she paid to do the work she did.

When she left British Intelligence, she had begun to think that the sum total of the prices she had paid and the things she had seen chipped away at her soul. More than once she had wondered how much could be lost before there was nothing left, at least nothing worthwhile.

It was at that moment that she had met Scott. Though she had fought it for weeks, there was no denying the force that drove them together. It was with him that she had learned that those lost pieces of herself could be found again in another person—or at least in Scott.

Though she and he had never discussed it, she liked to think that he had given her back most of herself. And because they were never apart for long, the process constantly renewed itself.

After waiting twenty minutes in their suite, Lily was about to call his cell phone when he came through the door.

As he approached and embraced her, Lily could see that two things were off about him. One, his expression wasn't its usual happy-to-see-her face. And two, he was wearing a suit, not his trademark black jeans and hoodie with a T-shirt, and not even the slacks and collared shirt he wore on their "date" nights.

He was wearing the charcoal suit she had had made for him in London, along with a black dress shirt and a dark tie. As she often did, she thought he was absurdly handsome. Secretly, she was glad he didn't dress like this often and kept it limited to their occasional special nights. It was like he reserved that part of himself for her.

After she kissed him deeply, she pulled back and said, "What's wrong?"

For a brief instant, Scott looked like he'd been caught at something. Then he shrugged and said, "There's some trouble at the new launch facility."

Studying his face, she replied, "I'm sorry to hear that, but congratulations on Project Stardust."

He grinned and said, "Thank you. *That* was pretty satisfying." Then, for an instant, his face lit up, only to be covered up again by the cloud that was hovering over him when he entered the suite.

"Did you bring me any of your stardust?" Lily said.

Scott winced and said, "Sorry. I did have something to show you but I got caught up in this new problem . . ."

Lily waved it away and said, "I'm just glad to see you. Are we going out?" Certainly, he was dressed for it. And she had dressed for the evening as well, just in case.

"Actually, I had planned on staying in," he said.

He hit a button on his phone and went to the bar. "Champagne?" he asked, and she nodded. As he was pouring, the suite doors opened and a parade of hotel staff invaded, pushing carts and carrying trays.

In less than five minutes, there was a beautiful meal laid out and lit by candlelight.

As quickly as they had come, the staff disappeared.

"If it's okay with you," Scott said, "I thought we would stay in."

His grin was back and she found that hers was as well. They ate and talked. He told her about the return of the Stardust rocket, and she told him about her mission with Alex Morgan in Eastern Europe. At least, she told him a version of the mission that she thought he could live with.

She didn't hide things from Scott. Not exactly. But she didn't want him to be exposed to all of the darkness she had seen. Though a massively successful CEO in the cutthroat world of tech, Scott was, if not quite innocent, spared the look into the dark corners of the world that she had seen. She was protecting him, but only partly. She was also keeping him out of those dark corners so he could continue to shine his own light on her. In her version of the story, they had saved dozens of women and taken out the bad guys. Her story was true, but it left out the hopelessness she had seen on the women's faces and the fact that though she and Alex had saved dozens, they had failed the hundreds if not thousands that had come before those women.

After dinner, Lily was pleased that whatever was bothering him, Scott's enthusiasm for her was not diminished, and she answered it with plenty of enthusiasm of her own.

However, in the morning, he had begged off from their planned day together, citing that problem at the new launch facility. They would have to get together later in the week when his problem was sorted out and she was finished with her meetings at MI6.

She'd kissed him when he left and knew with dead certainty that he was lying to her, or at least hiding something.

Lily had zero doubts about his feelings for her, but she couldn't shake the feeling that something was off.

Short of spying on him directly—which was a line she would not cross—there wasn't much she could do.

She did check the Zeta alert system to see if there had been any threats or even mentions of Scott, but there were only the ones she already knew about. Then she checked the Renard Tech security system to check for anything out of the ordinary, anything that would explain the change in Scott.

She gave up for the day. Lily would keep an eye on Scott and give him a chance to come talk to her on his own. If that didn't work, she would simply ask him.

After a room service breakfast, she dressed for her MI6 meeting. She left an English-language news channel on as she got ready. She was almost done when she heard a name on the news report that stopped her cold: General Shin Kwan Hyo.

That simple combination of sounds took her back years, to an empty Buddhist temple in the Dalian Jinlong Mountains of China.

Instantly, she could feel the profound cold of the floor of that temple, as if she had stepped across time and space to travel back there. But cold was not the worst thing she had felt in that temple; the worst things were caused by then Colonel Hyo, who had been in charge of her *interrogation*. She'd somehow managed to escape the temple to nearly die in the freezing mountain forest around it. She'd only been saved by a massive effort from Zeta, its allies, and Scott.

When her body had healed from that experience, she put it in a box and locked it away in her mind. Some things were better left alone. And there were pieces of herself that even Scott could not give her back.

Lily could talk about the experience superficially but she quickly learned not to discuss it around Scott. He wasn't able to lock away any of his feelings, and his hatred for Hyo was particularly strong.

For a time, Lily had assumed Hyo was dead. After all, his effort to acquire American cruise missiles had failed and he was disavowed by the North Korean government. He'd disappeared, and Lily assumed he had been swallowed by the North's gulag system and died there.

Then, two years later, a "rehabilitated" Hyo was back and had retaken his position in the North Korean military. Now, according to the news report, he had just been promoted to general and was overseeing joint maneuvers with the Chinese military. After that, he would attend a series of meetings in South Korea.

Lily felt surprisingly little at the news, and even less when she saw his image. Let him play soldier in the hellhole he'd helped nurture.

Suddenly, Lily understood Scott's behavior. He must have seen the report sometime in the twenty-four hours between the time they talked on the phone to set up their time in Paris and his appearance in the suite.

Scott's feelings about what had happened to her and about Hyo were not likely to have changed. He wore his emotions on his sleeve and had very little ability—or need—to compartmentalize experiences the way Lily did.

For the first time since Scott had turned up late, Lily felt a little better. Helping him work through a black mood was preferable to helping him fight off another dedicated assassination attempt.

For now, Lily decided that would have to pass as a victory.

* * * *

Conley tracked the white van, which stayed a few car lengths behind him. Dani had drawn her weapon and put in a fresh magazine.

He put on a little speed, just to keep his pursuers on edge. Conley cursed the fact that he was driving a rental. This was a run-of-the-mill, family-friendly blue SUV, not one of the armored miracles that came out of Shepard's shop. Between Shepard and Morgan, the Zeta motor pool had become a cutting-edge testing ground for armor, bulletproof glass, and additional "tactical" features.

This vehicle had none of those. And the radio presets were all for country music, which, ironically, Dani really enjoyed. On the plus side, the SUV came with the optional "family fun package." He wasn't sure what that was but there were television screens on the back of each headrest.

The bottom line was that there was very little between himself and Dani and the Iranian agents in that van.

Correction, in those *two* vans.

An identical white van had entered 635 on the last entryway. One van was something he and Dani could handle. If he kept the van on his right, the only person that could shoot at them was the driver, who Conley could keep busy.

However, two vans could keep Conley occupied, and if one of them got on his left, they would be free to shoot him, or shoot out their tires, which would amount to the same thing.

Conley had to admit that he worried about Dani in a way that he had never worried about Dan Morgan. In her own way, she was just as capable as Conley or Morgan. And he would have died for Dan without thinking twice.

And yet his feelings for Dani made things more complicated.

Conventional wisdom said that was a weakness, but Conley knew it just made him more determined.

He didn't have a lot of advantages in this confrontation, but he did have one. He knew these roads better than foreign agents ever would.

The fact was that the Dallas metro area was relatively new. The city and the state had grown at an astonishing rate, and because of that, it had the benefit of new technology in everything, including roadways.

Morgan had pointed out to him that Dallas had something on its highways that almost no other state in the union did.

Most cities, like New York and Boston, used a complicated daisy wheel system to change direction on a highway. You would exit the highway, follow a long circular arc, cross the road, and then follow another arc to drive in the opposite direction.

New Jersey used a similar system—as well as something called "jug handles" on local roads that drove Morgan crazy.

But Dallas had the best system that Conley had ever seen. From the service roads, you could access a simple 180-degree curve at overpasses that would allow you to change direction quickly and easily. It was called a Texas Turnaround and it was just what Conley needed.

Conley got onto the service road and put on a bit more speed when he saw an overpass up ahead. The turnaround was coming and Conley gave the SUV even more speed.

Checking his mirrors, he made sure the Iranians were matching him as he approached the entryway for the turnaround.

"Hold on," he said to Dani.

At the very last second, he cut the wheel hard to the left and entered the turn. He wasn't surprised when the closest van matched his move.

In fact, he was counting on that.

Once Conley had completed the turn and was in the straightaway leading back to the highway going east, he slammed on the brakes, stopping as hard as the antilock brakes would allow him.

It wasn't as sudden a stop as he would have liked but it was too quick for the van behind him, which braked just a little too late and hit Conley and Dani's SUV at a good enough clip to shake them and toss their vehicle forward.

There would be some damage, and Conley would likely lose his deposit on the vehicle. However, the SUV was still drivable.

The same couldn't be said of the van. Any head-on collision with a relative speed of over ten miles an hour engaged the airbags of the rear car, which would take the driver out of the fight for now. Plus, as Conley drove away, he saw steam rising out of the van's front end, which told Conley that the radiator was shot.

One down, Conley thought.

Before that thought was complete, Conley saw the second van had also made the turn.

Conley had to end this soon. He took the next exit and was soon on the service road.

There was a grassy hill to his right and at the top of that was a local road. Confirming that the four-wheel drive was engaged, Conley cut the wheel to the right and started up the hill.

This was not as unusual as it would have been anywhere else. He had found that drivers in Texas had the least patience of anyone else in the country for traffic. Add to that a high percentage of four-wheel drive pickups and SUVs, and you had drivers frequently crossing medians and climbing hills to avoid delays.

Conley's SUV climbed the hill easily, even with the unsettling rattle emanating from its rear end. At the top of the hill, he backed up a bit to give Dani a line of fire.

He looked past her to see the van struggling up the hill as Dani opened her window, pointed her gun, and emptied her magazine into the front windshield.

It was over in seconds.

The van froze for a second and then started rolling back toward the road.

Conley didn't stay to see what happened.

He was already calculating his way back to 635 and the airport. He knew that the faster they got out of Dallas the better.

Just before they got back on the highway, Dani asked him to pull over.

Then, without explanation, she hopped out of the vehicle, disappeared behind it for a minute, and then climbed back inside.

"You okay?" he asked.

She looked embarrassed and said, "That burrito . . ."

Conley pulled them back onto the highway.

Chapter 12

Bloch was pleased that Conley and Guo had retrieved the drone computer. The last thing the world needed was Iranian drones with that kind of cutting-edge flight control system, let alone the AI that drove it. If nothing else, the computer's ability to extend a drone's range and accuracy would make the Iranian regime much more dangerous. Then there were the dozen subsystems that had applications in other tech.

Bloch was looking forward to getting it back into the hands of Dallas Aerospace, though not until after Shepard, O'Neal, and their team got a look under the hood.

She was also glad that Conley and Guo were now free. She needed them in the Indian Ocean. Zeta's threat-assessment had been screaming that something was going on out there.

Renard Tech was on-site and engaged in deep-sea mining, so they were able to host her agents.

Bloch knew there was a risk that she was throwing resources at problems that might amount to nothing. That had certainly been one of Ares's strategies in the past: make Zeta chase their tail and expend resources on threats that never materialized.

The problem was that there was no way to know in advance which threats were real and which were decoys.

Even this operation in Dallas was part of the problem. It should have been a simple retrieval operation where stolen, classified tech was taken back from a scared and unarmed party. Instead, it had turned into a shootout between two of her agents and a group of armed and trained Iranian intelligence officers.

She wasn't happy with the risk to her agents, but even though they had come through unscathed, there was still the very real problem of cleanup. Local and state police would have to be managed, as well as the Dallas FBI field office. She could handle all of that, but it would take half of her day and use up favors she might need later.

Then there was the time and energy it took from O'Neal and Shepard's team, who now had to scrub a number of private and law enforcement databases of video and images of Conley and Guo.

Tying up herself and her agents was only one of the problems caused by the drastic increase in terrorist and general bad-actor activity. Eventually, Zeta would miss something or make a mistake.

In addition to all of that, a couple of dozen people were badly traumatized by seeing a bleeding man fall five stories and hit the ice. However, no one other than that man had died. In the last two years, Zeta had stopped operations that would have taken many thousands of lives, in some cases millions.

If any of Ares's major operations had succeeded, the survivors would have seen and experienced a lot worse. So Bloch buckled down and did her job.

She started with the NSA. They would be hardest to manage and would be the most out of joint if they found out about the situation from the FBI field office.

As Bloch worked through her list, she had the nagging feeling that she was failing in her most important job. She was failing her nephew, who likely needed her, and she was failing her sister.

* * * *

Lily would have preferred to surprise Scott. However, given the security she had put into place around him these days, that was impossible. Nobody entered a facility that Scott was visiting without being screened, videotaped, and confirmed as someone who was not a threat.

Scott had bristled at first, saying, "If someone wants me bad enough, Lily, all the security in the world won't stop them."

"Of course not, Scott," she had replied. "But I want to make them jump through a few hoops first, just to make it sporting."

Scott had found that funnier than she had.

She knew he was right. US President John F. Kennedy had said, "If anyone is crazy enough to want to kill a president of the United States, he can do it. All he must be prepared to do is give his life for the president's." Kennedy, of course, had been tragically right. However, Lily had tools that they didn't have in Kennedy's time, and she was deeply motivated.

The spaceport was sprawling on an island at the northern tip of Scotland. There was a central office building that looked like a flying saucer, which—with Scott—was not an accident. Then there were two hangars and a handful of large outbuildings for equipment and research, including what Scott maintained would be the largest wind tunnel in the world.

There were also four runways, two of which were still under construction. However, for Scott, the most important place was the vertical launch tower. This was where the new Renard Tech rocket would be launched. It stood near the edge of a large rocky cliff that overlooked the sea.

This was the centerpiece of Scott's plans. It was where the new super-heavy rocket would test-fire its engines. Lily liked that there were ruins of medieval stone buildings within view of her boyfriend's latest technological marvel.

As Lily made the walk from the central hub to the launchpad, she took a second to take in the sight of the nearly five-hundred-foot rocket that was fully assembled on the pad, ready for its test.

She saw someone leaving the launchpad and coming to meet her. Long before she could make out the man's features, she knew it was Scott by his walk. He was moving quickly, and Lily found herself matching his pace.

He embraced her when they met, and he said, "You're early." He smiled broadly and Lily could see that the clouds over him had lifted, and he was his usual self again.

"I finished early," she said. "I thought we could spend another night together before your test."

"Great," he said. "Come on, I'll show you what we've been up to."

He took her on a brief tour of the changes they had made since she was last there a few months ago. Before they headed back to the central hub, Lily pulled him into a small empty conference room.

"I want to talk to you about the other night and about General Hyo," she said.

His whole face darkened, and he suddenly looked as haunted as he had then. Lily was sad to see it, but there was something she needed to say.

"I want to put him and that part of our lives behind us," she said. "He was and is a petty monster, and he's irrelevant to us."

Scott's face was set in a way she had not seen before, in a way she found unnerving. "He hurt you, Lily. He tortured . . ."

For a second he couldn't speak and she saw real pain behind his anger.

"And you helped save me. It's been three years. I healed a long time ago," she said.

"Your knee still bothers you," he said.

"What?"

"When you've done too much and the weather is bad, your knee still bothers you," he said in a flat tone that she didn't care for.

"He didn't do that. It happened when I jumped from the balcony to escape," she said. She tried smiling to lighten the words.

"Are you really saying—"

"Okay, I'll grant the knee. But I'd been trained to endure much worse than he dished out. Forget about him. His punishment will be to live in the hellhole he helped create. And it will be a miracle if he survives the next military purge. The point is that I've moved on. I don't want him to have any power over either of us."

Lily gestured around them. "We both do what we do because we believe in the future. You are literally building the future in six different ways. In my job, I sometimes see things I wish I hadn't, but that makes it more important to me that those things don't touch you, don't touch *us*. So, for me, I'm asking you to let that part of the past go. And you'll get all the revenge you need when you and Renard Tech deliver the anti-missile system to South Korea next week. As of today, Bloch has put me on your security detail, so I can go with you."

"Really?" he said, visibly brightening.

"Yes, and you can stick it to Hyo and the tyrant he works for by taking away their power to do harm. I just want you to let go of the personal so they have no power over us."

The anti-missile system was important. In the years since Lily and Zeta had foiled Hyo's plans to acquire American cruise missiles, the North Koreans had dramatically increased their missile program. And given their close proximity to South Korea—to say nothing of Japan—the South Koreans needed an anti-missile system within insanely fast response times.

Scott exhaled deeply. "Okay, you're right. I did get a little preoccupied when he was preening for the cameras," he said. "I'm sorry if it ruined our night."

"That's not the problem. I just don't want you wasting a second of your precious time thinking about someone like him."

Scott put on a grin that only appeared slightly forced. "Okay, but I reserve the right to celebrate when he does get purged."

"*That* we'll celebrate together," she said.

His next smile was more genuine. "Come on, I want to show you one more thing that I hope you'll like."

Scott led her to the launchpad's control center, which had a dozen stations across from a wall full of monitors showing different angles on the rocket. Lily and Scott took a flight of stairs up to his office, which overlooked the space.

He closed the door, giving them privacy, though the glass wall allowed Scott to keep an eye on the control center.

But right now, all of his attention was focused on her. He gave a big, broad grin. It was genuine and one of his I'm-excited-about-something-new smiles.

In that moment, Lily was sure she had done the right thing by talking to him. This was the Scott she wanted to see all the time. This was the Scott that helped keep her own darkness at bay.

"I wanted to talk to you about this the other night, but we never got to it," Scott said.

Reaching into the pocket of his hoodie, he pulled something out. Before she could see what it was, he was lowering himself to the floor.

No, not lowering himself. Kneeling.

On one knee.

Lily's neck was hot and her mouth was suddenly dry.

She could also see something new on Scott's face. He was nervous.

"Lily," he said, looking up at her, "I've been thinking about the future too, and I want it to start right now. Will you marry me?"

Though years of training and experience had taught Lily to react immediately to any situation, Lily found she was speechless. She also did something she hadn't done since she was a teenager. She blushed.

As soon as she could find her voice, she said, "Yes."

His eyes went from nervous to relieved to happy in a second and then he was slipping something onto her finger.

He stood and kissed her, the kind of kiss that he usually reserved for when they were alone.

When they both came up for air, he looked her in the eyes and said, "Thank you. I hope you like the ring."

Looking down at her hand, she saw a flawless diamond that had to be at least two carats, in a classic round, radiant cut. The ring itself looked like . . . "Platinum," she said.

"Yes, I know it's your favorite for jewelry," he said.

That tickled something in her memory. Something from a press report about Scott.

"Where did the platinum come from?" she asked.

There it was, his broad, proud grin. "Glad you asked. It's from the first batch of material ever to be mined from an asteroid. I smelted and cast the ring myself."

"Of course you did," Lily said.

"It's made of stardust, Lily," he said.

There was another kiss, this one even longer.

When they finally broke, Lily realized that it felt completely right. For years she'd been telling herself that if it ever happened for them, it would have to come when things calmed down. When the world was safe from the bigger and bigger threats that seemed to come with more frequency than ever lately.

But now she understood that if they waited for some mythical "right time" to begin their life together, they might never actually do it. If Scott could let go of the past for her, she could embrace a future for him.

Over his shoulder, she could see a sudden burst of action in the control room. Three of the people there had converged on one station.

"Scott, there's something going on," she said.

He took in the scene and said, "I'm sure they can handle it. You know I only hire the best."

But she could tell he was worried. This project was one of his babies. It was very important to him, and she was wearing the proof of that on her left hand.

"Wouldn't you feel better if you were sure?" she asked. The question was just a formality. She already knew the answer. "Can't hurt to check," she added.

Scott led her out of the office, already in work mode but keeping her hand in his.

On the floor of the control center, he released her hand and conferred with the group at the troublesome console.

"The pumps are out, sir," the woman at the console said.

"Mechanical?" he asked.

"Maybe," she said, clearly unsure.

"It's okay, we have a day to sort it out," he said.

Turning to Lily, Scott said, "The water pumps at the base of the pad are out."

Lily knew what that meant. There were a series of pumps that worked like a steel-and-concrete showerhead, pumping large amounts of water up into the base to protect the structure from the massive thrust and fire generated by the rocket's engines.

"You said pumps," Lily said to the woman at the console. "How many are out?"

She checked a readout and said, "All of them."

"All twenty?" Scott said.

"Yes," said the woman, nervousness in her voice.

"Is there a chance that could be a mechanical problem?" Lily said.

"No," Scott replied. "They are independent systems, so no."

"I'm getting electrical surges in multiple systems," one of the other people called out from their console.

"Scott, we need to get everyone out of here, right now," Lily said.

Suddenly, it all made sense. The threat reports they had been getting weren't about just Scott. The attack they referenced was on the facility.

"Scott," she said as he studied the console.

"Everybody," Scott said. "Transfer control to the Hub and get out of here. Gerry, hit the alarm. We need to evacuate."

"More surges," someone called out.

"We'll deal with that from the Hub," Scott said. "Shut down power to your systems. . . . Wait. Is anyone up top?" he asked.

"Yes," someone called out. "There's a team on the nose."

"Keep power to the elevator and get out of here, now," Scott said. As the room burst into movement, Scott turned to Lily and said, "Please supervise the evacuation. Make sure everyone gets out. I just need to take the elevator up to—"

"No," Lily said. "You know these people. Get them out. I can take the elevator up and down before you're finished."

Lily saw that Scott would never let her do it. That meant he thought there was a real risk. And that was why she didn't want him to go.

Stalemate.

"Shutting down, but I'm showing pressure up slightly in engines twelve and fourteen," someone called out.

That was it. Lily's instincts were screaming that they needed to move. Now. They would have to do it together.

"Let's go," she said, taking his hand. "Let's get to the elevator."

Chapter 13

Alex slept most of the trip from London to Jamaica. She still felt strange flying first class, which her parents always thought was wasteful, but she was glad for the large seat, which was closer to a bed than a chair. It even had a curtain that allowed her to shut out the world.

Alex found that she needed the sleep.

She'd simply been up for too long with too much adrenaline flooding her system. The same mindset and focus that helped her survive missions like her time in Albania and Montenegro cost her later.

But after waking from a nine-hour sleep, Alex almost felt like herself. With the time difference, her early morning flight put her in Jamaica at ten AM. That meant that she'd have no trouble adjusting to the fast turnaround for the new mission.

The bright sun on her when she hit the ground in Kingston was in stark contrast to the dankness of every part of her last mission. Eastern Europe had been cold and rainy, but the worst places were the ones created by people—that warehouse and the inside of that awful train.

If anything could melt those memories away, it was the Caribbean sun, Alex figured. And, of course, she did take some satisfaction in the idea that the men who had created that world in Eastern Europe were gone from this one.

A car was waiting to take her to the Strathairn hotel, where a room was also waiting. The hotel was impressive and Alex regretted that she wouldn't spend even a single night there.

She found two duffel bags of clothing in her room that would be appropriate for her next undercover assignment: a deckhand on a marine salvage equipment trawler.

She showered, dressed, and grabbed the duffels. On the way out—in a supreme act of hope—she purchased a simple one-piece swimsuit from the hotel gift shop.

Then she took a cab to the marina, it was not one of the several yacht clubs or marinas that serviced the island's many pleasure crafts. This marina docked and serviced working boats used for fishing, moving small to moderate cargo loads, and transporting marine construction equipment.

It took some looking to find the ship; the *Shotton* was a forty-foot trawler, a work boat that was bulky in the front and smaller in the back.

There was a crane in the back and a lot of covered storage on the deck, which made sense for a working transport vessel.

"Hello?" she called into the ship.

"Coming," a voice said in a British accent, which was not a surprise; it was the most common accent on the island.

A man came up from below deck, wiping his hands on a rag. From the look of the rag, Alex assumed he'd been working on the engine.

He was young, maybe midtwenties. His features were somewhere between Western male and the exotic East, and his eyes were a striking pale blue. He was good-looking and extremely fit.

He didn't hide his surprise when he saw her. "Miss Morgan, it's a pleasure to see you again."

"You as well, Mr. Martin. The weather is exceptional, even for the island."

Devan Martin grinned and said, "That's the thing about weather; if it's not one thing, it's another."

There it was, the correct reply. Alex knew that Devan Martin was MI6, and she knew him both personally and professionally, but she took nothing for granted on her missions, and she wouldn't ignore protocols that might save her life.

"It's very good to see you, Alex," he said, stepping forward. For a moment, Alex thought he might kiss her directly on the lips. This would not have been unprecedented but had hardly happened often enough to be a given.

He merely lightly pressed his lips to her cheek and gave her shoulder a slight squeeze with one hand.

"I'm glad they sent you. At least I know you know your way around a boat," he said.

"Less than you think. My mom taught me a bit about sailing, but when we met I was a server on a cruise ship."

He smiled again, very effectively, she thought.

"As I recall, you showed you were capable in many areas," he said.

To an outsider, that would have sounded forward, but both she and Devan knew he was referring to her facility with mayhem and directed violence.

"I was a *very* good server," she said. "I consistently received the best tips on the lido deck." She gestured to his ship and asked, "Can I assume you also have some relevant experience."

"As you may recall, I am from Liverpool; I worked around boats when I was a kid. Didn't you grow up in Boston?"

"Yes," she replied. "Hence the sailing, but we really were more of a car family."

"You'll catch on," he said, leading her onto the ship. He took her below and said, "You can take the bigger cabin. I sleep on deck when I can."

Cabin was a generous term for the space, but it had a small bed and a door, so she wasn't going to complain. She tossed her duffels on the bed and met Devan on deck.

"Have you eaten lunch?" he asked.

Alex realized she hadn't. In fact, she couldn't remember the last time she had eaten. "No," she replied.

"There's a good place nearby. We can catch up, and then we can go meet a Saudi prince. We have a delivery to make."

* * * *

Lily could see the staff of the launch tower control room racing out as the elevator doors closed. Scott hit the controls and the elevator started its ascent. As soon as they were moving, Scott was on his phone.

"Gerry, everybody's out? Get to auxiliary control and shut down everything you can. As long as the flight system isn't affected, it'll be fine and we can keep on track, even if we lose a few days repairing the problem with the pumps. Okay, I'm losing you. As soon as we get down to the ground, I'll meet you at auxiliary control."

Putting away his phone, Scott said, "As soon as you get a few stories up, the launch tower interferes with cell signals. We use a hardwired system to communicate with the tower, but it seems to be down."

"Could that be related to the problem with the pumps?" she asked.

"No," he said. "It's probably related to the electrical problems, which could be behind the problem with the pumps. However, they are fully separate systems, so I'm not even sure how that could be possible."

"Scott, do you think . . ."

"Yes, I'm not ruling out sabotage, but it's a complex system, so I'm not going to make any assumptions until I can get with the team. However, I'll do my best thinking when we've gotten everybody away from the fully fueled, five-hundred-foot rocket."

Scott grinned and for a few brief seconds Lily felt better. She was used to stressful situations and danger, but this one was too far out of her control.

And then there was the problem of Scott. She wouldn't do *her* best thinking until he was far away from the launchpad.

As soon as that thought had formed in her mind, the lights in the elevator flickered and then went out for a full five seconds. When they came back on, the elevator stopped with a lurch and they went off again.

Scott reached for the controls, but before he could do anything, the lights were on and they were moving. They reached the top without any other problems, and the doors opened to a platform at the very tip of the rocket. Lily could see the crew capsule, and there were four people in Renard Tech overalls peering into the elevator.

"Mr. Renard?" one of the men said.

"We're evacuating," Scott said.

"We called down," the other man said. "Phones are out."

"We're having problems with the water pump system, and there are some quirks in the electrical systems. We'll head to the hub and figure it out from there. Come on in."

The four people stepped forward, looking at Scott as if they couldn't figure out why he was there. Lily understood. In what world would the CEO of a major aerospace company trudge up fifty stories to collect the staff in an evacuation?

"Um, thank you for coming for us, sir," one of the two women said.

Scott shrugged. "Happy to pitch in, but let's get out of here."

As soon as everyone was inside, Scott hit the control panel to take them to the bottom, and then the lights went out again and the doors stayed open. Scott worked the controls anyway, but nothing happened.

He picked up the emergency phone and said, "This is Scott Renard." Clearly, there was no reply, and he hung up the handset.

"I'm sorry to say that it seems we have to walk," Scott said. He seemed embarrassed, as if he was upset at inconveniencing his employees.

"We knew the risks, sir," one of the men said good-naturedly. "Thank you for coming for us."

They were all being brave, but it was fifty stories down and this would take a while. Lily quickly evaluated the staff. They appeared reasonably fit. With luck and a good pace, they would be on the ground in no more than thirty minutes.

Wasting no time, Scott led the group to the emergency stairwell. It was inside the structure of the launch tower, but since the tower was made of steel girders, it was open to outside. Normally, Lily had no problem with heights, but they were five hundred feet in the air.

At the top of the stairs, Scott said, "If the power comes back on, we'll grab the elevator on the way."

The group headed down and they were one floor down when an alarm sounded below them.

"Warning. Static fire in five minutes," an automated voice said.

Scott stopped and turned to Lily as the four Renard Tech people gasped. "Let's go back up," he said.

"Up?" Lily asked. All of Lily's instincts were telling her to run for the ground. "Shouldn't we just keep going?"

"No," Scott said. "We won't make it if there's an ignition."

He headed up the stairs. The rest of them followed. Lily was the last one to move and she didn't like the body language she saw on the tower crew.

At the top, Scott disappeared into the elevator. Lily saw him tap the controls . . .

Then hit them . . .

Then punch them.

When he came out, Lily saw that it was taking some effort for him to compose himself.

"Warning. Four minutes until static fire ignition," the automated voice said.

Scott winced at those words. "I'm sorry I couldn't get you out."

One of the women said, "Thank you again for coming for us, sir," she said, her voice solemn.

"What? What are you saying?" Lily said. "We have to fix this. We have to get out of here."

This was an elevator. She actually knew something about them. Lincoln Shepard had a favorite story about the elevator in the Empire State Building.

"You're all engineers or technicians," she said. "We need to cut the lines on the elevator, bypass the mechanical safeties, and then we can free-fall down. You have a piston system at the bottom?" she asked.

Lily knew that elevators had a safety system at ground level that was essentially a large piston in a vat of oil. In the event of a free fall, the car would hit the piston, which would absorb much of the impact.

Scott seemed impressed that she knew the technology but shook his head.

"Yes, but we have less than four minutes," he said. "Even if we could do what we needed to do to get the elevator to fall, we can't be at the bottom for any part of the ignition process . . . it wouldn't be safe."

"Will it be safe up here?" Lily asked.

Scott was clearly uncomfortable when he said, "We'll be *safer* . . . for a bit longer."

Lily definitely didn't like the sound of that.

"If there's a critical problem, the system will try to launch the rocket. That means it will disengage the tower and the rocket will head upward. If that happens, then there's nowhere on the launch tower that is safe." Before Lily could say anything, he continued. "And even if, somehow, that system is disengaged and the rocket is still attached to the tower during full ignition, then we'll be at the center of a big explosion."

"Warning. Three minutes until ignition," the automated voice said.

"Our best chance is that the ignition warning is an error," Scott said. "Or that if it isn't, the ground crew can stop it."

Lily didn't need her years of knowing Scott intimately to know that he didn't think either of those scenarios was very likely.

"I'm sorry, Lily," he said. His eyes focused on the ring on her left hand. Then he turned to the tower crew and said, "We haven't really met."

Stepping forward, he held out his hand to one of the women. "I'm Scott. This is my fiancée, Lily."

"Megan, nice to meet you, sir."

He repeated the procedure with Anita, Jeff, and Paolo.

"I want to thank all of you for your work. I . . . apologize for these technical difficulties," Scott said.

Then he took Lily's hand.

"Warning. Two minutes until ignition," the automated voice said.

All they could do was wait.

Lily knew that one way or the other, they wouldn't have to wait long.

Chapter 14

The Renard Tech helicopter was impressive. The Sikorsky S-76D was a solid aircraft, perfect for a mining operation. It was rugged, could haul a reasonable weight, and most important for their purpose today, it had a range of over seven hundred miles.

They were traveling almost that far out of Perth and into the Indian Ocean to land on the Renard Tech ship. Conley was looking forward to seeing what a mining ship looked like, especially one on which a bird like this could land.

As they approached, Conley could see that the *Demeter* appeared to be a large merchant vessel, with some key differences. It had a very big forward platform that was clearly the helicopter landing pad. As if to prove the point, there was another helicopter tied down on the deck.

Conley was pleased to see that it was a JetRanger.

That was a good omen for the mission, he thought. Besides being his favorite helicopter to fly, a JetRanger had helped him and Morgan get back from Antarctica in one piece.

There were also cranes and other heavy equipment on the side of the ship. And he could see at least one mini-sub in the back. This ship was a major investment, and if Conley knew Scott Renard, it would be state of the art and have more than one fun surprise.

On the helicopter, Dani seemed to waver between very interested and unwell. Dani maintained it was motion sickness, and he hoped it wouldn't flare up on the ship.

Since motion sickness had never really affected her before, he hoped it would pass. A large seagoing vessel was a lot easier on someone with that problem than a helicopter.

Since she'd been a little green around the gills, Conley had resisted sitting up front and talking to the pilot. His name was Randy, and Conley knew he'd come from the British Coast Guard. They were close enough to their destination that Conley allowed himself to leave Dani to move forward now.

"Impressive," Conley said, as they got closer to the *Demeter*.

"It's even better up close," Randy said.

"You log much time on the Ranger?" Conley asked.

"Some," Randy replied. "Theoretically, it's for search and rescue but that hasn't come up much. Mostly, we use it to ferry equipment to some of the smaller vessels."

They landed on the deck next to the JetRanger, and two men were waiting for them. One was in a white shirt and Conley guessed he was the captain. The other one was a solidly built man in late middle age with close-cropped gray hair. To Conley, he seemed like a career noncom in the Marines, the tough one you never wanted to cross and absolutely never wanted judging you in a court-martial.

The captain held out his hand and said, "Captain Taylor."

"Peter Conley," he said as they shook.

"Dani Guo," Dani replied.

"This is my chief of security, as well as my security staff, Mr. Slater," Taylor said.

When the second round of handshakes were done, the captain said, "I can't tell you how glad we are to have you here. Mr. Renard spoke very highly of you. Besides your special project with Mr. Renard, we're very glad to have your expertise. We're really a bunch of scientists. If any *unusual* circumstances regarding security come up, we're really not equipped to deal with them."

"We're happy to be the help you hope you never need," Conley said. "And Mr. Slater, please understand that we are only here to help, we don't want to interfere in any of your usual business."

"Feel free to interfere," Slater said. "I'm here just to break up fights and deal with pirates."

"Do you get many fights on board?" Conley asked.

"Never, but some of the discussions on Dungeons & Dragons nights get pretty heated," Slater said.

"Pirates?" Conley said.

"None so far," Slater said. "It's been four years since there's been an incident in the Indian Ocean, and much longer than that in the area where we have been working."

"I'll have someone bring your things to your stateroom, and Mr. Slater will give you a quick tour if you are not too tired from your trip."

"Dani?" Conley asked.

"Yes, I'd love to see the ship," she said, though to Conley it looked like she'd prefer to sit down. That made him nervous. Dani usually had more energy than he did.

"There's quite a bit to see. We have geology labs, marine life labs, and every type of sonar, radar, and remote imaging you can imagine. Plus, the food is pretty good, and I think you'll be surprised by the entertainment options."

"Entertainment?" Conley said.

"Mr. Renard likes to keep the crew happy. Movies, of course. Plus, video games and VR spaces. We also have a large swing space that is currently set up as a haunted house laser tag."

"A what?" Dani asked.

"Just what it sounds like. Mr. Renard is particularly proud of it. . . . There are zombies. It's actually quite a bit of fun and better than it sounds."

"I don't think that's possible," Conley said. He made a note to get Dani up early to try it out.

"However, I have been instructed to show you our new aircraft first," Slater said.

"Lead on," Conley said.

They headed toward an elevator at the rear of the landing area.

"It's been outfitted with state-of-the-art reconnaissance gear. That was my specialty in US Coast Guard intelligence."

"I didn't know the Coast Guard had an intelligence division," Conley said.

"That's how you know we're very good at our jobs," Slater said.

He hit a button and Conley heard the hum of hydraulics. Half a minute later, Conley took in the plane in front of him and thought for sure he was dreaming.

"You have a Harrier?" Conley said.

"Next generation. It's the F-35B. Vertical takeoff thanks to vectored thrust. This one has some features that even the Royal Air Force doesn't have. The Harriers have always had a low radar profile. Special coatings on the airframe make this bird even harder to see. No weapons, but the pulse-Doppler radar is state of the art and just the beginning of the technology you have on board. I understand that you'll be doing some air reconnaissance; I think you'll be pleased with what you see. And because of our core business, we have all the tools we need on board to analyze your data in real time."

Conley hoped that Dani started feeling better soon, because he also hoped they would be on board for a good, long visit.

* * * *

"Sir," Paolo said to Renard. "We were doing a final systems check. Everything in the capsule checks out, even the EES."

That got Scott's attention.

"EES?" Lily asked.

"Emergency escape system," Scott said. "It allows the crew to get out of the spacecraft in the case of a problem after launch. The capsule detaches and can come down to Earth on parachutes . . . if it clears the explosion of the rocket."

"Will it work if we're still on the pad?" Lily said.

"Not well, we're too low for the chutes to do much good, but it's something. Whatever happens, we'll be safer in the rocket," Scott said.

Not ideal, Lily thought, but Scott was right, it was something.

Scott was pulling at the handle on the side of the capsule.

Anita stepped up and said, "Let me, sir." She grabbed the handle and gave it a simultaneous pull and a twist, and then the door opened.

"I think I loosened it for you," Scott said, giving the group a smile. Actually, he gave them one of her favorites of his smiles, the one that made her first notice him.

"Of course you did, sir," she said.

Scott ushered everyone in and said, "Remind me to talk to HR later about giving each of you a raise."

Scott took what looked like a pilot seat and Lily took the seat next to him.

"Strap in, everyone," he said.

Lily studied the harness attached to the seat, but before she could begin to try to figure out how it worked, Scott was buckling her in.

Then he took his seat again and buckled his own harness.

"Warning. One minute until ignition," the voice said.

"Someone remind me to pick another voice for that alert," Scott said.

"If it comes to it, can you fly this thing?" Lily asked.

"Not at all, but to be fair, nobody can. She's a ballerina in space, but in atmosphere she doesn't fly so much as plummet."

Scott was scanning the controls, clearly unable to find what he was looking for.

"It's the big green button, sir," Jeff said.

"Thanks," Scott said, keeping his hand out, near the button.

"Does someone have eyes on the clamps? I need to know if they disengage," Scott said.

"I can see one clamp, sir," Anita said.

There was a thump and a rattle that Lily could feel through her seat, followed by a low hum.

"That's pre-ignition," Scott said. "This is happening."

"Warning. Thirty seconds until ignition," the automated voice said.

"Clamp is still engaged," Jeff said.

"I'm sorry, appears like we're going to lose the pad," Scott said.

Lily knew what that meant and the small spark of hope she'd maintained when they entered the capsule started to go out.

"Brace yourselves," Scott said, holding his hand over the large green button.

"I thought you said we were too low to use the system?" Lily said.

"We are, but I figure there's a 50 percent chance that we'll get tossed over onto the cliff side. If that happens, we'll have a few more hundred feet for the chutes to work. And then we'll hit water."

There it was, that very small spark of hope. It was still there because Scott was still there.

"Lily," he said, and she turned to look him in the eye. He gave her a smile. Her favorite smile, the one that she knew was just for her.

There was a countdown from ten. Lily resisted the urge to close her eyes and kept them locked onto Scott's.

She couldn't help but wince when the countdown got to "One" and then "Ignition."

At that point the rocket began to shake. Lily wondered how long it would take before the rocket and pad exploded.

It didn't seem like Scott was going to wait to find out. He hit the button and said, "Takeoff."

For a long second, nothing happened.

Then the world exploded around Lily.

After the initial blast, she was thrown down into her seat violently.

The world continued to explode, and the downward pressure on her was intense. It continued for several seconds and then there was the uncanny feeling of floating. They had reached the apex of their upward trajectory. A second later gravity took hold of them again, and Lily felt herself falling.

That feeling lasted for less than three seconds, and she was forced back down into her seat.

That would be the parachutes, Lily thought.

Now it would either be a too-short trip to the ground or a slightly longer trip to the sea, where they had a chance.

Lily held her breath for several seconds. Then a few more.

When they struck something, the feeling was much softer than she was expecting.

It took a second for her to process the sound the ship made. It was the sound of a large object hitting the water.

Looking around her, she was surprised and pleased to see they were still in one piece.

"Everyone okay?" Scott asked as emergency lights came on.

One by one, the tower crew sounded off.

Lily went last.

"Thank you for flying Renard Tech," Scott said.

Chapter 15

The press report said simply that the new Renard Tech rocket had exploded on the launchpad when a test fire of the rocket engines was triggered a few days early. There was discussion of a faulty fuel line and bad sensors.

There was no mention of anyone being on the launch tower—let alone inside the rocket—when it exploded. There was no mention of Scott Renard and his longtime partner, Lily Randall, being anywhere near the incident.

Rather, reports placed them in the launch complex swimming pool at the time of the incident. The story helped preserve Renard Tech's stock price, and—more importantly—it allowed Renard's people to conduct the investigation without the involvement of local police in a criminal investigation. No matter how well meaning, the police didn't have the expertise and knowledge of the launch system to conduct an investigation of the accident as an attempt on Renard's life.

And any criminal investigation would hold up a real investigation for weeks, if not months. Since Bloch was nearly certain that this was Ares, that kind of delay would ensure that Ares's trail would long go cold before Zeta could even begin to pick it up. And that meant that their next plot, or next assassination attempt on Scott Renard, would have a much better chance of succeeding.

Bloch's computer beeped, and she hit a button on the keyboard. A second later, Lily Randall's face appeared on the screen. She seemed normal, though for Lily normal meant that she looked like she could have just walked off of the catwalk at a fashion show or stepped off the red carpet at a movie premiere.

"Lily, I'm very relieved to see you. Thank God you and Scott are all right. How are the people who were with you?"

"Everyone is well," Lily said. "The Renard Tech doctors did a full workup and everyone checked out. Some of us picked up a few bruises climbing out of the capsule and onto the rescue ship but, otherwise, no one was injured."

"I'm glad to hear it. That makes me feel better about what I'm about to ask you. I need you to get Scott out of there."

Randall knit her brow. "He's going to want to oversee the investigation himself. This was, is, his baby. It's a setback and he'll want to know what happened."

"Anyone who knows anything about Scott would know that, and that means that anyone who might want to do him harm would know it. He's still needed in South Korea."

Nodding, Lily said, "If he knows he's a target, he'll grumble quite a bit, but he won't want to put anyone here in danger."

"Thanks, Lily, and again, I'm very glad you are all right," Bloch said.

"Thank you, Director," Lily said.

"Oh, and Randall, congratulations on the engagement," Bloch said.

Lily seemed genuinely surprised. "How did you . . ."

"Don't forget what business we're in, and the fact that I've been doing this much longer than you. Let me know when you've confirmed arrangements for South Korea with Scott," Bloch said, breaking the connection.

As soon as that was done, she heard Shepard's voice outside her door. "Director!" he said, then he was inside her office. His face told her that whatever he had to say, it was very serious.

"I don't think this was an attempt on Scott Renard's life. I just spoke to him; he wasn't officially supposed to be anywhere near the launchpad today. He is supposed to still be in Paris. He and Lily had a change of plans at the last minute."

"Maybe someone, Ares, tracked his travel," Bloch said. Even with all of their secrecy and travel protocols for Renard, it was still possible.

"Whatever happened on that pad was complex and would take months to set up. We'll be that long trying to untangle how they did it, if we ever can. I think the target was the launchpad itself."

That made sense. There were a number of parties—China in particular—who didn't want Scott Renard mining asteroids. Even if a successful program was several years or more out, the best time to put a stop to it would be now.

"If that's the case, then, unfortunately, their operation was a complete success," she said.

"I don't think they're done. There's a possibility that this will not be the only attack. They might not just be trying to stop Renard Tech. This may be a broader attack on space launches."

"All of them?"

"If you eliminated heavy lift launch capability across the board, then there are a number of things you could do that no one else could stop."

Bloch felt her stomach drop at that thought. That would be a big move, even for Ares.

"How many launchpads are there that have that capability?" Bloch asked, knowing that she would not like the answer.

"Thirty-five," Shepard said.

She knew she'd been right. She hated that answer. Just reaching that many different facilities in a short period of time would be very difficult.

"Do you have a list?" she asked.

"I sent it to you before I came over here," Shepard said.

As Bloch opened the message on her computer, she thought about her next move. To get a warning out quickly, she would need the president behind it. That meant her next call would be to Mr. Smith.

"Director . . ." Shepard said.

He pointed to the large monitor on her wall, the one that was always set to one of the twenty-four-hour news channels.

In one corner, there was the concerned face of a news anchor, but most of the screen was dominated by a large fire and a massive pile of twisted wreckage.

The text over the top of the screen read: *Massive Explosion in Florida.*

Bloch turned up the volume control on her desk. She could now hear the anchor, who said, "We have no reports about the number of lives lost but the devastation at the Kennedy Space Center is severe, and the launchpad has been totally destroyed. However, because there was no rocket on the pad, the damage was less serious than at the Renard Tech facility in Scotland. Rumors are already circulating that the two explosions are connected, but experts say there is no evidence to support those claims as of yet."

Bloch was still absorbing the fact that Shepard had obviously been right. The only bright spot was that other launch facilities would increase their security.

The image on the screen shifted to another fire and another pile of rubble. Over the image, the anchor's voice said, "This just in. We have video from the Baikonur Cosmodrome, the Russian spaceport that first launched the Sputnik satellite and is today the largest space launch facility in the world . . ."

What followed seemed endless. Two more sites in Russia. One in California, another in Alaska. Then China, New Zealand, England . . .

Shepard had warned her, but she hadn't had time to act on that information. The only satisfaction Bloch had was that whichever launch platform was still standing when this was all done would tell them quite a bit about who was responsible.

* * * *

"It hurts me. It physically hurts me," Devan said as they approached Prince Nasef's ship.

"That is a big ship for one person," Alex said.

"It's a hundred-foot super yacht. That's plenty of ship for a family of twenty, but that's not the problem."

He shook his head. "I mean, *look* at it," he said.

Alex didn't say anything. She had no idea what Devan was talking about.

"He built a ship that size with a fiberglass hull, which is terrible for structural strength, but he wanted speed," Devan said. "To make it worse, he insisted on a planing hull, which is great for speed but terrible when you're having a party on anything less than perfectly calm seas."

"Yes, he is a monster," Alex said.

Devan nodded.

"See the platform in the back? I read the specs on this ship. That was his helicopter pad. It's made of teak, which is idiotic for a landing pad, but it's criminal now that he's bolted cranes to it for his salvage work."

"Plus, there's the whole trying to recover enough bomb-grade uranium to level ten major cities," Alex added.

"That doesn't make his crimes against shipbuilding any better. Do you have any idea what the stress of heavy equipment, cranes, winches, and cargo has on a ship of those dimensions?"

Alex had no clue, but from Devan's tone of voice, she was sure it was terrible.

"I'm amazed it still floats," Devan said. "I'll be shocked if that hundred-million-dollar ship is still seaworthy in a year. You can't put that kind of stress on fiberglass, especially with all the heavy equipment in the rear." Alex simply stared at Devan. The man was genuinely upset.

He turned to Alex and saw her smiling. "You think this is funny. It's like taking a Triumph Rocket 3 motorcycle, swapping out the engine with a lawnmower, and using it for pizza delivery. It's worse, because that wouldn't break it in half like the *Titanic*. Plus, you'd be spreading joy and pizza."

"We not only have to stop him, we have to crush him," Alex said with a grin.

"That's the spirit, but try to hide your contempt. In our cover, he's an important paying customer."

"I will do my best," Alex said. "What are we delivering today?"

"New metal detectors," he said. "Plus, underwater sonar equipment."

"I hope you are at least overcharging him," Alex said.

"I am. I tacked on 20 percent for upgraded electrostatic circuitry," he said.

"What is that?" Alex asked.

"I don't know. I made it up, but he's paying through the nose for it."

"Wow. That is cold. . . ."

"I do have a dark side. I'm quite ruthless," Devan said.

"I see that you've dropped your London accent for this mission," Alex said. Once again he was gargling his *k*'s and drawing out his *t*'s.

"You know I'm from Liverpool. Prince Nasef went to school at Oxford," Devan said. "He'll be more comfortable if I'm clearly a commoner, which is how he'll see both of us because what we do is physical labor."

"An accent is like a disguise for the British," Alex observed.

"And mine is the best kind, because this is who I really am," Devan said.

"I can Boston-up my own accent," Alex said.

"No need. He'll look down on you simply because you are an American," he said.

"Great," Alex replied.

Devan pulled up to the ship. There was some shouting back and forth and then the ships were tied up together. Devan's boat was now partly under the rear platform of the yacht and directly under a crane.

"I'm going to have to run their crane. I don't trust anyone up there, and I'll be damned if I let these divvies ruin this ship. When I lower the hook, I'll come down and help you load the crates."

"No need. I can handle it. Just show me what goes up. I can also run the crane if you like," Alex said.

He smiled. "Not necessary. I'll take care of that. Just be ready," he said.

A few minutes later, the hook and chain came down and Alex attached the first load, calling out that it was ready.

Devan had a steady hand on the crane and lifted it slowly off the deck. They repeated the operation half a dozen times. Then Alex went up to help Devan unload the equipment.

"Now we do it all in reverse," Devan said. "We're taking the old equipment back. We'll pack it in the same crates."

"The prince only likes brand-new metal detectors?" Alex asked.

"He only likes overpriced junk not rated for the depths his people use it for," Devan said.

"More business for us," Alex said.

"And more chances to keep an eye on him," Devan said. "If he was competent, we'd have a harder time keeping an eye on him."

Two hours later, they had stowed and secured the old equipment on the *Shotton*.

"The crew didn't lift a finger to help; they didn't say two words to me," Alex said. "And it is *their* equipment."

She thought of her father, who would always pitch in when receiving a delivery of parts for Morgan Classic Cars. And her mother would never sit still while the host cleaned up at a party.

"We are manual labor. Even the salvage team see themselves as being on another level. If the prince's limo gets a flat, the driver won't change it. They'll wait for a mechanic."

Devan disappeared onto the ship and returned with an envelope. "I'll say this for oil-rich princes: at least they pay in cash. And more importantly, the prince's personal secretary wants to talk to us. Of course, we'll have to change first. We can't meet him in work clothes."

"Heaven forbid," Alex said.

Alex cleaned up quickly and threw on capri pants and a button shirt, the nicest things she'd brought given that she'd expected to be working as a deckhand.

On the deck of the yacht, they were approached by a well-groomed man in early middle age who was wearing casual slacks and a crisp, white shirt. He extended his hand to Devan, who shook it. He nodded to Alex, and she understood. He would not presume to touch a strange female that he was not related to.

"I'm Mr. Salam. I want to thank you and express the prince's gratitude for your efforts and assistance in his endeavor. He would like to invite you to dinner this evening. Will six o'clock be convenient?"

Mr. Salam spoke with a polished London accent.

"Of course," Devan said. "Alex?"

"We'd be delighted," she said.

"Excellent, we'll see you in just under two hours, then," Mr. Salam said.

Back on Devan's boat, Alex said, "Seems like we've found a way to get close to the prince."

"That was a surprise," Devan said. "I've made three deliveries and never got a dinner invitation. You must have the touch, Miss Morgan."

"I'm glad we get to see inside that yacht. The last time I was on a ship bigger than yours, I was bringing fries and chicken nuggets to ten-year-olds. It will be nice to see how the other half lives."

Chapter 16

Dani wasn't feeling well in the morning, so she went back to the room after breakfast, and Conley met Slater on the flight deck.

The jet was waiting for him.

"Have you flown one of these before?" Slater asked.

"No, but I'm also a helicopter pilot and I've logged some time on simulators," Conley said.

He'd logged a lot more than "some" time, at least on simulations of the Harrier II, the previous-generation model. He'd had about a dozen hours on the new F-35Bs simulators though.

Conley knew he was ready. The big challenge for most pilots was the vertical flight capability, which is why Harrier pilots were usually jet pilots who were also trained on helicopters. At first, the RAF had tried to cross-train helicopter pilots as jet/Harrier pilots, but for whatever reason, that had not worked as well.

Fortunately for Conley, his experience made him a good candidate to fly his dream aircraft.

"I didn't bother asking the crew to set up the ramp. I thought you'd like to go vertical your first time."

Conley found that he was liking this Slater more and more. Though the Harrier family could take off and land completely vertically, you paid a cost in fuel. The compromise that pilots made most of the time was to use a short ramp for takeoff. It meant you didn't need a full aircraft carrier deck, and the fuel savings would extend the flight range of the aircraft.

Today, Conley wasn't worried about any of that. This was a getting-to-know-you flight for the jet and the special equipment.

As soon as the ground crew was clear, he started the engine and the power shook the airframe. Knowing he was showing off a bit, Conley made sure his takeoff was smooth. He hovered over the deck for a few seconds and then gained altitude.

At a thousand feet, he adjusted the thrust vectoring from beneath the aircraft to the rear.

The sudden acceleration forced him back in his seat as the jet leaped forward. He increased his speed further, then decided to play.

He did the reverse vectoring maneuver that had made the plane famous, dropping his speed dramatically and subjecting him to several g's of force.

In a dogfight, that maneuver would put an enemy on your tail in your sights nearly instantly. Then he took a few minutes mastering the more subtle vector shifts that gave the aircraft its remarkably tight turning radius.

After a half hour, he decided that if he ever went into combat again, he'd want to be flying one of these.

Of course, it wouldn't be this plane, specifically.

The Renard Tech jet had swapped out its weapons systems for sensor and tracking equipment. *Fair enough, on a civilian aircraft,* Conley thought, *especially one that was going to be used in mining surveys and this kind of stealth reconnaissance work.*

In a few minutes, Conley knew it would be time to get on the radio with Slater to calibrate and test the new sensors, but there was one more thing that he wanted to do before he got to work for the morning.

Conley realized that he'd never actually flown at supersonic speeds before. He put some distance between himself and the *Demeter* and then slowly increased his airspeed.

As it edged up to Mach 1, Conley prepared himself. When he passed the threshold, there was no shaking or noise. From the pilot's point of view, nothing really changed. However, outside the plane, he knew the sonic boom would be heard for miles.

He took the plane up to Mach 1.5 and tried a few gentle maneuvers. That was when he felt the difference between normal and subsonic flight. The forces on his body and the airframe were dramatically stronger at the higher speed.

Slowing the bird to cruising velocity, he turned and headed back to the ship.

He hit the radio. "Slater, are you ready to go to work?"

* * * *

Bloch saw that the death toll was in the hundreds. Though no one had perished at the Renard Tech facility, that was unusual compared to the other sites. Most launch facilities suffered at least a few casualties, and one of the Chinese pads had lost nearly fifty people.

It was all over in less than thirty minutes. As the launch sites fell, Bloch physically checked them off of her list. The last one was in New Zealand. *The last one.*

It took a second for that to fully sink in for Bloch. As Shepard had explained it to her, the reason to do this would be to achieve some sort of temporary dominance in space launches.

But now *no one* could launch.

She had no idea what that meant.

Shepard and O'Neal sat in front of her desk. While the reports had been coming in and the launchpads were being turned to rubble, Shepard seemed like each one was a personal loss—like he was losing friends.

As the numbers increased, he looked more and more anxious. Now he simply seemed baffled.

Bloch knew how he felt.

"Can you think of any advantage to doing this?"

"Absolutely none," Shepard said.

Someone just grounded the world's spacecraft. That wasn't on the long-range wish list of any crackpot government, terrorist organization, or extremist group in the world.

And yet someone had gone to a lot of trouble to do just that.

Bloch asked the only question she could think of that might have an actual answer. "Why the delay between the attack on Renard Tech's facility and these?"

From the expression on his face, Bloch could tell that Shepard had been thinking about this issue.

"Karen and I came up with two possibilities. The first is that the timetable on Renard's facility was sped up somehow because the enemy found out he was on-site. I'm not completely comfortable with that theory, given the complexity of this whole operation."

"The second possibility, then?" Bloch asked.

Karen O'Neal spoke, in her customary businesslike tone. "The attack on Renard was meant to send a message. It may have been intended to give Zeta a taste of what was coming. Certainly, Ares knows how closely we work with Scott Renard and his people."

It was ridiculous, but it fit the facts better than anything else Bloch could think of. The problem was that it was too personal. Even in war, nations fought over ideology, territory, and resources. Yet here, someone was shaping global events and still taking the time to, what, gloat? Threaten? Why? Because Zeta had beaten them a couple of times?

Bloch decided that though it seemed absurd, Ares was in fact making this fight personal.

* * * *

Mr. Salam greeted Alex and Devan warmly on the deck. "Very nice to see you both. The prince looks forward to meeting you. Now, if you'll follow me, I'll show you where you can change."

Instead of following him, Devan said, "I'm sorry, but we expected to work today. This is all we have brought."

The older man gave Devan a patient smile and said, "I'm sure we have something for you." They went below, and Mr. Salam led them to two doors. He pointed out which room was Devan's and which room was Alex's and said, "You'll find what you need in the closets. Dinner is at seven sharp. I will meet you five minutes before and take you to the dining room."

Inside the room, Alex found the closet and in it were five cocktail dresses in her size. Before she could begin to choose, there was a knock at a door that she realized connected her room to Devan's.

She opened it and he said, "Just making sure you are all right."

"Fine but what is going on?" she asked. "Are they just being generous or are we about to be the subjects of some crazy rich person's game or a deadly hunt?"

"I think a hunt is unlikely. The ship is big, but for a proper human hunt, you need a forest."

"That is a relief," Alex said. "So what is this about?"

"I have no idea. I've never been invited to dinner with a Saudi prince on his super yacht. I do know that Arabs are famous the world over for their hospitality. Maybe this is what hospitality looks like for the oil rich."

That actually made sense but Alex resolved to keep her Smith & Wesson in her purse, just in case. She closed but didn't lock the connecting door, also just in case.

Alex chose her dress. She went with the Ferragamo, which had a long sash that gathered at one shoulder. Red in the center, it morphed into yellow on top and a burnt orange at the bottom. The dress was amazing, and she knew it cost as much as a decent entry-level BMW motorcycle, like any of the G310s.

Her pistol fit nicely into the matching purse, which she decided she'd be taking back with her to Devan's boat. She chose the red Manolo Blahnik shoes, which she'd also be taking with her.

If Devan could overcharge the prince, she could defund global chaos in her own way. She carefully put her phone and ID in the Ferragamo purse as well. If she had to, she'd leave behind the clothes she came in.

Mr. Salam was at her door promptly at five minutes before seven, and then they collected Devan. He stepped out into the hallway in a white dinner jacket. Alex was struck by how handsome he was, especially out of his work clothes.

"Alex, you look lovely," he said.

"Thank you," she replied, and then they both followed Mr. Salam to the dining room.

At the head of the table, the man Alex assumed was the prince was waiting. He was maybe thirty and blandly good-looking, though he seemed a bit soft in his features and in his build. He was also wearing a white dinner jacket, but this one had gold-edged lapels.

The prince stood up and opened his arms in a grand gesture. He approached them and shook Devan's hand. "Mr. Martin, I am Nasef bin Fahad," he said. "And very nice to meet you, Miss Morgan. You look lovely." He did not extend his hand to her, which was now not a surprise.

"Thank you for inviting us to see your remarkable ship," Alex said.

"Yes," Devan said. "It is really . . . something."

"Once, not too long ago, it was a toy. Now it's a working vessel. As you know, we search for treasure, but the treasure is a byproduct. We are searching for history, and we have found quite a bit. But before we go any further, I insist you call me Nasef."

"In that case, I'm Devan."

"And I'm Alex."

A slight man with salt-and-pepper hair entered. "This is my friend Roan Berisha. I present Alex Morgan and Devan Martin."

"Very good to meet you. Call me Roan," he said.

Alex heard some Eastern Europe in his voice, but she'd need a few more words from him to narrow it down.

"Albania, is it?" Devan said.

"Yes," Roan replied, surprised.

"I'm from Liverpool," Devan said. "I have an ear for accents and, living in a port city, I've had a lot of practice."

"And this is my business associate, Sergei Ivanov," Roan said as another man entered. This one was tall, very fit, and very well groomed.

"It is very good to meet you," the man said. "And I insist you call me Sergei."

His voice dripped of Russian with what she thought was a Moscow accent. She found there was something odd about him, something she didn't trust. Alex just couldn't put her finger on the reason.

Of course, obviously, she had just recently had experience with Russians and Albanians together, but that single experience was not a basis for any hard conclusions.

At least not yet.

Chapter 17

After breakfast, Slater was waiting for Conley on the deck. "How, exactly, do you mine the ocean at this depth?" Conley asked. "I get drilling for oil, but how do you root around down there?"

Slater thought for a second before he answered. "You know that you are asking the person on board with the least amount of knowledge on this subject."

"Just the basics, then," Conley replied.

"It's not mining like you are thinking," Slater said. "Well, the surveying is similar, some of the geology. We need to know where to search. But really what we do is vacuum up sediment from the ocean floor, filter out anything larger than a small pebble, and pull up what we get. There's a surprising amount of useful metals in very small pieces. We process it up here, separate the ore, and that's it.

"Because it's Scott Renard, there's also a whole team of biologists looking for and cataloging any life we find down there. They've already discovered a number of new species."

"I guess with the accident at the launch center in Scotland, you guys have just become more important," Conley said.

Conley had only seen the press reports about the accident, but he'd been glad to see that no one was hurt at Renard Tech. He was sure there was more to the story—especially given the other launchpad explosions that followed—but Bloch would brief him and Dani when she was ready.

"The asteroid-mining is promising but it would have been years off if there hadn't been a setback. This is the future, at least for the next decade or so," Slater said.

Conley was up in the air quickly. And with the introductory flight out of the way, they were able to get right to work. Keeping the speed down, Conley managed his fuel carefully and got in about two hours of flight time.

He used it to start a grid search, relaying sensor information back to Slater. Besides the radiological sensors, they were searching for submarines, unregistered drilling platforms, and underwater structures.

There was nothing out of the ordinary, but Conley was not surprised. There was a lot of ocean to cover, and Conley knew they would be at it for a while.

When he got back to the *Demeter,* he found Dani looking well and in good spirits. They had lunch, and she remained fine. He assumed she'd adjusted to the ship and whatever trouble she was having with motion sickness was over.

After lunch, she had suggested they try Renard's haunted house laser tag. Conley found that, though fun, it gave them a surprisingly good workout. Conley found it surprisingly challenging.

Part of that was, of course, because Dani was so competitive and he'd had to bring his A-game to keep up with her.

They had dinner with Slater at the captain's table. They talked a bit about the mining operation and it was clear to Conley that Dani was completely up to speed on what they were doing.

Some of the discussion went over his head, since it involved details that he and Slater hadn't discussed, but it was clear that Dani understood and was fascinated by the whole process.

At the end of the meal, the captain brought out a rare Chinese whiskey that he offered to them.

Conley said yes, but to his surprise, Dani declined. She liked whiskey and had really taken to Kentucky bourbon, claiming it was a lot like some of the blends from home.

"No thank you," she'd said simply.

Of course, she wouldn't discuss her stomach problem with the captain or Slater. She barely would talk about it with him.

And at that moment Conley realized how stupid he had been.

It was his business to keep and uncover secrets. He wondered how this one had gotten by him, and he wondered how long Dani had known she was pregnant.

* * * *

Once everyone was seated at Nasef's table, two women appeared from outside. They were young, attractive, and wearing very small bikinis. The only nod to modesty was their sheer cover-ups.

Roan and Sergei seemed immune to the young women, as did Mr. Salam. Devan, who was seated across from Alex, had to make an effort to look away.

The women leaned over Nasef and fussed over him. He good-naturedly endured their kisses; then he whispered something to each of them. Looking up at Alex and Devan, he said, "This is Alina and Zaneta. Ladies, these are my new friends Alex and Devan."

The women smiled and said, in a chorus, "Nice to meeting you."

Alex could hear the Polish in their voices.

"Unfortunately, they do not speak very much English," Nasef said. "But they are very good company." With a nod, the women disappeared back outside.

What was that? Alex wondered. Was he showing off? Or maintaining his cover as a royal playboy? Both perhaps?

"They will not be joining us for dinner. They have already eaten."

Based on the way they wore those bikinis, Alex seriously doubted that was true, or that they ate very much at all.

Alex had noticed that, before they left, both women looked at Roan, who gave them a slight nod. Strange. What was he to them? Her brief and unpleasant time recently in Albania made her think she already knew.

Alex would have normally rejected the idea of a coincidence except this was not really a coincidence. Albanians and Russians had together run the human-trafficking operation Zeta had just broken up. And the idea of using a treasure hunt as a cover for a weapons-grade nuclear material recovery operation had all the earmarks of an Ares operation.

Alex decided that she and Devan needed to be very careful.

* * * *

Two very serious and very efficient male servers appeared and poured absurdly expensive champagne into the glasses of everyone but the prince and Mr. Salam. They drank something out of a different bottle; Alex was nearly certain that it was sparkling cider or something else nonalcoholic. That suggested that, playboy or not, Nasef and Salam were devout Muslims.

In and of itself, that meant nothing, but it did seem to contradict his behavior with the models. Of course, those contradictions were nothing new among devout people of any religion.

"A toast to new friends and new adventures!" Nasef said.

The table raised their glasses and Alex sipped her champagne. Not surprisingly, it was excellent.

"Miss Morgan and Mr. Martin, I would like to present you with a small gift, a memento of your time with us," Nasef said.

Two servers appeared, one next to Alex and one next to Devan. Each of them held a small platter on which rested a single large coin. A gold coin.

A very old gold coin.

"From one of our successful recovery efforts," Nasef said. "My gift to you both."

Alex picked up the coin. It was heavier than she would have thought. There was a cross etched into the center, and what appeared to be Latin words decorated the outer edge.

Alex had no doubt that it was worth even more than the outfit she was wearing. Suddenly, she understood something. What if the treasure hunting wasn't just a cover? What if it was a source of funding for Ares?

Certainly, Nasef had massive wealth, but even he had a family that might ask questions and a government that might not approve of an arrangement with a group like Ares.

"This is very generous indeed," Devan said. "Thank you."

"Yes," Alex said. "Thank you very much."

"It is my pleasure to share the bounty of the ocean with you. These were from a Spanish galleon that sank not far from where we are now."

"You mentioned new adventures," Devan said. "Are you searching for any particular ship now?"

"We only have a few more weeks in this location, but I am hoping it will be productive, thanks to the new equipment you so kindly brought us. Sadly, I have other commitments, and I will soon have to bring my treasure-hunting career to a close."

Alex held up the coin. "Though clearly not without some success."

"True," Nasef said. "But we never seem to have time for all we wish to accomplish. I do intend to make the most of the remainder of this expedition. And I hope you can accept our hospitality for the night and tomorrow."

Devan gave Alex a look, and she said, "We would be delighted."

Dinner passed pleasantly. Nasef spoke at length about his successes in finding and salvaging historical shipwrecks. He asked Devan a few polite questions about his work with ships. He even asked Alex a few questions when he'd learned that she worked with exotic motorcycles. Surprisingly, he even knew a bit about Italian bikes.

After dinner, they retired to their rooms. Devan opened the door and they exchanged pleasantries. Both knew enough to avoid saying anything suspicious until they could sweep their rooms for listening devices.

Devan disappeared into his room and Alex took out her phone. As soon as it turned on, Alex received her first major surprise of the night. She resisted the desire to tell Devan until she had swept the room.

It was clear. In her room, at least, they could speak freely.

"I'm clean," Devan said, popping his head into the room. "You?"

"This is one of those good news/bad news situations. First, the good news is that my room has no listening devices. But the bad news is that the gold coin the prince gave me is radioactive."

"What?"

"Our tech team built a Geiger counter into the phone, and as soon as I turned it on, I got an alert. Bring me your coin."

Devan reached into his pocket gingerly and handed Alex his coin, she brought it up to her phone and said, "Yeah, yours too."

"You don't seem panicked, and I don't want to be a baby about this, but *how* radioactive are we talking?" Devan said.

"Not dangerous, but about the amount that would show if the coins were stored near weapons-grade uranium or plutonium."

Chapter 18

Devan looked like he couldn't believe what she had just said. Alex barely believed it, and she was studying the readout on her phone. The coin was definitely mildly radioactive, about the amount Shepard told her to watch for as she hunted for items that might have been exposed to enriched nuclear material.

"The prince is a clown," Devan said. "Is that a ruse? What he's done to this ship . . . everything. Is he really a mastermind of some kind?"

"I don't think so," Alex said. "I think he is probably exactly what he looks like."

"Then how?" Devan asked.

"An operation like this fits the profile for Ares. What do *you* know about them?"

"The one time I faced a threat from Ares, I was with you on a cruise ship. Everything else I know came from intelligence reports that I assume were recycled from Zeta briefings to MI6. I know Ares tends to use local extremist or terrorist groups as part of a larger strategy."

"That's our understanding," Alex said. "I just came from breaking up a human trafficking operation in Montenegro, in which Albanians were working with very competent, well equipped, and highly trained Russians."

"You think those Russians were Ares?" Devan asked. When Alex nodded, he said, "Why not ex-KGB, Russian mob, or just freelancers?"

"They were too well trained. And when we got one of the bodies back to Zeta, the team confirmed that it carried the cyanide tooth that every Ares agent we have recovered has in his mouth."

"Okay, so we've got a Russian who may be Ares, an Albanian, and a spoiled prince. Plus, of course, two women who kept looking at the Albanian as if he was their boss."

"You noticed that?" Alex said.

"I'm not your sidekick," Devan said with a grin. "We get a little training at MI6 before they throw us out into the field."

"Well, obviously, we have to search the hold and see if the . . . nuclear material is still on the ship. Whatever happens, they can't leave with it. If we have to, we sink this thing and let our organizations sort it out later."

"Anything else you want to do while we're here?" Devan asked.

"Yes, I want to talk to the women. If they are here against their will, they come with us," Alex said.

"Sounds easy," Devan said, grinning.

"I thought so too until I realized that the Russian may not be the only Ares agent on board. They might have embedded an agent into the crew, the salvage team, or both. Come to think of it, it would be nice to take one of those agents alive."

This time, the grin melted from Devan's face. "You want to take one of these highly trained Ares agents alive? So we have to somehow subdue him and knock him out before he activates his poison tooth. Can I assume you have a plan on how to do this?"

Now it was Alex's turn to grin. "Yes. First, I need to change. Second, we search the hold while avoiding any bad guys. After that, we grab any dangerous nuclear material and subdue anyone who has a problem with that."

"Alex, that is not a plan. It's a to-do list," Devan said.

"Fair enough," Alex said. "But we're going to have to hurry if we want to get it all done by morning. And the first thing on that list is that I have to get out of these shoes."

* * * *

"What is it?" Karen O'Neal said, looking over his shoulder.

"I've been through every database I can think of. I've searched all the relevant FBI, CIA, and NSA files—as well as any relevant Department of Justice files. I've followed the chain of evidence and, as near as I can tell, all relevant Friends of Feynman material was dropped into a vault and never seen again."

"Which seems to contradict the fact that their plans keep turning up as real-world operations," Karen said.

"Exactly," Shepard said. "And the survivors were watched for years. They haven't had any contact with any extremist organizations, let alone international terrorist groups, or anything on the scale of Ares."

"That leaves the dead ones," O'Neal said.

"I ruled them out," Shepard said.

Karen simply looked at him, as if he would elaborate.

"I went to Alison's funeral," he said. "It was an open casket."

"And Kurt was killed in a car accident; he had a closed casket. There was a fire, and there wasn't enough left of him to identify the body. . . ."

Even as the words left his mouth, Shepard realized that he had been a fool. No, worse than a fool, he'd been actively stupid.

Chapter 19

"You think he's still alive?" Bloch said.

"Yes," Shepard said simply. "One of our first projects was creating false identities."

Shepard could feel Karen's eyes on him. He said the next part for her benefit, since Bloch already knew it.

"It was just a game, to see if we could do it. The idea was to create an identity to slip into if we ever got into trouble. As you know, even when I was questioned by the FBI, they never found it, though I disclosed it to you when you recruited me. It really was simple. We found people who were born around the time we were but died shortly after birth, before they had applied for a Social Security number. We applied for the number and built the identity from there. Years ago, that would have been it, but it's gotten trickier in the years since 9/11. You have to hack a few government databases to keep yourself off the radar, but we were primarily hackers, so that wasn't much of a challenge."

"You think this Kurt Richter disappeared into his alias?" Bloch asked.

"At first, but I remembered the name and checked. It's been dormant since he was declared dead. If he's still alive, he could have created another one. I've already started searching for signs of breaches in government databases at that time. The problem is that after a couple of system upgrades, the trail would be cold."

"I can call Mr. Smith if necessary. We could get the cooperation of any agency you might need," Bloch said.

Shepard could see that Bloch wanted to help, to do something, but he couldn't afford to waste any time on false modesty.

"Honestly," he continued, "any agency IT personnel would likely just get in our way. We have the run of any or all relevant federal and state systems. Most people in those government jobs don't stay in one place long enough to have much of an overview, but because Zeta has been moving in and out of the systems for years, we have more reliable long-term information."

The director was clearly frustrated.

"I can follow up on some personal angles, places he might have interacted with in his previous life. He was an only child and his parents are both deceased, but there is extended family and some friends."

"But we have to assume that he will be as good at covering his tracks as you are at uncovering them," Bloch said.

As upsetting as that was, Shepard could not deny it. "Yes, for all intents and purposes, we have to assume that—if he's still alive—he's as good as I am."

Shepard saw something in Bloch that he had never seen before. She seemed uncomfortable. In some ways, that was a compliment, but the stakes were too high for that to matter to him.

"There's something else, Director," he said. "Kurt has something personal against me."

"Personal?" she asked.

"Yes, he hated me, hates me," Shepard said.

"I was the one who shut down the group's activities and was the first to cooperate with the FBI when they came knocking. There was also something with Alison, the young woman who committed suicide. He blames me for her death and actually hit me at her funeral."

He didn't have to look to feel Karen's eyes boring into him.

"She . . . liked me, and I didn't return her feelings. And Kurt had feelings for her. Somehow, he blamed me when she didn't return them," Shepard said.

Bloch looked at him as if she couldn't believe what he was saying. "Are you telling me that all of this, all of the worst threats we've faced, are over a . . . college girl? A college girl you weren't even interested in?"

"Partly, yes," Shepard said. "But more importantly, he blamed me for her death. Later, I found out that she'd always had problems with depression and had been hospitalized three times during her teenage years. When the FBI started investigating some of our group activities,

Kurt wanted to deny everything and cover up whatever we could. I insisted on cooperating and then did. He thought the extra pressure is what drove her to suicide."

"You think that all somehow led him to . . . what? Found Ares?" she said.

"I don't think so. He's not a leader; he's not that person. If I had to speculate, I'd say that he got involved somehow and has been working with them in the way I work with Zeta."

"I can't believe I'm saying this," Bloch said. "But it sounds like you're suggesting that you have an evil twin working for the other side."

"Yes, and based on what we've seen in the last few years, whoever it is, this person is very dangerous and is happy to kill millions."

Bloch got up from her desk and led both Shepard and O'Neal to the small conference table on the other side of her office.

"Okay, Mr. Shepard, it's time to tell me everything about what they might be planning."

* * * *

Dressed in her capris and button top, Alex stuffed the dress, shoes, and coin into a plastic laundry bag she found in her closet. Her instinct was to put the coin in her pocket, and while the Geiger counter on her phone said it was safe, she didn't see the point in taking any chances.

She was closing the bag when Devan came in.

"Taking the dress as a souvenir?" Devan asked.

Alex looked up at him and said, "And what will I find if I peek inside your bag?"

"The jacket is Armani, and it's a perfect fit!" Devan replied.

Alex suppressed a smile and said, "Come on."

On deck, Alex was pleased to see that there was no one at the rear of the ship. They walked casually, keeping their cover if anyone did show up. Then they saw Devan's ship, still tied up where they had left it.

"She seems okay," Devan said as they both tossed their bags onto the smaller ship's deck.

Alex realized they had never been offered a tour of the prince's ship. When she'd come on board, she'd thought nothing of it, assuming that it was a super-wealthy thing.

Now she realized that it might have been because the prince was worried about revealing the ship's true purpose. Now she realized that she didn't have any idea where to start.

As if he could read her confusion, Devan said, "Come on, I think I can get us there." He led her to the front of the repurposed helicopter pad. There was a door there that Alex could see had been widened to accommodate a set of industrial-looking double doors.

"The companionway," Devan said, pushing open one of the doors and holding it for Alex. They were in a small vestibule with a regular-sized door about twelve feet in front of them. On the right was a heavy-duty elevator and on the left was a set of stairs.

Devan pointed at the elevator and said, "That will take us directly to the hold."

But Alex remembered Peter Conley's many warnings and would never get into an elevator in a tactical situation if she could avoid it.

"No, the stairs," she said.

"With the engines running, the noise won't—"

Alex ignored him and headed for the stairs. A second later, he was behind her.

Since they were on utility stairs and about to enter a cargo hold used to store illicit nuclear weapons, Alex decided that the jig was up on their cover. She drew her Smith & Wesson from the shoulder holster under her light jacket. They descended two levels and were standing in a large open space that Alex realized was the hold.

There were racks of equipment, some of which Alex recognized, and other racks of what appeared to be junk that had been salvaged from the sea floor. There was something odd about the artifacts; they appeared staged, and Alex had the uncanny feeling that they hadn't been touched in some time.

Alex brought up the Geiger counter meter on her phone's display and started running it over each rack. They all showed higher than normal radiation, hovering around the level of the gold coin.

But Alex noted that the numbers increased as they moved forward, toward the bow. As she reached the forward bulkhead of the cargo hold, the numbers quadrupled.

"This is it," Alex said.

The problem was that while the readings were exactly what Shepard had told her to expect when she found the place where one or more nuclear weapons had been stored, this section of the hold was empty.

Both sides of the door that led to the main passageway were giving her high readings, but there was nothing there.

"They must have moved them," Alex said.

"Or they removed the radioactive cores, dumped the casings, and have the nuclear material somewhere else on board."

Perfect. Sneaking around a mostly empty storage compartment was one thing, but conducting a room-by-room search of the vessel might attract some attention.

"I think it's time to talk to the prince," Alex said.

"I can find his cabin," Devan said. From her look of mild surprise, he said, "I memorized the ship's original blueprints."

That material wasn't in the Zeta mission briefing material.

"Like I said, I'm not a sidekick," Devan said with a grin.

Once they were in the main passageway, they both kept their weapons in hand but mostly hidden under their jackets.

They walked up one level of stairs at the end, and then Devan indicated the door on the right. He motioned to her and started lifting his foot when Alex stopped him with a wave.

Instead of kicking the door in, Alex gently tried the doorknob. It opened easily and Devan gave her a sheepish grin.

Once inside, they found Nasef and Mr. Salam huddled over a dining table off to the side of the lavish stateroom. The men looked up in surprise, still dressed in their evening clothes.

"Hands on the table," Alex said to the two men.

"No noise, no movement, and no one gets shot," Devan said.

"Some ground rules for both of you," Alex added. "Go for a weapon, and I'll kill you. Sound an alarm, and I'll kill you. Do anything I don't like, and I'll kill you. Fair warning, tonight I'm feeling particularly on edge and I won't like *anything* but brief, truthful answers to my questions."

"What questions?" the prince said, seeming progressively more nervous by the second. Mr. Salam, on the other hand, seemed remarkably cool.

"Where are the nuclear bombs?" Alex asked.

"The what?" Nasef asked, visibly sweating now.

"The nuclear bombs you meticulously tracked and salvaged from the ocean while you were picking up gold coins," Devan said.

"Yes," Alex added. "*Those* nuclear bombs."

"This is outrageous," Mr. Salam said, starting to get up from his chair.

"Sit down!" Alex said, training her weapon on the center of his chest. Mr. Salam froze in place, and while keeping his eyes fixed on Alex's gun, he slowly sat back down. Just as he touched the seat, his hand shot onto the table, grabbed something, and then in a flash of movement he swept his hand under the table.

"Hands!" Devan said as Alex fired her weapon. At the last second, she shifted the gun to hit him in the left shoulder. The impact forced him back into his seat.

While Alex kept her gun on Mr. Salam, Devan stepped forward and pulled the table out of the way. There was a knife sticking out of the prince's thigh.

A baffled Nasef stared at the knife.

Alex focused her attention on Mr. Salam. He was clearly the only threat.

"Clever," Salam said. "I wonder, how did you find us?"

Then he made an odd chomping motion with his jaw and almost immediately started to convulse. It was over in seconds.

"Cyanide," Alex said. "I guess we found the other Ares agent."

After taking several seconds to process what had just happened, a baffled Nasef looked up and said, "He stabbed me."

Alex put the barrel of the gun against his cheek and said, "Tell me where the bombs are or that will be the best thing that happens to you all day."

"I don't—" he started to say but stopped when Alex dug the gun into his cheek.

"Ivanov would come and take them," he said.

"How many?" Alex asked.

"Four in two years."

That surprised Alex, and she heard Devan gasp.

"And where did he take them?" Alex said, pushing the barrel even deeper into his cheek.

"I overheard him speaking to an associate in Swiss. I speak a little. He didn't know . . ." Nasef said, his breathing getting labored.

"Where!" Alex demanded.

"An atoll somewhere . . . somewhere in the Pacific," Devan said.

"We need more!"

"I don't know. If I knew, I would tell you," Nasef said.

Alex believed him.

"I think . . . I think I need help," Nasef said.

"Your personal secretary severed your femoral artery. If we were in a hospital, I don't think there's anything they could do." She checked her watch. "You have maybe two more minutes of consciousness, and it won't be much longer after that."

The prince looked at her uncomprehendingly, and then her attention was drawn to a beeping sound coming from Mr. Salam's watch.

Devan was there first, holding up the man's hand. Salam was wearing a smartwatch that had a flashing red dot in the center.

"Alex?" he said.

"An alarm," she replied. "Maybe he tripped it, or it engages when the heart stops."

Alex was on the move. She grabbed Devan by the elbow, and then put him and herself on opposite sides of the door.

"If it's an alarm, it won't take Ivanov long to get here," she said, lifting her weapon.

"Let me handle him," Devan said. "You want him alive, right?"

There wasn't time for a discussion, so she just whispered, "Fine."

As if on cue, a large male figure raced into the room with a gun drawn and scanned the dead bodies in front of him. With surprising speed, Devan stepped forward and with his left hand slapped Ivanov in the neck and held his hand there.

Ivanov started, straightened up, and then crumbled to the floor.

Alex kept her focus on the space behind Ivanov. If there were any more Ares agents coming, she couldn't let them inside the room.

She waited several seconds and then closed the door to be sure.

Devan took the man's pulse at the neck and said, "He's alive."

"Wow. That is impressive. We only captured one of them alive and he died before we could interrogate him. Okay, I officially propose we take turns being the sidekick," Alex said.

"Fair enough," he replied.

"How did you do it?" she asked.

He held up his palm, revealing a disk with a short needle sticking out of it. Turning his hand over, Alex saw that Devan was wearing the device like a reverse ring.

"You took him out with a gadget?" she asked.

"And years of training," he replied.

"You do realize that it looks like a joy buzzer," Alex said.

Devan frowned. "It worked, and now we have someone to interrogate, someone who knows where the nuclear bombs are. Let's get him to my ship and get out of here."

"What do we do with everyone else?"

Alex spared a glance at the prince, who wasn't moving. She had no doubt that he was gone.

"Once we get him on board," Devan said, "I'll disable the engine and have them all picked up. The HMS *Mersey* is less than two hours away. They will tow the ship and detain everyone for a proper . . . debriefing. And the two women will be well taken care of."

They wrestled Ivanov onto Devan's ship and then Devan returned to disable the super yacht. Alex waited a tense several minutes for him to return. He finally reappeared and cast off the ropes binding them to the prince's ship.

They pushed off the yacht with two large poles. Devan waited until they had drifted a couple of hundred yards away from the larger ship before he started his own engine.

It was probably an unnecessary precaution but Alex agreed that it was better to be safe than sorry. The information and the captured man had to be secured.

Just in case something went wrong, Alex filed a quick report to Zeta HQ as Devan found a pair of pliers and removed the man's cyanide tooth. When Alex was finished with her report, she sat behind Devan as he piloted the ship.

"How long will he be out for?" Alex said.

"A man his size, at least two hours. And we'll be back at the marina in forty-five minutes."

After thirty minutes Alex had to force herself to stay alert. It was getting late, and she was feeling the letdown after an adrenaline surge.

A few minutes later, Ivanov twitched and then in a movement almost too fast to follow, the hands that were zip-tied together on his lap grabbed at something in the pocket of his slacks. He took hold of it and jammed it into the side of his neck. By the time Alex's hands were reaching to stop him, he was stabbing himself again and blood was spurting out of what she realized was his jugular vein.

"Damn," Alex said. She pulled a flat, semi-flexible metal band out of his hand and reached around for something to stop the bleeding. She came up with a rag and pressed it against the man's neck.

As soon as she touched him, he grabbed her blouse with hands that were surprisingly strong and said, "Tell Shepard."

That stopped Alex cold.

"Shepard?" she said.

"Tell Shepard . . . Tsar Bomba."

Chapter 20

September 2001

Lt. Diana Bloch had to force herself to focus on the briefing. Her aide, Lisa Garrity, had prepared it, and Bloch didn't want to show her impatience. However, Bloch's headache had returned, the remnants of last night's excursion to the local bar called The Jolly Roger.

"The Borei submarine is less than five years old and has become a cornerstone of Russia's efforts to modernize their submarine fleet after the 1991 breakup of the Soviet Union . . ." Garrity continued.

Bloch found the tackiness of the pirate-themed bar she had been to last night amusing. It catered mostly to the American tourists and naval personnel, like Bloch, from the Crete naval base.

From the cradle of civilization to a tourist attraction that wasn't even about Greek culture in just a few thousand years, she thought.

"The recent deployment of a Borei to the Mediterranean," Garrity continued, "is clearly a show of force meant as a response to the recent US carrier group maneuvers."

That was definitely true. The problem was that when your "show of force" was a single sub playing hide-and-seek with a US carrier group, it just telegraphed your weakness.

The Soviet navy was still reeling from the loss of their Kursk submarine just a year ago. And they had all but ceded the Mediterranean to the US and NATO.

In a way, deploying an ineffectual Borei sub was a perfect epitaph for the Soviet empire.

Of course, that said something about the importance of Bloch's posting. She ran a naval intelligence office of three people who watched the Russian efforts in the Med to show the flag for their fallen empire.

However, Bloch wasn't worried about her career. She had plenty of time, and there were much worse postings than a Greek island.

Plus, the drinks at Jolly Roger's were cheap, and in just over an hour she could start work on tomorrow's hangover. And there was a handsome British naval intelligence officer she knew that was visiting, and she had promised to show him the local nightlife.

Garrity continued, and Bloch nodded along.

Bloch noted the sign that was behind Garrity. She'd had it made up and was particularly proud of it. It read, "IVAN WATCH COMMAND," and underneath it read, "WE WATCH IVAN SO YOU DON'T HAVE TO."

"So it's safe to say that the Russian deployment is simply saber-rattling and represents no actual threat to our carrier group or to commercial shipping."

Bloch nodded her approval, but before she could speak, someone outside shouted . . . or screamed. There was the sound of commotion, and through the glass she could see people running back and forth.

Then there was another scream.

As the highest-ranking person in the room, everyone looked to her, so she did the only thing she could think of, she stood.

At that moment, one of the base commander's aides opened the door and barked, "Duty stations. New York has been hit."

For a second, Bloch was too shocked to move. New York had been hit? How? By whom? Was it a last, desperate strike from the failing Russian bear?

Or was it China?

Why would anyone hit New York now?

Then she realized that the "hit" was most likely a terrorist attack. But the last terrorist attack in New York was more than eight years ago, and the people responsible were either in jail or dead.

It had been a bomb in the parking garage of the north tower of the World Trade Center. This was years before her sister Jackie had started working in the same tower. Even if New York had been hit again, Bloch told herself that lightning would not strike the same tower twice.

"Stations, everyone," Bloch said to the room, and then she was out the door and heading for her office. There was more commotion outside, and Bloch could see that groups were huddled around televisions all throughout the floor.

She resisted the urge to investigate. Instead, she turned into her office, waving off something Garrity was trying to tell her, and closed the door.

It took a few seconds for the picture on her office television to flash on, and when it did, Bloch assumed she was hallucinating. She had to be; what she was seeing was clearly impossible.

The television showed the World Trade Center, and it was burning. More specifically, the north tower was burning from a gaping hole somewhere near the top—very near where Jackie worked.

And then her heart nearly dropped out of her chest.

In the very next instant, her phone rang. She stared at it like she was seeing a telephone for the first time. She would have ignored it, but the display said the call was coming from the United States.

Picking up the phone, she put it to her ear and heard Jackie say, "Diana."

Bloch felt her heart jump back into her chest, and she said, "Jackie, thank God."

"Oh, Diana . . ." her sister said.

"Where are you?" Bloch asked.

"I'm at work," Jackie said.

"But it's early," Bloch replied as her mind rebelled. Her sister couldn't be there, not in the place Bloch was watching on TV. It was not only impossible, it was ridiculous.

"There's a fire here," Jackie said. "Felt like a bomb went off."

No . . . No . . . No . . . No . . . No . . . Bloch's mind screamed.

"Diana?" Jackie said.

"It wasn't a bomb, it was a plane. . . . A plane hit the building," Bloch said, just a moment after reading the text crawl saying just that on the television. "Why are you there so early?"

"Jeffrey has a concert later at preschool. He'll be singing . . ." Jackie said, her voice trailing off.

"It's going to be okay. Jackie, I need you to do something for me. I need you to get up and get to one of the stairwells. Get down to the ground as quickly as you can."

"I tried," Jackie said. "One of the stairwells is gone. The others . . . you can't get through."

"Okay, stay low and, if you can, stay close to an open window," Diana said.

"You can't open the windows, but on one side they're all gone . . ." Jackie said.

"Someone will come. Just sit tight," Bloch said. She was thousands of miles away, and Diana Bloch had never felt more helpless.

"I don't know, Diana. It wasn't so bad at first, but there's a lot of smoke," Jackie said.

"Don't worry, someone will come. Just stay low and cover your mouth with something," Bloch said.

"Okay . . ." Jackie said. "I'm scared, Diana."

"I know you are but—" Bloch couldn't finish. She was watching the screen when there was a flash of what looked like a plane, and then there was a large explosion in the other tower.

She would not have believed it if she hadn't also heard a loud thud come through the phone.

"Diana!" Jackie screamed into the phone as Bloch simultaneously called her sister's name.

There was a terrible silence on the other end of the line, and then Jackie said, "Diana, are you there?"

"Yes," Bloch said, amazed that her sister was still on the line.

"Something happened. . . . There was an explosion," Jackie said.

"Yes, there's a problem in the other tower," Bloch replied.

"Hang on," Jackie said and then the line went silent. After nearly a full minute, Jackie came back on and said, "Diana."

"I'm here, Jackie," she said.

"Jeffrey is going to need you," Jackie said.

Bloch felt tears coming up. She fought them, knowing that if they came, they wouldn't stop.

"He needs *you*," Bloch said.

Jackie coughed and said, "We both know I'm not getting out of here."

"No, you are. You just have to wait," Bloch said, struggling to keep her voice from breaking.

"The smoke is getting worse . . . and it's getting hot. There are flames coming out of the stairwell," Jackie said.

She stopped to engage in a coughing fit.

"Diana, I don't want to . . . to burn. I don't want to be a coward, but I don't want to burn," Jackie said, her voice amazingly composed. "Please take care of him."

"*You'll* take care of him," Bloch replied.

"Promise me you'll take care of him," Jackie said.

The fight went out of Bloch. "I will. You know I will."

"He likes you better, you know," Jackie said.

"No, no, you're his mom."

"Oh, he loves me more, but he likes you better. It's hard to compete with fun Aunt Diana," Jackie said. Then her sister took a sputtering breath and said, "Some people are talking about jumping . . . if the fire gets too bad. Jumping instead of . . ."

"No," Bloch said, giving up her fight against the tears.

"I love you, Diana. Take care of our boy," Jackie said. Then the line went dead. Not silent but truly dead this time.

Bloch sat in silence for several minutes, shooing Garrity away twice and locking the door.

She made a series of calls to the United States to take care of the immediate details and to make sure someone came to get Jeffrey. Then she got up to talk to the base commander.

He would be busy, very busy, but there was nothing he or the rest of the base could do to help in New York. A time for help might come, but right now, the entire US Navy was as useless as Diana Bloch felt.

They had been playing hide-and-seek with a Russian ghost, while the real threat had lain in wait for eight years right under their noses.

There would be time for recriminations later, Bloch realized. At the moment, she had urgent business and someone in New York who needed her.

* * * *

The Present

On the day Diana Bloch had lost her sister, she had sworn that if she were ever in a position to make a difference, she would not be distracted. She would not turn away from the real threat, the real problem, whatever it was.

Now all she wanted to do was to send every agent she had and call in every favor she could to go after Jeffrey.

However, she knew she couldn't do that. There was too much at stake. Too much of the world that could suffer for such a selfish act.

And yet she had made a promise to a better woman. And there was someone in Antarctica who needed her.

Some of the old feelings of helplessness came back, but she realized that she wasn't completely helpless. There was one place she could still go, one person who might help.

It was a long shot, but so was everything she did these days.

And as she had learned a long time ago, when you had one option, you took it.

* * * *

Dan Morgan turned on the lights in his shop for the first time in months. He and Jenny had both enjoyed their trip, but he knew his wife was as glad to be home as he was. They had been talking about the Morgan World Tour for almost their entire marriage.

At first they had put it off because of Morgan's work with the CIA. Then when he retired from intelligence work to focus on his family, Alex had been too young for the couple to go away together.

When Alex was grown, he had already started working for Zeta and it had been one international crisis after another. Finally, when Alex was established at Zeta herself, Jenny had put her foot down.

It was time. And more importantly, Jenny maintained that Alex would never reach her full potential if Morgan was always looking over her shoulder.

Now, nearly five months after they had left, the world was still there, and Alex had just successfully completed another mission.

Valery Dobrynin had kept the wheels turning at Morgan Classic Cars. Now that he was back, Morgan was already looking forward to doing the advance work on the New England Classic Car Show that he had founded.

And there was a rare 1967 Impala in Vermont he was eager to go see. The four-door hardtops were hard to come by, at least original ones. Most collectors these days had to make do with converted Caprices.

But those plans had all changed at dinner last night. Morgan had been surprised when Jenny told him that Lincoln Shepard and Karen O'Neal would be coming over.

Morgan liked both of them, and he and Shepard had seen a few things together, but they had never been to the house. In fact, he had never seen them outside of Zeta headquarters, except during a couple of active operations.

As far as he knew, they mostly lived in the lower levels at Zeta, which everyone called the Basement. He knew they had carved out a very comfortable apartment for themselves out of that space and used it when they were chained to their computers or labs during extended crises—which seemed to happen more and more lately.

Nevertheless, they had shown up at the house last night and the two couples had all enjoyed a roast. The most unnerving part of the evening was seeing Shepard in a button shirt instead of his usual T-shirt and hoodie—and seeing O'Neal in a skirt instead of her usual jeans.

Morgan had bet on some big, personal event in their lives. They were getting married, or having a baby, or both. But when the conversation had gotten to the reason for their visit, Morgan had been genuinely surprised. He also mentally cancelled any plans he had made for the next month at least.

He had just gone through his mail when there was a knock at the door. He opened it to find Diana Bloch standing outside.

"Morgan, could I have a word?" Bloch said.

A few days ago, Morgan would have been shocked to see Diana Bloch at his door, but after last night it almost made sense.

He had planned on going to headquarters tomorrow to check in, and this just hurried the process along. Dobrynin could handle the car show details for that long, and Morgan hoped the Impala would still be there when he got back.

"Director, of course," Morgan said, ushering her inside. They headed to the back of the shop to his office and he took the seat at his desk, leaving her to sit in what he thought of as the "client" chair.

He knew he would remember this as the strangest part of their encounter, Diana Bloch sitting in his office, in that chair.

Morgan understood in that instant how hard this trip must have been for her. Bloch was a good boss, probably the best he had ever had, but he had never seen her anything less than completely in charge.

"Director, I was about to make a pot of coffee. Would you like some?"

"Yes, please," Bloch said in a smaller voice than he had ever heard her use.

Morgan really did need a cup of coffee, and it would make her more comfortable.

A few minutes later, he handed her a black coffee and sat down with his own.

"Morgan, I'm here to ask for your help, but I have to warn you that this isn't Zeta business. It's personal," she said.

"You know my answer is yes," Morgan replied.

"Wait until you hear what I'm asking," she said. "As you may know, my nephew is with Naval Intelligence. He's undercover doing signal work and attached to a scientific outpost in Antarctica. US intelligence agencies have been keeping a careful eye on the continent since you and Peter Conley's mission there a quarter century ago."

That made sense. The Russian bear might hibernate from time to time, but he never ceased being dangerous. And embedding a signal man with a group of scientists was a good and low-profile way to watch over things.

"The problem is that the station has been completely out of contact for almost a week," Bloch said.

That was bad, Morgan knew. A lot could happen in that cold in a week.

"The base is fairly remote," Bloch said. "And officially, it's a civilian base, so intelligence and military can't take too eager an interest in the situation. Plus, the assumption is that the base may already be lost."

Bloch's voice caught a bit on that last phrase.

"I'll go, of course," Morgan said.

"Thank you for offering, but I need you to know all the risks first. This won't be a sanctioned mission, not even by Zeta. And winter is beginning in less than three weeks. By the time you got down there . . ."

Morgan understood what she was saying very well. In Antarctica, if you missed the last flight out before the start of winter, you'd be looking at six months on the ice before flights resumed. And if the cold wasn't bad enough, you would live in perpetual darkness in which the sun never rose.

That was why the summer population of Antarctica was about five thousand people, and the winter population was only one thousand. Bases ran with skeleton crews as people hunkered down for the winter.

"Morgan, this is a lot to ask. If you get stuck down there . . ."

"I'll have to make a point of finding your nephew and getting on a plane out of McMurdo by February 15," Morgan said.

"I'm sorry to ask . . ." Bloch said.

"Don't be sorry," Morgan said. "He's your family, and I'm happy to do it. Honestly, I'm already regretting that our last stop on our trip was Tunisia. It was just too damn hot. It will be nice to be in the snow."

Morgan smiled. This time of year, Boston was plenty cold for his taste, but this was hard enough for Bloch.

"Of course, I'll cover any expenses and make your travel arrangements," Bloch said.

"No need. The arrangements are all taken care of," Morgan said.

Then, for one of the very few times in the years that he'd known her, Diana Bloch looked genuinely surprised.

"What? How?" she asked.

"Shepard and O'Neal met with Jenny and me last night. Shepard told me that you've had him monitoring communications out of Antarctica, and why. And I knew that we had a February 15 deadline. Jenny is packing my things now, and I was going to talk to you about this tomorrow morning at headquarters. And as for travel arrangements, there's a Renard Tech jet standing by at Logan."

For a few seconds, Morgan thought that Bloch might lose her composure, but her iron will reasserted itself, and for that, Morgan was grateful—for both their sakes.

"Dan, I don't know what to say."

"Director, there's nothing to say. It was worth it just to see that we had surprised you," Morgan said.

Bloch actually laughed at that. "Well, I have been distracted," she said. "And please, call me Diana."

"Sure, Diana," he said, but even as he said it, he knew that that would never happen outside of his shop or his home.

He made a very brief call to Jenny and then said, "Diana, Jenny would like you to stop by the house on the way to headquarters. She has a few questions for you about the trip."

That was, of course, a ruse, but he hoped it would get Bloch to the house. Jenny and Bloch had a surprisingly warm relationship—as close to a personal relationship as he suspected that Bloch had in her life.

Morgan might be able to find her nephew—he prayed that he could. Yet Jenny could sit with her and talk and offer her something more immediate that would help Bloch face whatever came in the next few weeks.

"Of course, I'm asking her to make a sacrifice as well. I'll tell her whatever I can," Bloch said as she rose to leave.

Chapter 21

The last thing she needed was a sentimental American in her head, Jenya Orlov thought. Even if that American was her sister.

The simplest thing to do would be to jump the maid and knock her out, or—better yet—silence her permanently.

But Jenya knew that her sister Alex would not approve of either option. *Kashmar,* she thought. Sometimes it was better when she had no family to worry about.

No, that wasn't true.

She'd had very little family. There was her mother's father, a cold, distant soldier whom her mother had rarely seen and Jenya had met only a handful of times.

There had been an uncle she barely remembered.

And, of course, there was her mother, who had been taken from her much too early.

At first, she thought that finding Alex was a blessing. Not that Jenya was religious, at all, but her family at one time had been simple and devout villagers and Jenya accepted that some reflexive thoughts in that area were unavoidable.

The Bolsheviks had seventy years to beat superstition out of the population, and they had failed. Her mother had told her a common joke about the five-year plan: Progress is slow, but work continues.

The result of all of the voice's interference was that she stayed her hand because she knew her sister would not approve of hurting a hotel maid.

Of course, Alex would never know what happened in this hotel room tonight, but that was the problem with voices in your head. They didn't follow the normal rules of logic.

However, they could be predictable. And rather than face the recriminations from Alex's voice later, Jenya decided to wait. Acting rashly might have been more expedient, but it would mean dealing with the voice later.

So Jenya did one of the few things she was not good at. She waited.

She knew housekeeping's routine in this hotel; she'd been staying there for a week. What the maid was doing was not normal, and the service she was providing was also not something the hotel usually offered.

That meant that this had been set up separately with the concierge. From her vantage point on the balcony, Jenya could see the maid placing fresh flowers throughout the suite.

Then there were plates of fruit, cookies, and other goodies.

Even Jenya, who had become quite accustomed to the good life and five-star hotels, thought this was a bit much.

Fortunately, Alex's voice was silent about the theft Jenya had planned. The couple who was staying in this penthouse suite had made a considerable fortune cutting down rain forest to plant soy so that Europeans could make synthetic fuels.

The fuels were expensive, inefficient, and worse for the environment—making this what they called in the decadent West a home run.

Relieving these two of this particular piece of property was very nearly a public service.

Finally, the maid completed her work and left the suite, and Jenya wheeled her suitcase back inside.

The hard-shell Prada suitcase had been specially modified to bear some extra weight. The wheels spun smoothly and, more importantly, quietly.

When she reached the closet, she opened the door and considered the safe. It was good, very good. In fact, it was so good that the owner wasn't crazy to think the necklace was as secure in the suite safe than it would be in the hotel safe.

However, they had not considered Jenya when they did that calculation. True, it would be impossible to open the safe without the combination, outside of a workshop with specialized tools and hours to spare.

Fortunately, Jenya had both.

She went to work removing the intricate moldings that hid the mount which set the safe inside the wall. Removing the bolts that held the safe in place challenged her strength.

In the end, the bolts gave way. She lifted the safe out of the wall and put it on the carpet. Then she pulled the duplicate out of her suitcase and lifted it into place. In less than fifteen minutes, the bolts were tight and she was resetting the moldings.

They required a bit of extra time, and Jenya had to touch up the gold paint that had chipped in a few places. The paint would dry in a couple of hours and the open windows would take care of the smell.

When the owners tried to open the safe, they would find that it had not been locked and they would also find a very good replica of their Burmese ruby necklace.

The original, now safely in Jenya's suitcase, had ninety carats of rubies and diamonds. It really was an attractive piece, though Jenya was not tempted to keep it.

It was too famous, and eventually, the theft would be found out—sometime in the next year when the couple's jewelry collection was reappraised. When that happened, it wouldn't do to be seen wearing the original.

Jenya could try to pass the original off as a replica, but she had standards, and the Formula One driver and sometimes model Jenya Orlov never wore replicas.

She'd sell it through an intermediary to a private collector, who would pay about half of the ten million it was worth.

That was fine with Jenya. The money would be nice, for the day's work, but the pleasure of separating these two from their treasure was more than worth it for Jenya.

In the bathroom mirror, she checked her appearance. Between the large sunglasses and the wig full of dark brown hair, even people who knew Jenya would have trouble recognizing her.

Jenya smiled pleasantly to the people in the elevator. She didn't worry about the security cameras in the elevator car or in the hallways or lobby. It would take weeks or months for the owners to realize the ruby treasure was missing.

When they found the safe open, they would likely assume one of them had left it that way and would consider themselves lucky that the necklace was still there. Weeks or months in the future, when they did discover the loss, any security footage would be long gone.

Outside, she hailed a cab, which took her to her rented workshop and small office. She would open the safe tonight and leave Brazil tomorrow afternoon. Though she loved Rio, it was best in small doses, and after a week she was ready for something else.

Before she unlocked her office door, her phone gave a beep that she immediately recognized. It meant that there was news about Dan Morgan, a special kind of news, the kind that she had long been waiting for.

Inside, she rushed to her computer station and read the report. It looked like Dan Morgan was going on a trip to Antarctica of all places.

That would be a perfect place to put an end to him.

She had sworn to do it years before. And she remained committed to the task, even after meeting Alex and her sister had taken up semi-permanent residence in her head.

The one concession she had made to family was that she would not do it in the family home. She preferred to do it overseas when he was away from Alex and her mother. The problem was that for months Morgan and his wife had been traveling together, and while he had been vulnerable many times, he was never alone.

Jenya cared nothing for the woman, but the woman was Alex's mother, and for that reason, she received some consideration.

Jenya realized that this was not just good. In fact, it was perfect. In that cold and desolate place, it would be very easy to find Dan Morgan and to kill the father who had taken everything from her. And best of all, on the ice it could be made to look like an accident.

Alex's voice in her head tried to speak up but Jenya forced it down. That voice would make a lot of noise, no doubt, when Jenya did this important work and likely for some time after.

However, eventually the voice would quiet, and Jenya would finally have paid her last debt to her mother.

Part 3

Enemy Action

"The real war will never get in the books."
—Walt Whitman

Chapter 22

Lily could see that Scott was restless.

"What is it?" she asked.

He was pacing around their suite at the Grand Intercontinental in Seoul as if he were caged.

"I need to be there," Scott said. "At the launch site." He grimaced and then corrected himself, "The *former* launch site."

Lily gestured to the impressive multi-monitor and multi-CPU workstation he had set up in their suite. The setup took up half of their living space, and she knew for a fact that it rivaled anything he had anywhere.

"Is there anything you could do there that you can't do here?" she asked.

"For one, I would be there. The staff would see me, they would know I was working with them to figure out what happened and how we're going to reestablish launch capability. As you know, it's not just Renard Tech that can't launch. There isn't a single functioning heavy-launch facility in the world."

Lily was getting frustrated. "Okay, let's play this out. Assume you were there, right now, working with your engineers. Let's also assume that the incident that nearly killed us both really was—at least partly—an attempt on your life. Let's further assume that the bad guys would find out in one minute that you were back. You would have just painted a target on the backs of your people."

That stopped Renard cold. Using his feeling of responsibility toward his staff was an obvious manipulation. However, everything she said was true.

Scott had been a target too many times recently to pretend that it wouldn't happen again.

"Scott, I know this was a setback, and it set back your asteroid program," she said.

"It cost us *years*," he replied.

"Yes, but before you can start rebuilding, you and your people need to figure out how Ares got so deep into your systems. And that is what you do. I know you want to fix it and move forward, but you need to do it armed with the knowledge to keep it from happening again. But for any of that to happen you need to not make yourself and the site in Scotland a target again. Give it some time. Your people know their jobs. Let them do what you hired them to do."

She watched the struggle play out on Scott's face. She wished she could help him more than she was, but what had happened was as bad as it got. However, since she couldn't do more to help him fix the situation, she'd decided to settle for keeping him alive.

"And you are personally overseeing the deployment of the Renard Tech anti-missile system. That's one area in which you are doing some good now. De-fang the North and everyone can breathe easier," Lily said.

That was as close as she had come since Scotland to mentioning General Hyo. Scott was deeply enmeshed in the Scotland situation, which was now the first incident in what was a global catastrophe for human space travel. However, there would be months of sorting through that rubble. The best thing for Scott was to have a problem to solve now, something forward-thinking. And if it directed his feelings about Hyo to something good, then all the better.

A light seemed to go on in Scott's head. "Okay, you're right. And now that heavy launch is off the table, the systems that protect against smaller, weaponized rockets are more important. And there have been serious glitches in the software."

There it was. Lily could almost see the instant when his mind had switched focus to a new problem—one that he could start solving today.

"Okay, but I'll have to go to the meetings in person," Scott said.

Lily knew her expression betrayed how she felt about that. His attendance wouldn't be on any publicly available schedule but would not stay secret long.

He just shrugged. "If I'm going to do this, I need to do it. This isn't make-work to keep me busy while you go out and keep the world safe. Half this hotel is either a Zeta asset or your handpicked Renard Tech security. We'll have to make this work. If I do this right, we can move on before the bad guys even know I was here."

Lily grinned tightly and said, "Of course, just coordinate with the team outside and give them enough lead time to actually sweep any meeting sites."

Scott smiled, and Lily knew she had achieved her goal.

"I'm going to my NIS meeting. Call me if you need anything," Lily said, kissing Scott and turning to leave the suite. She didn't enjoy lying to him. There was no NIS meeting. She had exchanged messages with the South Korean National Intelligence Service, but she had no meetings planned with them.

Everything on her agenda today had only to do with Scott's personal security. The lie bothered her a little. Okay, more than a little.

Since she had started at MI6, remaining absolutely truthful in her personal life had become very important to her.

But she would have to forgive herself for this one, as long as Scott stayed safe.

* * * *

Morgan's pilot wasn't happy. One look at his face told Morgan that. Of course, even if Morgan couldn't see his face, the pilot's voice made his displeasure perfectly clear.

"The only reason I'm landing in this is because I've got three sick people to fly out of McMurdo," the pilot had said to him when he boarded.

It was bumpy outside, and though not exactly a whiteout, visibility was low. The pilot wasn't wrong, but at the moment neither of them had a choice.

Morgan made a promise, and he would be bringing back Bloch's nephew. He hoped it would be alive, but the boy would be coming home no matter what.

Everything else was detail.

However, based on the weather for the last week out here, some of those details would be tricky.

Since Morgan had taken the Renard Tech jet to Chile, he had a strong feeling that he had forgotten something.

That feeling had only gotten worse when he boarded this charter to take him the rest of the way. Now he realized that he hadn't forgotten anything, he'd left something behind. Rather, he'd left *someone* behind: Peter Conley.

The last time Morgan had been here, he and Peter had succeeded in their mission, but the fact was that the only reason Morgan had come back from that mission at all was because of Peter.

And Morgan had been very glad to come back knowing that Natasha Orlov was waiting for him. Of course, things had fallen apart with Natasha very soon after that.

Not only did the life he had envisioned with her never materialize, but the last time he spoke to her, she'd had him bound to a chair with barbed wire.

Surprisingly, that was not the most vivid memory he had of Natasha, far from it.

He couldn't bring himself to regret what had happened at the end because it had all led to Jenny, and later to Alex. Those women had become his life—at least the only part of it that mattered.

Yet Morgan thought about Natasha and, very occasionally, dreamt about her. There were regrets, but only about what she had believed about him at the end.

Morgan mentally shook off the thoughts. The last time he had been in Antarctica, he had been thinking about Natasha more than was healthy on a mission.

He'd come through it because of Conley, but he was here alone now and whatever happened next would require his complete focus.

As if to prove that point, the medium-sized prop plane he was in shook and then dropped in the air for a few seconds.

The pilot's voice echoed through the cabin. "Make sure you are buckled up, Mr. Morgan. We'll be on the ice in just a few minutes."

Now comes the hard part, Morgan thought.

* * * *

"Let's start with Tsar Bomba," Bloch said across her conference table to Lincoln Shepard and Karen O'Neal.

"Literally, it means Tsar Bomb," Shepard said. "It was the largest, most powerful nuclear weapon ever built. The Russians tested it in 1961, and the fireball was five miles in diameter. In fact, the shockwave nearly crashed the plane that dropped it when the aircraft was almost thirty miles away. Overall, the blast was 1,500 times more powerful than the Hiroshima and Nagasaki weapons, combined."

"The Russians actually built and tested this?"

"On an island in the Arctic circle. It turned out to be a bad idea. The mushroom cloud was forty miles high, and the only reason there wasn't worse nuclear fallout was that the stronger than expected shockwave kept the fireball from hitting the ground."

"Okay, so why is an Ares agent connecting this with you?" Bloch asked.

"It's possible that Ares learned I work for Zeta and are taunting us, but I take it as proof that Kurt Richter is still alive. One of our thought experiments involved dropping a nuclear weapon of that size into the Marianas Trench in the Pacific," Shepard said. "We didn't come up with that. It was a question that had been studied by scientists for years. We did the math, however, to try to model the devastation. People have theorized that the detonation could crack the Earth's crust, but we proved that wouldn't happen. However, there would be massive earthquakes and tsunamis with catastrophic loss of life in Asia and Australia, as well as the western United States. The total devastation would involve a significant percentage of the world's population."

"You think that Ares built this bomb?" Bloch said.

"We certainly can't rule it out. We know they have at least four thermonuclear weapons, or the enriched uranium from four weapons. There may be others, and they may have other sources of uranium."

"Okay, but why do it at all? Threats? Blackmail? And who would they threaten, the world?" Bloch said.

"I've given this a lot of thought, and I have grave concerns here. We know that Ares was behind the Russian virus operation that involved Karen and Alex Morgan. The problem there was that even just creating the virus—especially in an unofficial desert lab without proper HAZMAT procedures and equipment—was literally crazy."

"Yes, we still have no idea why they did it," Bloch said. "No intelligence organization in the world even has a workable theory."

"I don't think we can rule out the possibility that they really want to destroy everything," Shepard said.

For a second, Bloch was speechless. Even the usually very hard to read Karen O'Neal seemed mortified.

"Why?"

"Pick your crazy agenda," Shepard said. "You have your religious sects that want to bring about the end times. We know there was an environmental angle on the creation of the virus—though we don't know if it was genuine. And most theories about organizations that seek massive destruction is that they want to seize power over what's left. But what if they don't want anything to be left?"

"Oh my God," Bloch said.

"An overly complex form of personal, group, or global suicide may be at work here," Shepard said. "And that changes things. One of the reasons that suicide bombing is so devastating is that the bomber doesn't have to worry about an escape plan. What if that is what Ares is doing, the equivalent of some massive suicide bomb? What if they just want to burn it all down, and not to build it back in their image, just to destroy it?"

"But who would want that?"

"I know that Kurt Richter believed that was the flaw in most terroristic, political, or religious acts of destruction—that the plotters were trying to achieve a primary goal. He always thought that this attitude limited the ultimate destructive power of the plot. Before, I always thought he was just eccentric and using that belief for thought experiments. Now I'm much less certain."

"And with Ares he might have found like minds," Bloch said.

"That is what worries me," Shepard said.

"Okay, Mr. Shepard, because *I* don't have enough to worry about, tell me what else they may be working on."

"The virus was one plot, we know. And, of course, there is the Tsar Bomba possibility. Then there are two others we modeled. One was the idea of knocking out space launch capabilities. Once you'd done that, you could do a number of other destructive things. Destroy satellites. Establish dominance in space. And there was one other possibility. At the time, it was science fiction, but now . . ."

"What?" Bloch asked.

"Redirect an asteroid to Earth. The farther away it is, the less you have to move it. Anything bigger than a mile wide would cause massive devastation. Anything bigger than fifty miles would destroy all life on Earth."

"Could that be done? I mean, physically, would it even be possible?"

"Theoretically, but there are a lot of variables. Size and makeup of the asteroid, for one. Also what you use to move it. The only thing we have going for us is that no one has any heavy-lift launch platforms left, as far as we can tell."

Bloch took a second to absorb that.

"Don't just look for finished platforms," she said. "Scan for components. Or even any hidden industrial capability to make those components. Let's assume Ares has thought this through and has a plan to assemble both a rocket and a launch facility quickly."

"We'll start now," Shepard said as Bloch started to get up. "But there is one more."

Bloch had to force herself to sit back down slowly.

"The other operation would be to melt a significant portion of Antarctic ice. If you did that, it would relieve surface pressure on the massive volcanic system in Antarctica. There are a number of super-volcanoes which—"

"I'll stop you there. I think I can guess. Massive regional if not global devastation?"

"Yes," Shepard replied. "At a minimum we'd be looking at a two-hundred-foot rise in sea level within years, and that's not the worst of it . . ."

"As you know, Dan Morgan is in Antarctica now. What you don't know is that he and Peter Conley had a mission there more than twenty-five years ago for the CIA. They found a secret Russian underground nuclear waste site and buried it under a mountain of stone and ice."

Shepard clearly didn't like the sound of that. And Bloch didn't like the look on his face when he heard it. "I'll send you the report," she said. You tell me when you've had a chance to review it."

Silence fell over the room. Bloch took another deep breath and asked, "Anything else?"

"No, Director," Shepard said.

Then Bloch got up to leave as Shepard and O'Neal followed suit.

When they were standing, Bloch stopped and said, "Thank you. I know this is hard, but there is no one else that can do this work, at least not as well as Zeta can. If we can get through this and put an end to Ares once and for all, then we can go back to worrying about wars and terrorist attacks."

"Yes, Director," Shepard and O'Neal said in unison.

Chapter 23

When the helicopter touched down on the deck of the *Galene*, Devan stepped out, and then Alex quickly followed. Someone that Devan obviously knew greeted them and led them off the platform.

Once they were clear, the helicopter took off again, and Alex looked around at the deck.

Now this looked like a research ship, not like the prince's insane, mutant super-yacht-salvage-boat.

The *Galene* was 225 feet of busy people, large cranes, and at least one mini-sub that she could see.

A man in a blue jumpsuit approached them and extended his hand. "Devan, good to see you."

If Alex had to guess, she would say the man was in his indeterminate forties, but his shaved head made it hard to make an accurate estimate.

"Good to see you, Nathaniel," Devan said.

And then Alex realized where she knew him from. This was Nathaniel Blake. He'd made a fortune in manufacturing equipment for England's North Sea drilling operations.

"And you must be Alex," Blake said.

She extended her hand, and he shook it. "Mr. Blake," she said.

"Please call me Nathaniel."

"It's very nice to meet you. I'm pleased to meet a—" Alex had to stop herself from saying *billionaire*. "Someone in your position who *isn't* trying to get into space."

He smiled at that. "If we're all looking in the same direction then . . . well, I'm not sure, but it can't be good. I'm very glad to meet you. Our young master Devan speaks very highly of you. And he almost always shows good judgment."

"Almost always?" Alex asked.

"He's quite committed to Liverpool FC," Nathaniel said. "Even though everyone knows that Manchester United is a far superior club. Do you have a preference?"

Without blinking, Alex said, "The Red Sox."

Nathaniel laughed at that one. "Of course, Devan mentioned that you were from Boston."

That left Alex wondering about the level of detail that Devan had given Nathaniel about her in their discussions.

"I'll have someone take you to your quarters. Once you're settled, we can meet for dinner, and then I'd like to invite you down to the trench tomorrow morning."

"The sub's ready?" Devan said, clearly excited.

"Just got out of dry dock. Repairs are finished, and you're welcome to join us," Nathaniel said. "Ms. Morgan?"

"You're going down to the trench?"

"Yes, and you can be among the very few that have seen what we are about to," Nathaniel said.

"Um, that is very generous," Alex said. "But no training is required? Special suit?"

"Nothing like that. I know what I'm doing, so does Devan for that matter. It's all very civilized. Just wear something reasonably comfortable."

"You said the sub was in the shop?" Alex said.

"Routine maintenance and a few upgrades," Nathaniel replied.

Alex didn't see another option, so she simply said, "Then thank you. I'd love to go."

"Brilliant," Nathaniel said.

Once they were settled in their rooms and Alex had a chance to change, Devan came to get her.

"Alex, it's okay if you're nervous. You don't have to come along," Devan said.

"I'm not nervous, just surprised. I didn't expect to be diving . . . at all, let alone so soon," Alex said.

"I've seen you fight off armed pirates with tablecloths," Devan said. "It's okay if you don't like submarines."

"It's not that I don't like them. I've never thought about it. And didn't that sub that visited the *Titanic* just . . ."

Devan nodded in understanding. "This is completely different. For one, we're going much deeper than they did." He clearly realized that this was not the tack to take with Alex. "I mean that that sub was nothing like these. They were an accident waiting to happen. It was tragic for the passengers, but the people in charge did the equivalent of going to space in a garbage can. In the sixty-year history of this sort of deep-sea exploration, there hasn't been a single other death . . . in legitimate research vessels."

Alex had thought they were going to remain on ship to provide additional security and then get involved if an Ares ship showed up with a bomb. She didn't expect to actually go underwater, but they were here so that no one dropped a few tons of trouble into the deepest place on the earth. It wouldn't hurt to visit the site they were there to protect.

Pushing down her concerns, Alex said, "Let's go, I'm excited to see what it looks like down there."

* * * *

Peter Conley appreciated the shower after their latest session of haunted house laser tag. According to the crew, it was supposed to be fun and not necessarily particularly competitive, or much of a workout.

But they had never played with Dani.

Conley enjoyed her style of play and appreciated the workout, especially since he and Dani had stopped their normal martial arts sparring sessions. She had claimed that it was due to her "motion sickness" on board, but in the past he'd found that she would train harder when she was sick or had a minor injury.

Of course, he knew the reason but would let her tell him in her own time. He also knew that meant he needed to be prepared to wait.

Dani had opened up quite a bit since they had been together, but it had taken time. She'd also learned to keep to herself while working her way up in the Chinese government after the party had taken her parents from her.

He knew that motherhood was seen as a weakness in official Chinese circles, an area in which she regularly had to compete with men for position.

However, he couldn't help but be happy. He knew she would get there, and then they could talk about the future.

Given his past and his track record with women and relationships, her pregnancy should have scared him, but it did not. He found himself looking forward to it.

The fact was that their lives wouldn't be much different. They kept their own apartments, but they rarely spent a night apart.

No, he decided, the future would only be a little different, but—he realized—it would be better. And then there would be a baby.

Suddenly, the life that Dan Morgan chose decades ago, the life that Conley had never thought was for him, was not only possible, it was now inevitable.

While Dani was still getting dressed, he received a message on his phone. They had a surprise conference with Director Bloch in ten minutes.

It looked like that future would begin after a slight delay.

When the time came, he and Dani sat in front of her laptop and Bloch appeared on the screen. The story the director told was . . . remarkable. The potential plots she described were horrific.

"Does this focus our search?" Conley asked.

"Not really. We still don't know what role the Indian Ocean might play in any of Ares's plans. It could be an assembly area for nuclear weapons, the potential site of a launch platform for a rocket, or something else we haven't thought of. The mission remains unchanged. Scan for unidentified submarines or drilling platforms. Do your radiological scans and keep your eyes out for anything that looks or feels wrong. Also, be wary of any potential threat to the mining ship itself. I wish I could tell you more, but I wanted you both to know the stakes here."

"I appreciate that, Director," Conley said. "Any chance we could get some help from the US or British navies?"

"I've made a case to both United States and British intelligence agencies, but what we have is thin by any normal standards. And even though we have friends in both organizations, getting military assets reallocated . . . just isn't feasible."

Bloch took a breath and for a second she seemed . . . tired . . . distracted. Conley found that unnerving.

The slip was momentary, and then the director's iron grip was back.

"I also don't know that naval resources would help you much. They might widen the search, but I understand the sensors on your aircraft are better than anything currently in the navy. And you are covering quite a bit of ground. In any case, you both are what we have to work with right now."

"I understand, Director. If there is something to find in these waters, we will find it," Conley said.

"Good hunting," Bloch said and disappeared from the screen.

Conley was pleased they had spoken. It gave him no information he could act on, but it helped to steel his resolve. After all, he had more to fight for than he had ever had before.

* * * *

"What can I do for you, Mr. Morgan?" Childs said, holding out his hand.

Morgan shook the man's hand and then took a seat when the older man did.

"Initiate an immediate search and rescue operation at the Daystrom Base," Morgan said.

"Let me put it another way," Childs said, softening what was about to come with a smile. "What *else* can I do for you?"

Childs was a tall, relaxed African American man about ten years older than Morgan himself. He was dressed in khaki slacks and a plain blue oxford shirt that said he was serious but not stuffy.

Morgan had noticed that a lot of the higher-up administrators at McMurdo Base dressed like that. No suits and ties at any level for this group.

And there was no one higher up the food chain than Childs, the administrator of McMurdo Base, the largest community on the continent.

"There is nothing else I need. This is an emergency. The base has been cut off for over a week," Morgan said.

"I know that very well, Mr. Morgan. I know the base manager personally. The problem is that it is one of a dozen bases that are officially out of communication because of the weather."

"I understand," Morgan replied. "But I have to get out there."

"Look, I don't know who you are, but I do know that before you came, I got a call from my boss, the director of the United States Antarctic Program. She told me to give you any assistance within my power to give. And after we were done talking, I got a call from the director of our parent organization, the National Science Foundation—who, by the way, was appointed by the president of the United States. He stressed how important it was that McMurdo be at your disposal and that you have anything you needed."

Wow, Morgan thought. *Diana Bloch must have called in every favor she could for this one.*

"And just to be clear," Childs said. "In a pinch, the director of the National Science Foundation can talk to the president anytime he needs to and could have requested an emergency search and rescue operation conducted by the US military, but he didn't and for the same reason that I'm not going to: it's just not safe. It's whiteout conditions and seventy degrees below zero, with hurricane-level winds."

Morgan understood. No one who had a choice would go out there, or order anyone else to go. The problem was that he hadn't been ordered, he'd been asked, and asked by someone to whom he owed more than loyalty. He owed Diana Bloch his life and, more importantly, his daughter's life.

"That's a long way of saying that I would help you if I could," said Childs. "And let me be very clear about this, I would help you even if I didn't have people who regularly met with the president leaning on me. This is what we do. McMurdo is the biggest base on the ice and everyone out here depends on us—even the groups that don't like Americans very much. Plus, as I said, my friend runs that base."

"I understand, but I still need to get there," Morgan said. Then, before Childs could speak, he added, "All I'm asking for is advice."

For several long seconds, Morgan could see Childs wrestling with himself about what to say next. "Okay, I get that this is personal. There's one pilot who might be willing to take the trip. Now remember, the plane you came in on barely got out of here, and things have only gotten worse. We're battening down. But like I said, there's one pilot. Otherwise, it's ground transport if you can find it, and if possible, that's a worse option than air at the moment. Sixty miles is too far to go on the ground in this weather. If something happens out there, no one can get to you."

"I'll take what I can get. Where can I find this guy?" Morgan asked.

Twenty minutes later, Morgan was out in the cold following a guideline that had posts every dozen feet. The wind was brutal, and he was depending on his goggles and face mask to protect him because exposed skin would suffer frostbite in under a minute.

From his survival training more than two decades ago, Morgan had learned about the dangers of total whiteout, in which the snow in the air reduced the visibility to less than ten feet.

In those conditions, it was nearly impossible not to get lost, even in familiar surroundings. Hence, the guidelines. If you kept hold of them, you could get point to point relatively safely.

In this case, he'd left the administration building and followed a line that connected to a hangar two hundred yards to the west. The hangar was one of the buildings that wasn't there when Morgan first visited.

McMurdo had grown to one hundred buildings and now had three airfields instead of just the one.

The base was also having weather that Morgan had only heard about. In his single two-week visit last time, he'd seen cold and some snow but none of the extremes that were happening now.

Though he could not have imagined it then, the last time he had come he'd been lucky, at least with the weather. And even the business with the Russians had turned out all right, thanks to the fact that Conley was with him.

If Peter were here, Morgan had no doubt they would grab a plane or a chopper and figure it out from there. Lacking Conley, Morgan found himself negotiating with the only pilot Childs thought might even consider a charter in this weather.

"Is your name really Crash?" Morgan asked.

"Yeah, but it's an honorary title," the man of about thirty said.

"Honorary?" Morgan asked.

"More like ironic. They call me Crash because I fly in anything and I have never . . ." he said.

"Crashed?" Morgan supplied.

"Well, not yet," Crash said with a broad smile.

"Then I'm in the right place. I've been told that you are the only one crazy enough to take a helicopter out in this and get me to Daystrom Base today," Morgan said.

The man's face fell. The humor left it, and the expression that remained was deadly serious.

"I may be a little bit crazy, but I'm not stupid," Crash said.

"I will pay you what you make in a year," Morgan said. If this was a negotiation, he was determined to make it quick.

"That sounds good, but it would be pointless if I wasn't around to spend it, which I would not be if I did what you want. In fact, neither would you."

Morgan could tell by the man's face that there was no angle here. Crash wore a solemn expression and had clearly decided not to live up to his name.

Then the man seemed apologetic. "I really wouldn't be doing you or whoever you are going to see any favors. Reports say that the weather will clear in five days. If it's even remotely safe, I'll take you for one month's salary."

Five days was more than enough time for Jeffrey Bloch to die in the cold if he was even still alive. Hell, five minutes in this cold would kill someone who was already even moderately injured.

"I appreciate your time," Morgan said. "Can you point me to somewhere I can get ground transport."

Crash seemed surprised. "Listen, you really don't want—"

"Who do I see?" Morgan said seriously. "I need to get underway as soon as possible."

Chapter 24

As soon as Lily left, Scott Renard got to work looking over the deployment and testing phases of the anti-missile system. It was remarkably complicated, with sensor, laser, and ballistic components. It also required massive data-processing resources.

Renard made some notes for tweaks to the algorithms that underpinned the threat-identification and targeting software, and then focused on his real concern, which was overlapping the times and places for the anti-missile meetings and General Hyo's schedule in Seoul.

The man was a monster, with numerous human rights violations and other crimes that would have been war crimes if they weren't perpetrated against his own people.

Of course, the South Korean government had numerous political and other concerns that drove their behavior. Often, Renard knew, politicians had to lie down with monsters to achieve their ends. It was a distasteful truth about running a country.

But Scott Renard didn't run a country, though Renard Tech employed many thousands of people across its various divisions—and its market cap was significantly higher than the value of the North Korean one, as well as a number of other actual functioning nations.

As a private citizen and businessman, Renard didn't have to worry about politics or currying favor with despots. His only concern was solving problems, and he regarded General Hyo as a problem.

The man had hurt Lily, and if he'd had the opportunity, he would have hurt her much worse and then killed her.

Renard and Diana Bloch had mustered all of the resources of both his company and Zeta Division to try to rescue Lily, and it had almost not been enough. In the end, it had taken intervention from Mr. Smith himself, a member of the board of the Aegis Initiative, which oversaw Zeta.

With some changes in Renard Tech's anti-missile project schedule, Renard saw that there were three times when he could arrange to be in the same building as Hyo.

The key was to do it in a way that didn't set off red flags in Lily's carefully wrought security for him and the Renard Tech team.

There was no doubt that if Lily got wind of what he was planning, she would shut it down.

He wasn't comfortable deceiving her, but she didn't understand what drove him. In her mind, he was somehow above or separate from the kind of moral compromises that she had to make in her own work. What she didn't understand was that something had happened to him when he had nearly lost her.

He had never taken a life with his own hands, but he had provided the tools that Zeta agents had used to eliminate people who would have done great harm to others. He had done that knowingly and without regret.

Whatever happened with Hyo, Scott knew that he would have no regrets.

* * * *

Conley had one more flyby of an offshore oil rig and then it would be time to go back to the *Demeter*.

Of course, not *straight* back.

He always made sure he had enough fuel for some maneuvers in this beautiful aircraft. It really moved like nothing else he had ever flown, or really anything else in the air.

The same vectored-thrust capability that allowed it to take off and land vertically also gave it the ability to change speed and direction like no other plane.

He was putting so many regular flying hours on the aircraft that he wanted to make sure his combat flying skills were as strong as his normal flight skills.

Of course, since this fighter had traded its usual armaments for an extensive sensor array, it wasn't likely that he would be taking the aircraft into combat. However, as Dan Morgan always said about carrying a weapon, it was better to have the skills and not need them, than need them and not have them.

Plus, pulling extreme maneuvers in this aircraft was without a doubt the most fun Conley had ever had in a cockpit.

Conley used the tactical system to lock the aircraft onto the offshore oil platform up ahead. Though the jet didn't have any actual weapons, it still had all of the offensive targeting equipment—which was useful in directing the jet's sensors.

He lowered his speed as he always did when approaching a platform. Since he was coming in at a lower-than-normal altitude, he didn't want to scare the people working there.

He transmitted the standard friendship message, tailored to the language of the crew on the platform—which Zeta had identified as Sri Lankan. The message identified the Harrier as a civilian aircraft conducting a scientific survey of atmospheric conditions and ocean currents.

Shepard had designed the message so that it was scientifically accurate and extremely detailed, so much so that the practically minded rig crews never replied with more than a simple acknowledgment.

One at a time, Conley approached the platform from each of its four sides, breaking off when he was about a quarter mile out.

The platform had been there for five years, some sort of joint venture between the Sri Lankan government and Iran.

Conley brought the jet around and prepared for his fourth approach. When he was finished, he would start his normal grid search of the nearby waters. This would show any submarines or hidden structures under the surface.

Conley had just switched over the sensors and had begun his last run when Shepard's voice was in his ear.

"Conley, break off," Shepard said.

This was the first time he had spoken to Shepard since they had tested the sensors on his first survey flight.

"What's wrong?" Conley asked.

"Not sure. There was something strange on the infrared. It might be nothing, but if it's something, I don't want to put anyone on notice. Why don't you just come in, refuel, and we'll look at the data. Like I said, it might be nothing."

* * * *

"Can we please skip the part where you tell me it's too dangerous?" Morgan said.

Jerry of Jerry's Garage wasn't intimidated by Morgan's tone or posture. He just shook his head and said, "No, this is the part where I tell you I'm not going to rent you a vehicle that I know for an absolute fact will never be coming back here."

Fair enough, Morgan thought, but he couldn't leave without a Snowcat.

"I'll buy it from you," Morgan said.

"You'll buy it?" Jerry asked.

"Yes, I'll buy it, in cash, right now."

"You carry around that much cash, or do you need to go to an ATM first?" Jerry said. His tone had shifted to wary.

Morgan opened up his small Renard Tech duffel and pulled one stack of hundreds and held it out. Jerry stared at the cash as if it were an alien creature. Then Morgan showed him how much more was in the bag.

After three full seconds, Jerry looked up at Morgan and said, "Let me show you what I have."

"This is search and rescue, so I'll need to bring gear and I'll need enough interior space to bring back at least one injured person."

"Any special equipment?" Jerry asked.

"No. I brought medical supplies, an Arctic survival kit, some tools. I have it all in the administrative building and McMurdo. From you, I'll need some diesel."

"How much?" Jerry asked.

"As much as the Snowcat can carry. I'll want to run the engine if I get stuck, and I want extra if the base has run out."

Morgan knew that sounded absurd. Any base on the ice would run out of food before they ran out of diesel. But he also knew that hitting the tanks and generators were his and Conley's first move when they took out the Russian base the last time he was here.

"The trade-off is that the heavier the unit, the more likely it is that you'll run into trouble . . . sinkhole, crevasse, that sort of thing."

"I understand. Let's see what you have," Morgan said.

There were eight Snowcats in the garage. Two had the interior space he needed, and Jerry pushed him toward the older model.

That made Morgan smile. The man didn't want to lose the nearly new vehicle.

"It's solid, and it's been in the cold longer than I've been alive. I just rebuilt the engine myself. It's the closest thing I have to bulletproof," Jerry said.

The pitch was pretty good. More importantly, Morgan found that he believed Jerry. "How much?"

Jerry thought for a minute and said, "How about forty?"

That was fair, Morgan thought, and he liked Jerry a little more for that.

"Can you have the Cat fueled, loaded, and prepped while I get the rest of my gear?"

Jerry agreed and twenty minutes later he helped Morgan load his things into the interior space, which was mostly full of five-gallon plastic jugs of diesel.

"I also gave you as many spare blankets as I could find and some water," Jerry said. "I know everybody thinks the snow will be enough, but sometimes you just need a drink without having to heat up snow."

"Thank you," Morgan said.

"You've been on the ice before?" Jerry asked.

"Yes," Morgan said.

"Then you know these things go faster than is safe under normal conditions. If visibility is bad and you hit volcanic rock too hard and you blow a tread, your trip is over. Same with crevasses. Your best defense against falling into one is going slow. If you start to tip forward, you can pull back."

Morgan cracked the one case he hadn't loaded onto the Snowcat. He pulled out a small satellite dish.

"Uplink to the crevasse-detection satellites and local ground-penetrating radar system," Morgan said.

Jerry seemed impressed and then frowned. "That's okay for mapping and will help you avoid known hazards but you really need real-time warnings in this weather."

Morgan pulled out his last piece of equipment and put it on the Snowcat's dash. It was about a foot across with a nine-inch screen.

"That's why I brought this. It's a portable radar unit," Morgan said.

Jerry appeared shocked. "The only 'portable' units I've seen are carried on trucks and extend twenty-five feet in front of the vehicle on steel booms."

Morgan shrugged and said, "I have a guy."

"You do realize that is *fish* radar," Jerry said.

"What?" Morgan replied.

"It's for a boat. It's to find fish," Jerry said.

Morgan saw the Catch Master logo on the side, and as he put additional sensors on the far ends of the dash, he said, "It's been modified. My guy is very good."

He wasn't sure that was enough for Jerry, but it had to be enough for Morgan. He trusted Shepard and his team. With luck, the software Shepard's people were still working on to run the unit would be ready anytime now, and then Morgan would receive it through the satellite uplink.

Jerry handed Morgan the keys to the Snowcat. "Any chance I can talk you out of this? It's not too late for a full refund."

"No, but thanks for trying. I'll tell you what, I'll let you buy it back from me when I return."

Morgan got into the Snowcat and turned the key. The engine caught right away.

That was a good sign, Morgan thought.

It wasn't much but he would take it.

* * * *

Bloch rarely left her office, and even more rarely went down to the Basement. However, at the moment, she judged that Shepard and O'Neal's time was more valuable than hers.

"The infrared readings were not consistent with any conceivable use for an oil platform," Shepard said.

"Okay, the infrared is showing something odd," Bloch said. "What does that tell you?"

O'Neal looked up from her computer in the couple's shared workstation and said, "It tells me that we are on the right track. At first, we were studying oil platforms as potential heavy launch facilities. On the macro side, we've also been reviewing shipping manifests for both supply ships and oil tankers to see if there was anything out of the ordinary. We've been checking to see if any oil rigs have been getting too many supplies and not offloading enough, or any, oil. That would tell us if that platform has another purpose."

That was clever, even by the standards of high-end intelligence work. The Basement was one of the few places in the world where Bloch sometimes felt genuinely out of her depth.

"And we've calibrated sensors for the oil platform surveys to make sure the rig is a functional oil platform and that it doesn't have any unusual structures. The platform Conley just surveyed didn't have any of those red flags, but it was generating a lot of heat in two locations, much more than you would need for any use I can think of but one, manufacturing."

"So they are building something," Bloch asked.

"Specifically, they are generating the kind of heat you would need if you are making something out of steel or a composite material."

Bloch had to stop and think about that.

"Why would you manufacture anything literally in the middle of nowhere, in the ocean?"

"The only reason to do it would be that you absolutely wanted to hide it. And they have done a masterful job of doing so. Unless you surveyed the platform from the air with sophisticated sensors, you'd never see it. You certainly would never see it with satellites."

"Well, it's a good thing we have someone in the area with the equipment to find out what they are trying so hard to hide. How soon can we get Conley back out there?"

"Not long," Shepard said. "I just have to recalibrate our sensors now that we know what we are searching for."

Bloch looked forward to giving the other side a bit of a surprise. If this was Ares, for once, it appeared that Zeta had the jump on them.

Chapter 25

Though the Zeta staff called it the War Room, it was really just a conference room with a large monitor on one wall and three smaller monitors on either side of that one. At least that was the current configuration.

The main screen was split down the middle. On the right was a satellite-eye view of an oil platform. On the left was a view from Peter Conley's cockpit.

With their audio plugged in to Conley's radio, Bloch could hear her agent running through his preflight routine. Someone on the deck gave Conley a thumbs-up and Bloch could hear the low rumble of the jet's engine firing.

Within seconds, the view shifted slightly as the aircraft rose smoothly from the deck. Clearly, Bloch's agent had mastered the plane in his short time on the ship.

"Conley, this is Shepard. I'm here with Director Bloch for this survey."

"Glad to have you with us, Director. How sure are we that this is an Ares facility?" Conley said.

"It's our best guess right now, but I think you are about to find out for sure," Bloch said.

"Understood," Conley said.

"Standard oil platform survey pattern to start," Shepard said. "We'll fine-tune the sensors and then you can start getting closer. By the time you're done, we'll know what cereal they are having for breakfast."

"Good. And it's not like they can go anywhere," Conley replied.

"If it looks like Ares, feel free to get close. Very close," Bloch said. "They have been taunting us. If they are building something dangerous out there, let's let them know that we know."

"Affirmative," Conley said.

Bloch could see the platform in the distance from the wing camera. The plane approached and then broke off before it got too close, repeating the operation from the three other sides.

"That's good. Infrared is lighting up," Shepard said. "I'm also getting some interesting readings on the spectrograph."

Bloch could see two of the monitors around the main screen come to life and show graphs and numbers that Bloch couldn't begin to read. Two of the other displays were showing what Bloch recognized as the fighter's various instruments.

"Ares or not," Shepard said, "someone is hiding something on that platform. Feel free to get as close as you want."

"Permission to buzz them, Director," Conley said.

"Buzz at will," Bloch replied.

Bloch could see through the cockpit camera that Conley was dropping altitude, so much so that he seemed only slightly higher than the top of the oil platform, which was barely two hundred feet above the water.

The sense of speed in the image was great, and slightly disorienting. The plane was coming in very fast, and at the last instant it gained a hair more altitude and barely cleared the top of the main tower on the platform.

"Haaaa!" Conley said.

Before his whoop was finished, one of the War Room's smaller monitors began to flash red.

"I've got something on my panel," Conley announced.

"On it," Shepard replied.

"My board is screaming that they have me on Radar Lock," Conley said.

"I'm sure they are just trying to scare you," said Shepard.

"Fair enough," Conley said. "I shook them pretty good. I'll come around and do it—"

His voice was interrupted by a klaxon in the cockpit.

Another screen on the wall came to life. It blinked the words "Active Missile Lock."

"You see that, Shepard?" Conley said.

"I do," Shepard said, typing furiously onto his keyboard.

"Did you and Renard's engineers leave me any missile countermeasures in this thing?" Conley asked.

Shepard hesitated before he replied, "No."

"On the plus side, the warning system seems to be fine—" Conley began, but he was interrupted by another alarm.

"Missiles away," Conley said.

"Use your speed! Now!" Shepard said.

"Afterburners on," Conley replied. Then the cockpit view began to shake. "But I can't outrun the missiles, can I?"

Bloch didn't need to check the satellite overview to see the answer to that. They all knew it.

"No," Shepard said. "You can't."

* * * *

Morgan had to fight the urge to go faster than ten miles an hour.

He'd been forced to start slowing down the first time the Snowcat hit a small piece of volcanic rock sticking out of the snow. He hadn't seen it. Though, to be fair, he often couldn't see anything at all.

The winds were regularly gusting at ninety miles an hour and sometimes hit well over 150.

Though the Snowcat was heavy, and fairly wide between the tracks on each side, the stronger winds sometimes rocked the Cat if they hit the vehicle on its side. Fortunately, he never had to turn into the wind to keep the vehicle from tipping over. That was something.

But since all he could see was the white snow in front of him, he had to watch his speed and use Shepard's radar to avoid large rocks and more than a few crevasses of indeterminate size.

When the visibility was less than ten feet, Morgan dropped his speed even further but never stopped. He knew that if he just kept moving forward, he would get there eventually.

He only hoped it happened in time to do some good.

Checking his coordinates, he saw that he was halfway there. Just a little less than thirty-five miles to go. With luck, he could make that in another four hours, and if the weather cleared, he would make even better time than that.

Just as he had that thought, the wind picked up and pummeled the side of the Snowcat, rocking it harder than it had any time since he'd started.

The weather was reminding him who was boss. That was fine with Morgan; he'd dealt with difficult bosses before.

* * * *

Conley's first maneuver was to fly for the sun. Since the missiles were likely heat seeking, conventional wisdom said to give them the biggest heat source in the sky.

When he'd confirmed that the missiles were on his tail, he kept on course and then banked hard to his right.

With luck, the missiles would keep on their trajectory and race for the sun until they ran out of fuel.

Putting on speed, Conley watched the tactical display that told him where the missiles were. He watched them continue in a straight line for a few seconds and then turn toward him.

Damn, he thought.

"They're still on you," said Shepard.

"I need a speed and collision analysis," Conley replied.

"Working on it . . ." Shepard said. Then he added, "You've got a solid ninety seconds."

That was a decent lead, provided he could come up with something fast.

"We're trying to identify the missiles to estimate range and fuel," Shepard said, with very little hope in his voice. Conley appreciated the effort, but it was a Hail Mary. Missiles like these were designed to catch fighters, and that meant that pilots very rarely succeeded in avoiding them by making them run out of fuel.

As for these specific missiles, Conley already knew what he needed to know about them. He had a good estimate of their reaction time and their turn radius.

Those were two areas in which he knew he could beat them, especially in a Harrier-class fighter. The key was to stay alive long enough to exploit those advantages.

His internal clock told him that he had just over a minute.

Conley decided that he wasn't going to wait that long and began throttling down his speed.

"Conley . . ." Shepard said.

"I'm trying a maneuver," Conley replied. Shepard said something after that but by then Conley was completely focused on flying and on the tactical display that showed him how close the two missiles were to his aircraft.

When he guessed they were less than twenty seconds away, he took his left hand off the stick and took hold of the thrust vector lever.

One of the best things about this plane was the brilliant simplicity of its additional controls. Pilots adjusted the angle of the thrust with a single lever.

Like many things about flying, the operation was simple enough but required a lot of practice and perfect coordination. Fortunately, Conley had spent every second he could putting the jet and himself through their paces.

With the missiles seconds behind him, Conley vectored the thrust about eight degrees forward and then pulled the stick.

Now the aircraft did the thing that made the Harrier famous; it turned practically on a dime.

Pulling about as much g-force as he could without passing out, Conley straightened out his thrust and throttled up his speed as he came out of the turn.

No missile in the world could match that maneuver, and these two didn't even come close. They continued straight on Conley's former course for a solid five seconds . . . before they began to turn.

Conley muttered and then Shepard spoke aloud the realization that hit Conley. "They are not heat seekers," Shepard said.

"No," Conley replied, then he muttered a few other terms under his breath.

Watching their arc on the tactical display, Conley realized that they might not be heat-seeking missiles, but they were operating in tandem.

That was something he could use.

"We're still trying to calculate their range and fuel," Shepard said, but the young man's heart wasn't in it. Playing cat-and-mouse with jet-killing missiles was not a game with much of a future.

"You've got maybe a minute on them," Shepard said.

"More than I need," Conley replied. He heard the confidence in his own voice. There was one thing he could still do.

For good or bad, this encounter would be over in less than a minute.

Altering his course, Conley made straight for the oil platform.

"Mr. Conley . . ." It was Director Bloch's voice on the radio now.

"Not to worry, Director. I'm going to give them back their missiles," Conley said.

As he raced for the platform, Conley banked left and then right.

Each time, after a short delay, the missiles mirrored his movements. That was, of course, what the missile operators were trained to do.

Initially, Conley had thought the lag time in the missiles' maneuvers was processing time, but he quickly realized that it was the operator's reaction time. Reluctantly, Conley had to admit that the operator was very good. To be that good, they had to remain hyper-focused on their target—which Conley was counting on.

Conley kept adjusting his weaving pattern to make the operator earn their money. Each shift also gave him crucial information about the person he now thought of as his opponent.

With the platform appearing to come up fast, Conley cut his speed. For this to work, he'd need the missiles to be close.

"Conley . . ." Shepard said, but Conley once again tuned out the voice.

When he was practically on top of the oil platform, he clocked the two tallest structures. The first was the oil derrick itself, which resembled a tubular steel pyramid. The second was the flare boom, which was angled out over the ocean and looked like a large construction crane.

Banking hard to the left, Conley straightened his trajectory out and then rolled the fighter so its wings were vertical when it shot through the space between the two structures.

A fraction of a second later, Shepard said, "Conley! Conley!"

"I'm still here," Conley said.

"We just showed two detonations," Shepard said.

Conley smiled. Based on what he'd learned about the operator, he guessed that both missiles hit the oil derrick solidly in its center.

Unable to resist, he pulled the jet around and vectored down the thrust to keep the burning oil platform in view.

"Mr. Conley, that was very impressive," Bloch said.

"Thank you, Director," he replied. "If you like, I can make another run on the platform with the sensors now."

"That won't be necessary," Bloch replied. "We'll let the US Navy examine the site directly. With luck, they will get there around the time Ares gets the fires out."

As the smile formed on his lips, a large explosion radiated out from the center of the platform. It was much bigger, he knew, than the one made by the two anti-aircraft missiles.

Instinctively, Conley vectored his thrust forward and started turning away from the explosion just as he could see a good-sized mushroom cloud form over the crumbling platform.

A blast wave hit the plane hard enough to rattle it and then Conley was speeding out of the area.

"What was that?" Conley asked.

"A large explosion," Shepard said. "Conventional. I'm guessing it was intentionally triggered."

"So the whole platform just took a cyanide pill," Conley said. "I'm sorry, Director. I know it would have been useful to examine the platform."

"It looks like there will be nothing left of it," Bloch said, but there was no regret in her voice. "Better them than you, Mr. Conley. Better them than you."

Chapter 26

"It looks like a seahorse," Alex said, pointing to the submersible.

"Yes," Nathaniel said. "And it stays vertical when it's in the water."

"You've taken it all the way down?" Devan asked.

"We have, several times in the last month," Nathaniel replied. He turned to Alex and said, "When Devan was last with us, he accompanied me to the seafloor, but we had not yet entered the trench."

Turning to Devan, Alex raised an eyebrow.

Devan shrugged and said, "It was a mission. Nathaniel was kind enough to let me dive with him in this beautiful machine."

"We were still in testing phase, and not to worry, Alex, the *Ometz Lev* passed all of her tests and has been making runs to the bottom of the trench for weeks now."

"*Ometz Lev?*" Alex asked.

"Hebrew for courage. Literally strength of heart," Nathaniel said. "I hope you don't mind working, Alex."

"Never," she replied.

"The *Lev* sails with a three-person crew. I'll be piloting. Master Devan will co-pilot and monitor systems. You'll be on the arms. That's those," he said, pointing to two mechanical arms that jutted from what would be the bottom of the sub when it was in the water.

"Simple joystick controls. You'll have plenty of time to practice on the way down. We'll be four hours down, four on the floor of the trench, and four back up. We have a full day planned."

They waited as a crane lifted the submersible into a vertical position and lowered it into the water, leaving the top third above the surface. Climbing down a short ladder, they stepped onto a platform that led to the hatch on top of the sub.

It was open and Nathaniel offered his hand to help Alex step in. "You take the ladder down to your seat at the bottom. It's a tight squeeze to get past the pilot and co-pilot seats but you'll have a bit of room once you're settled."

Climbing inside, Alex worked her way down a ladder that took her to her seat. Getting down was very tight, even with one of the seats above her station folded to one side.

It's a good thing I'm not claustrophobic, she thought.

Once she was sitting, the men got into position above her. She looked up to see Devan waving.

"You okay, Alex?" he asked.

"Fine," she said.

"Splendid," said Nathaniel. He shouted something to the crew outside, and then there was a loud clang as the hatch slammed shut.

It sounded very solid. That was something, she thought. *At least it's strong.* On the other hand, it also sounded like the closing of a crypt door in more horror films than she could count.

"Brace yourself," Nathaniel said.

She heard the clang of metal and felt a short drop as the larger ship released the *Ometz Lev* into the Pacific Ocean. She felt the sub tilt and bob briefly, then right itself.

There was a mechanical whir, and then the *Ometz Lev* began to descend.

* * * *

Shepard seemed almost upbeat when he entered Bloch's office.

"Good news?" she asked. She had counted Peter Conley's survival as a win. They might have lost the Ares facility, but they had tracked a major Ares base and handed the enemy a serious setback.

If nothing else, Zeta had turned an expensive enemy asset to molten metal and ash.

Shepard sat and said, "Not quite yet, but I think we're getting close. At first, I couldn't figure out how the base kept itself hidden, given how carefully we've been watching shipping in the Indian Ocean. But they were right down the line on the number of supply shipments they received and the barrels of oil they shipped out."

"But you found something?" she asked.

"Yes, the number of incoming and outgoing shipments was correct, but when we looked closer, we saw that the weight of the vessels that serviced the platform had been tampered with."

"So they were sending out less oil than they claimed?" she asked.

"Yes, and by itself that would be difficult. There were many oil tankers from several shipping companies, plus there are records at the receiving ports. And that's only part of it. As near as we could tell, the supply ships had their numbers fudged as well."

"Any idea what Ares was shipping out?" she asked.

"None," he said. "And it will take some time to untangle this mess, but we have somewhere to look. I have the team on it, and we're getting a lot of support from the people at Renard Tech. Eventually, we'll be able to trace their shipments, and I'm hoping to back-trace those orders to other Ares bases of operation."

That was more than Bloch had even been hoping for. They'd been able to take the fight to the enemy only a very few times, but this was potentially big. Perhaps a game changer.

"Thank you, Mr. Shepard. Very well done," she said. Then, because she could see that he was anxious to get back to his work, she added, "I won't keep you."

Shepard got up from his seat like she had just announced an early recess.

Bloch was taking her wins where she could these days. She had heard from Morgan when he hit the ice in Antarctica. She hadn't heard anything since, but she had faith in Morgan. If anyone could bring Jeffrey home, he could.

She had just begun to place a call to Peter Brown at MI6 when her assistant buzzed her and said that Karen O'Neal was waiting outside.

That was more than odd, especially since Shepard had just left.

"Send her in," Bloch said, and then Karen took a seat in front of her desk.

Immediately, Bloch could see that something was wrong, though usually Karen O'Neal was notoriously hard to read.

"Yes?" Bloch said.

"I've been monitoring the threat-assessment system. And something has happened," O'Neal said.

Bloch steeled herself. She wasn't sure she could handle one more crisis.

"It's something that we haven't seen before, not since we developed the system . . ."

Bloch had to force herself not to hurry the young woman along. That would only make it harder for O'Neal to get to her point.

"Since we started tracking threats, especially ones with regional and global potential, they have only gotten bigger and more frequent. But this is . . . unprecedented."

"A new threat?" Bloch said.

"No, the opposite. It's like someone flipped a switch. The system isn't picking up anything new or ongoing. There are the usual terrorist operations and relatively small blips, but nothing that we would call Ares-scale."

"And you think this is a bad thing?" Bloch asked.

"Yes," O'Neal said simply, and Bloch had the growing sense that the young woman was right.

"You think they have figured out how to game our system?" she asked.

"No," O'Neal said, shaking her head definitively. Bloch sensed a touch of pride there. Fair enough. The system was O'Neal's and there was nothing else like it in the world.

"We've gotten very good at identifying the false positives that Ares used to fool our system, but even those have stopped. I think they have gone inactive."

"But why . . ." Bloch said, but even as the words left her lips, she knew the answer. "Because whatever they are doing is already in motion and is so big that they've ceased all other operations."

"Yes," O'Neal said simply.

Given the scale of the plans that Shepard had warned her about, that was frightening. A huge, space-born attack. A giant nuclear bomb in the Marianas Trench. And then there was some sort of super-volcanic eruption in Antarctica.

As far-fetched as they sounded, any one of them would be devastating. The fact that Ares was so confident in them was very concerning.

"Thank you for bringing this to me," Bloch said.

"I haven't told Lincoln yet," she said. "Even though he shouldn't, he's felt responsible every time Zeta has confronted anything like one of those plans from college."

"He's been instrumental in helping us defeat every significant Ares action to date," Bloch said.

"I know, but he still feels it," O'Neal said.

"Then there is something we can do to help both him and everyone else. Please do whatever you can to help him track down Ares. If he can do that, we may have a real opportunity to cut them out at the source. Maybe your metadata analysis and processing algorithm that runs the threat-assessment system can be useful there."

That seemed to spark something in O'Neal. She stopped moving and didn't even blink for a full thirty seconds.

"I think it could," O'Neal said. The young woman smiled, actually smiled, and said, "Yes, I think it could."

"Excellent," Bloch said. "Then I won't keep you."

Chapter 27

When Morgan reached the location that the GPS told him the Daystrom Base should be, there was nothing but white.

Of course, that didn't mean it wasn't there. The whiteout conditions meant that visibility was about ten feet. If he was a foot more than that away, the base might as well be on the moon for all that Morgan could see.

When he and Conley first trained for their CIA mission to Antarctica, they had taken Agency cold-weather training, which was even more intensive than the training given to residents at McMurdo.

Both versions used the white bucket test, in which the trainee wore a five-gallon bucket over his or her head and tried to navigate on the ice. It actually did a good job of simulating complete whiteout conditions, in which you sometimes couldn't see your hand in front of your face.

By that standard, the ten-foot visibility was pretty good, and the wind was now down to less than seventy miles an hour.

Morgan stopped the Snowcat and put on his parka, gloves, and facemask. Last were his goggles. With this temperature and wind, any exposed skin would be frostbitten nearly instantly.

Leaving the vehicle running, Morgan stepped outside, the wind suddenly pulling at him. He tied one end of his nylon rope to the door handle of the Snowcat and let it out slowly.

Without a guideline, in this weather you could freeze to death a few feet from safety and never know it. Morgan headed straight for where he estimated the front entrance of the base should be.

His guess turned out to be pretty good, and he saw the double doors less than two seconds before he walked into them—or would have walked into them if they had been closed.

Morgan could only assume they had been propped open intentionally. There was literally no other reason to keep a door open anywhere on the ice. That meant one thing, Daystrom Base had been breached. And the attack had been successful, or at least successful enough that this part of the base was lost. Snow filled the large vestibule almost to the ceiling.

Digging through would take hours in good weather and would be impossible with the wind replacing the snow as fast as he could shovel it.

Morgan's only option was to try another entrance and hope there were survivors somewhere inside. He cut and tied off the guideline from the Snowcat, attaching it to one of the doors.

Then he tied a new line to the same door and headed clockwise around the base. He'd studied the layout. It was a simple T design, with four equal wings.

The second section also had the doors propped open.

Morgan tied off his line and started another one. When he reached the third set of doors, they were closed. That was promising. At least it meant that there was a chance.

Morgan opened the outer door, and the vestibule appeared untouched. Once he was inside, he turned on his flashlight, keeping the beam low. If there were people alive in the base, the odds said they were the attackers.

Any force aggressive and organized enough to hit a bunch of civilian scientists taking ice core samples would likely prevail. Correction, the base held a bunch of civilian scientists and one undercover naval officer.

Even so, it wasn't hard to win an engagement when you took your enemy by surprise and they didn't even know they were at war.

Morgan felt anger rising up inside him and pushed it down. There might be a time very soon when he would need it, but now it would just get in the way.

Out of the wind, Morgan took off his outer gloves, which were basically heavily insulated mittens. The thinner, inner gloves allowed Morgan the use of all of his fingers and, most importantly, allowed him to draw his weapon.

He pulled back his hood and took off his goggles and facemask. Now he could see and hear properly.

Keeping the flashlight beam small and low, he pushed open the inner door as quietly as he could with the hand holding the flashlight—all the while keeping his Walther ready in his right hand.

Once on the other side, he closed the door as quietly as he could.

Now that he was in the hallway, it was easy to see where he needed to go. He could see light up ahead. Everything was dark, except a single transom window above one closed door on the right. He was also nearly certain that he could hear low voices coming from inside.

Keeping himself against the wall, he approached the door slowly and quietly. When he was a dozen feet away, he put away his flashlight and followed the dim light from the transom.

When he got to the door, he realized how handy Conley would come in this situation. Morgan hated rushing into rooms without backup the way his partner hated using elevators in a firefight.

However, under the circumstances, he had no choice here. In a single motion, Morgan opened the door with his left hand while he raised the gun with his right, and then he stepped inside.

Scanning the smallish room for movement, Morgan saw that there were just two people sitting at a table . . . with playing cards in front of them.

One of the people was a young woman Morgan did not know. The other was Jeffrey Bloch.

They looked at him in surprise, and Morgan lowered his gun.

"Jeffrey Bloch," Morgan said.

"Yes . . ." The young man leaned forward, as if he could somehow protect the woman, but the motion was awkward from a seated position.

"My name is Morgan. Your Aunt Diana sent me."

"What?" the young man said, looking like Morgan had just announced he was Santa Claus.

"Diana Bloch," Morgan said.

"Wait, you're Dan Morgan. My aunt, she's mentioned you," Jeffrey said.

"She thought you might be in some trouble," Morgan said.

"How did you get here?" Jeffrey asked.

"I've got a Snowcat running outside."

"Is there anyone with you?"

"No," Morgan said.

"You came out here, by yourself, in a Snowcat, in that weather?"

"Your aunt was very concerned, and looking at the base, I think she was right to worry. Where is everyone?"

"They're dead. We were attacked," Jeffrey said. "I'm the only survivor. I don't know why me, but—"

"Don't do that," Morgan said. "Don't ever feel guilty for surviving. It's one thing we have over everyone who has ever died. We're all just lucky to be here."

Morgan's antenna was up. If Jeffrey was the only survivor, who was the woman with him? She was studying Morgan closely. There was also something in her eyes. Was it . . . fear?

"Hello," he said, nodding at her. "I'm Dan Morgan."

She studied him warily. Then said, in a thick Russian accent, "I am Olga."

"Sorry," Jeffrey said. "This is Olga. She's the only survivor of a Russian base just two miles from here that was also attacked. It's a miracle she survived, and as big a miracle that she made her way here."

Olga said, "My English . . ." and then shrugged.

"She doesn't speak much English, but she's killing me at cards," Jeffrey said, smiling for the first time since Morgan had entered the room.

"How did you survive, and how are you still here? I see the generator and the heat are out," Morgan said. Scanning the room, he saw large metal cans filled with something burning. Whatever it was, it was actually keeping the room reasonably comfortable.

"It's hand sanitizer. It's the same, chemically, as the fluid they use in those fake indoor fireplaces."

"Good thing you had a good supply. You've been cut off for days," Morgan said.

"The base commander is . . . I mean was . . . a bit of a germophobe. During the pandemic, he really stocked up."

"Can you even get sick down here?" Morgan asked.

"Not really," Jeffrey said, shrugging. "And we had a lot of sanitizer to start, but we don't have much left now. If you didn't show up, I knew we'd have to start conserving, but I was afraid of letting it get too cold. There's a danger of falling asleep, and if you do . . ."

"What's the status of your generator?" Morgan asked.

"They sabotaged it. We fixed the damage, but they emptied the diesel tanks."

"Then it's a good thing I brought some diesel," Morgan said.

"Oh, thank God," Jeffrey said. "Otherwise, we'd have to chance your Snowcat, and it's really not safe to be out in this."

"That's what Jerry at the garage says. He doesn't think he's getting his Snowcat back. I really just came out here to prove him wrong."

"I doubt that," Jeffrey said. "I know what it must have taken." The young man extended his hand again. "Thank you."

"It really was my pleasure," Morgan said.

"You know, my aunt told me about you, quite a bit, actually—at least for her," Jeffrey said.

"In my defense . . ." Morgan replied. "Well, first you'll have to tell me what she told you. Whatever it was, I'm sure I had a good reason."

The young man laughed out loud at that, and Morgan saw Olga looking at them like they were both crazy.

"Come on, I left the Snowcat running. We can shut it down, get some fuel in the generator tanks, and get your base back on its feet."

Jeffrey suited up and Olga started to follow him. Morgan shook his head and said, "She can stay and keep the fires going. We'll need them until we get the heat back on and the temperature up in the base."

Morgan wanted to get Jeffrey outside. The fact was that there was a stranger on the base, shortly after an attack that killed the entire staff—except for one.

And it wasn't lost on Morgan that she was Russian. Jeffrey accepted her as a refugee from the Russian base, but Morgan couldn't shake the memory of his last encounter with Russians in this part of the world.

And the fact was they were now less than twenty miles from the volcanic tomb of the Russian nuclear waste.

It might not be fair to paint her with that same brush—given that she would probably not have been born at the time of that mission. Yet his gut told him that there might be trouble there, and Morgan didn't argue with his gut.

Chapter 28

Alex found that there was very little sensation of movement once they got going. That made sense given the fact that they were traveling at about one and a half miles an hour and heading straight down.

"How deep are we going?" she asked.

"About thirty-six thousand feet," Nathaniel said.

Alex marveled at that.

"It's about three times the depth of the *Titanic*," Nathaniel continued.

"And deeper than Mount Everest is tall," Devan added.

"It's the closest anyone can get to the center of the Earth, Alex," Nathaniel said.

The only illumination outside was from the bright lights outside of the sub. After a few hundred feet, she stopped seeing any fish at all. After three thousand feet, the last of the sunlight disappeared and Nathaniel had turned on the sub's powerful exterior lights.

However, there was nothing to see outside of their craft. Nathaniel explained that 90 percent of all sea life lived in the top six hundred feet of water, and they had left that behind some time ago.

At about the same time, Alex felt her nervousness disappear. Nathaniel explained that the sub's hull was reinforced titanium and that it was rated for even greater depths than the bottom of the trench—even though there were no greater depths on the planet.

In any case, when he had explained that if there was a problem—and the only problem worth worrying about was a sudden implosion—it would happen in about a thousandth of a second. This was, of course, much faster than human nerve conduction velocity.

So even if she heard a creak, they would be smashed to atoms before she had time to think about it.

Instead of making her more nervous, it had the opposite effect. Alex never worried much about things she couldn't control. On a mission, that kind of anxiety could be deadly.

She decided to just enjoy the ride.

After what felt like much less than four hours, Nathaniel said, "Alex, it's official. You are now at the deepest point in the ocean."

From above, Nathaniel slowly swept the ship's powerful lights downward. Alex suspected there was a bit of showmanship there, but she respected that. The view was amazing.

The lights now illuminated a hundred feet or so out of the bottom of the Marianas Trench. To Alex, it looked like the surface of the moon, desolate and nearly colorless—just a uniform gray/brown.

"It's called the Challenger Deep," Devan said. "It's a small part of the trench, but about fifty times the size of the Grand Canyon."

"It's your first time," Nathaniel said. "Look around for a bit and then we'll get you to work."

Alex was aware of Nathaniel and Devan speaking, but she was absorbed by the alien-looking world around her. There was the colorless bottom, with small rocks here and there, and then large rocks, some smooth and some with jagged shapes.

She caught movement and then saw what seemed like a dozen or so nearly transparent shrimp that were about an inch long. *So there is something alive down here,* she thought.

"Alex, are you ready?" Nathaniel said.

As if waking from a trance, Alex said, "Yes."

After a good amount of practice on the way down, Alex was confident about her skills with the two grabber arms. They used a control system that was familiar to her from the console video games she sometimes played with Shepard and Spartan.

She was surprised at how smoothly they moved and how fine the controls were. She found out why when she grabbed what appeared to be a flower growing out of a rock. She picked it up gently, put it in a small bio-container, and then put that container in a bin on the side of the sub.

Next was a scoop of what looked like sludge that Nathaniel said contained a rare bacteria.

After more than three hours, Nathaniel seemed very pleased with their haul, and he and Devan began preparations for their ascent.

On the way up, Devan announced that he couldn't reach the ship. Nathaniel was more annoyed than concerned and blamed the transmitter receiver on the sub.

"I thought we had licked that problem," the man said. "Something about the acidity of the water down here. We'll have to come up with a new unit."

The men chatted occasionally on the way up, but like Alex, they mostly remained thoughtful.

"We are right above you," a voice said on the radio.

Alex presumed the transmitter had sorted itself.

"Susan, where's Gregory?" Nathaniel asked, sounding a bit concerned.

"He had to take care of something," she said. "He will be on deck to meet you."

Alex didn't know Susan. In fact, she didn't think she'd met the woman during the brief time she was on board, but something wasn't right about her speech. It was too slow, too formal.

"Tell Gregory that he can't avoid me forever and I haven't forgotten that he owes me money," Nathaniel said. His voice, Alex noted, seemed normal.

"He hasn't forgotten, sir. It's all he talks about," she said.

Cutting the signal, Nathaniel said, "There's something wrong. Susan is under duress. No one would *ever* lend Gregory money."

"Alex," Devan called down. "You ready?"

"Yes, any idea what's going on?" Alex replied.

"None," he said. "Did you bring your weapon?"

"No," Alex said, cursing herself. "I honestly didn't think I'd need it."

"Me either. We may have to improvise," Devan said.

For the first time since she'd gotten onto the sub, Alex felt claustrophobic. If the situation got tactical, she would need to move fast, but that would be impossible if she had to shimmy up that tight space to get to the hatch.

Doing it under fire would be suicide. Of course, if the situation became a one-sided firefight, staying where she was would also be suicide.

Alex and Devan had come to the Pacific to find an Ares cell out to cause trouble. Now she was afraid they had just found one. Of course, it could be pirates, but that was, by far, the least likely possibility.

Looking up, she watched as Nathaniel released the hatch and pushed it open. He took one step up to put his hand outside and said, "I don't know you, sir, but we have a strict rule on this ship: no AK-47s. And I see five of you breaking that rule."

Good, Alex thought. Nathaniel was giving her and Devan intelligence. Unfortunately, though good to know, there wasn't much either of them could do with the information.

On the plus side, whoever it was hadn't fired any shots. In fact, the person talking to Nathaniel hadn't even raised his voice. Alex couldn't make out his words but the tone was even, if not polite.

"Okay, I'm coming out," Nathaniel said. "Let me just tell my crew what's going on."

He took a step down and then stage-whispered to Devan, "Close the hatch behind me and get out of here."

"But, Nathaniel—" Devan said.

"Just get yourselves somewhere safe and report," Nathaniel said as he quickly stepped up and out of the sub.

"I understand," Devan said. Then there was some sudden movement and the hatch slammed closed.

Moving quickly, Devan hit the seal and said, "Alex, get ready, I'm going to manually release the clamps."

He hit a switch somewhere and the sub dropped again, bobbing in the water before settling.

There were the pings of gunshots hitting the hull of the sub.

"They're shooting!" Alex exclaimed, immediately embarrassed to be stating something so obvious. But she was frustrated to be stuck, unable to move freely, let alone help.

Devan chuckled. "They are adorable. The titanium hull is designed for pressures that make gunshots seem like angel kisses. Still, Nathaniel did instruct us to get out of here."

He manipulated the controls and the sub started descending, a bit more roughly than when Nathaniel was piloting, and in less than a minute they were a few hundred feet under the surface and well out of reach of any weapons.

"What now?" Alex asked.

"Let's put a little distance between us and them. We used up most of the battery power getting down and then up again, so no long cruises. We only have a short time to figure out our next move."

Devan switched to the pilot's seat and Alex took the co-pilot's. Soon they had only moved a quarter of a mile or so from the site of the *Galene,* and Alex was wondering how long they should wait before surfacing and trying to see if the ship was still there.

The problem was that the submersible didn't have a periscope, and it wasn't designed to surface like a military submarine. Once it was above the water, docking clamps would lift it to the platform so people could enter and exit. The same clamps would then lift the sub, by crane, to its docking station on the larger ship.

If they opened the hatch when they were bobbing around in the ocean, they would almost certainly take on some salt water, which wouldn't do the delicate electronic equipment any good.

"Devan, do you have any active radar on this ship?" Alex asked.

The MI6 agent snapped to attention and said, "This is why I'm the sidekick at the moment. I didn't think of that." He flipped it on and said, "The *Galene* is still there." He worked a panel in front of him, and a rough, green-hued image of two shapes appeared on a screen between them. "Rough, sonar-based imaging. It's used to identify large marine life and shipwrecks."

Alex realized that she was looking up at the shapes of two vessels seen from their angle under the surface. Mostly she saw the bottom of the ships and she wasn't sure which was the *Galene.*

"The *Galene* is the smaller one. My best guess is that the other ship is a large fishing trawler."

Before Alex could wonder out loud why the ships were still sitting there, the radio came to life and Nathaniel's voice filled the sub.

"Guarantee the safety of my crew. Then I'll listen to your demands," Nathaniel said.

"We have no intention of harming anyone on board this ship," a man replied. His voice was calm and sounded almost reasonable, with a hint of a European accent. "And we have only two demands. One is that when we leave you, you report what has happened here today."

Alex assumed they were on the bridge of the ship and she guessed that Nathaniel had switched on the radio link to the *Ometz Lev* to give Devan and Alex whatever information he could.

"I have no idea what's happening here today," Nathaniel said.

"You will because you will witness it," the other man said. "And second, I want you to give a message to your friends at Zeta to tell Shepard the following: Tsar Bomba."

"What does that mean?" Nathaniel asked, and Alex felt a ball of lead drop into her stomach. It was impossible. She looked at Devan as he also realized what they were talking about.

"It's the name given to a Russian nuclear explosive device, the largest ever built. The one you see being moved by the crane on our ship is similar but larger in yield. Very soon we will deploy it into the ocean."

"Why?" Nathaniel said.

"In a few hours, you will see. In fact, you and your crew will likely be the first people to see what happens," the other man said, his voice sounding shockingly reasonable.

"Okay, we'll deliver your message and watch whatever it is you want us to see. Now will you get off my ship?"

"Keep your eyes on the water," the other man said.

There was rustling, the sounds of movement on the other side of the radio, and then silence.

Alex looked at Devan and knew that her eyes probably had the same slightly desperate appearance as his. If the two of them were on the *Galene,* there might be something they could do. Here, trapped in *Ometz Lev,* they were cut off from taking any action that might make a difference. All they could do was watch the sonar imaging screen and wait.

They didn't have to wait long. Within a minute, a third object appeared in the water. It was much smaller than the two vessels and had a cylindrical shape.

"Oh my God, they did it," Alex said out loud.

The object started its downward journey, and in less than thirty seconds they were watching it from above as it descended.

"If only we'd been on board . . ." Devan said. "I should never have listened to Nathaniel and stayed in here. At least then we would have had a chance, some chance."

"Actually, we do have a chance. In fact, I think we represent the *only* chance," Alex said.

He looked at her like she was crazy and said, "Alex, we're stuck in . . ."

"The only vessel on earth that has a prayer of reaching that thing and preventing what we both know will happen," Alex said.

"Alex, even if we could catch it, what would we do? And our battery power . . ." he said.

"We can't solve all of that now but there is one thing we can do. Devan, follow that nuclear bomb."

* * * *

"Help me understand what is happening while Alex Morgan goes chasing after this . . . thing," Bloch said to Shepard as he sat in front of her desk. When she told him the message she'd gotten from the *Ometz Lev*, he looked like he might pass out. Even now, he seemed like he would fall over if he were standing instead of sitting.

"You know this person, the person behind this. What do they want? We haven't received any demands. No one's called the president or the UN to ask for anything. So I'll ask again, what do they want? I know you have been focused on stopping these disasters, but now we have to face the real possibility that this one, at least, is very likely to happen."

"Director," Shepard replied, "I've thought quite a lot about this and I don't think they want anything."

Bloch didn't have an immediate response for that. Then she said, "They must want something."

"I think they want the attack to succeed. I think they just want to destroy," he said. "This may be proof of the theory I mentioned before."

"That this is some obscene suicide plot?" Bloch said.

"I've always been troubled by the Ares agents' suicides. We only captured one alive, and he died as soon as we administered standard interrogation drugs. So we have never had an opportunity to ask any member of Ares what they want."

"They do go to a lot of trouble to commit suicide," Bloch said.

"And that's not that unusual. Early astronauts were given cyanide pills to be used in certain hopeless situations. The CIA gives cyanide teeth to black-ops agents facing torture and certain death. I know that Dan Morgan had one implanted when he started at the Agency and never had it removed. But I don't think Ares uses suicide solely to prevent their operatives from suffering. Certainly, there's a security element, but there's something suspicious about how *enthusiastically* they plan for death and engage in it."

Suddenly, Bloch missed the Cold War and the War on Terror when all you had to worry about were people and groups committed to deeply flawed and dehumanizing beliefs.

For one thing, their systems tended to be destructive and self-limiting. Secondly, they always wanted their idiotic ideology and system to survive.

"So Ares may be a murder-suicide cult after all? How would you recruit anybody worth a damn for that?"

"I would bet that not everyone in the organization knows. They may have been offered the usual: wealth, power over others, the promise of building a new system that will finally right the world."

"How do we fight them? And how do we help Alex stop that monstrosity they've dropped into the Pacific? If she catches it, can you help her disarm it?"

Clearly, Shepard didn't want to just say no, but that was obviously what he was thinking.

"I'll look over the specs of the submersible she is in. Let me see what its robot arms can do. Once they are close enough to get some pictures of the bomb, I can try to work up an approach."

Then the real problem hit Bloch, probably the same issue that was troubling Shepard. Why would anyone build a bomb like that, that they intended to use, and even leave the possibility that it could be disarmed underwater?

Damn, she thought.

"Karen and I will put our heads together and see if we can . . . we'll see if there's anything that might work."

Bloch didn't like the expression on his face. He had the look of someone who had just been handed a task that he knew was impossible but would try anyway.

Chapter 29

"Why isn't it falling faster?" Alex asked.

Devan studied the screen and said, "They can't just drop it. I assume it's designed like this sub, but you still can't descend too quickly or you'd have an implosion that would damage . . . the device."

"Well damaging the device sounds pretty good to me," Alex said. "If we catch it, maybe we can take out its propulsion."

Devan thought about that. "That might help somewhat, but if I were building something like that, I would only have propulsion for minor course correction, not for descent. Better to have a passive system using buoyancy to make it fall at a steady rate. But even if that wasn't so, we have another problem, Alex. We're at ten thousand feet now. At our current relative speed, I'm estimating we would be able to catch it at maybe sixteen or seventeen thousand. The problem is that we'll be out of battery power before then."

"Leave that to me. Just follow the bomb," Alex said.

"What do you mean, leave it to you? Did you bring industrial lithium-ion cells with you?"

"Not exactly," Alex said. "But there's more power in the existing cells. I'll explain later, I just need to know what you have for a toolkit around here."

Alex was impressed by what she found in the kit. Besides the basic hand tools, it had what she really needed, spare wire and a soldering iron. There were four cells and one extra, the only battery that still showed full power.

That was good, she'd need that later, but first she'd need to create some bypasses and borrow some resistors from somewhere to create a hot-swapping station.

By wiring the two batteries in series and shifting their order while the system was running, she was confident that she could create a sudden "draw" that would coax the 20 percent or more power that was thought lost when lithium-ion cells had been recharged a few dozen times.

The power should still be there, but inadequate power management systems usually left it dormant in the battery.

Alex was sure it would work. Okay, almost certain, but since it had to work, Alex decided she would will it into functioning.

When she performed her first hot-swap, she watched the charge indicator on one of the "dead" cells vacillate between 1 and 2 percent to a solid 22.

"Alex, whatever you did, you just gave me more power. I can increase our speed. If you can keep the power coming, we may get there faster."

That was good. However, it created a problem of a different sort.

"How is the communications link with my people coming?" Alex asked.

"The *Galene* is setting up some sort of relay so that you should be able to talk to them over our system in a few minutes," Devan said. "It should work at any depth we reach. Now can you explain what you just did? I thought you specialized in *motor* vehicles."

"Yes, but I had a client who bought a 1933 Harley Davidson in mint condition. However, his wife thought it was too loud, and he found some butchers to convert it to electric. They turned the engine housing into a casing for an electric motor and batteries."

The situation still gave Alex the chills almost a year later. "I know," she said. "It's a war crime. The problem is that it didn't even work as an electric—at least not well. So I had to learn the system so I could help live the zombie half-life of a vintage electric Harley."

"Alex, I have Zeta headquarters for you," Devan said.

The next voice she heard was Lincoln Shepard's. "Alex, are you there?"

"I'm here, Shepard. We're ahead of schedule; now I need to know what to do when we catch the bomb."

* * * *

"Tell me the truth," Lily said as she stepped into the suite she shared with Renard.

"About what?" Scott asked as he turned away from his workstation and toward her. He had his I-just-got-caught-but-I'm-innocent face.

"You've been working on the launchpad problem," she said.

"Lily, you know I can do two things at the same time," he replied.

"That's not what I mean and you know it," Lily said. "It's just that we both know it's too early to do any good in Scotland. They'll be collecting data for weeks."

"So you don't want me spinning my wheels?" he asked.

"You know that's not it either. What happened in Scotland was bad, very bad. It's okay to grieve. And I know that being here is a different kind of stress."

Once again, that was as close as Lily would come to talking about Hyo, but from Scott's face she could see that was enough.

"We both know that the best thing you can do for yourself is to throw yourself as deeply as you can at a single thing."

Scott smiled at that. The first smile since she'd arrived.

"Lily, are you prescribing work as therapy?"

Lily returned the smile and said, "Absolutely."

Scott stood up, his expression suddenly serious. He put both hands around her waist and pulled her toward him.

"I was thinking about an entirely different kind of therapy," he said.

Lily replied with a stern expression of her own. "See, that is the opposite of what I am saying. You just added a *third* thing for yourself to do."

Scott leaned in and kissed her. "Not at all. I can only think of one thing I want to do, and it's something that will require all of my attention."

He wasn't wrong. Scott could be *very* focused on certain things. And it occurred to her that she might benefit from some therapy herself.

* * * *

As Morgan and Jeffrey walked down the hallway, Morgan kept his light on at full brightness as Jeffrey did the same. This time, Morgan noticed an unusual detail on the door of a room across the hallway from Jeffrey and Olga's safe haven.

There was a neat hand-drawn cross.

"I moved everyone to that room. Maybe I shouldn't have, but I couldn't leave them where they were." Then, before Morgan could ask, he added, "They were all shot, except for McMurtry. He was a lab technician and an incredible pastry chef. He must have fought; he was stabbed more than once, and then I think they broke his neck."

The young man took a second to collect himself. "There was also some blood near his body that I think wasn't his. I like to think it wasn't his."

"How did you avoid what happened to them . . ." Morgan asked.

"Dumb luck. Bad luck really. Every month we have a poker tournament. I'm usually near the top of the pack, but I've never won. This time the cards were against me. I came in dead last . . . and the loser has to sleep outside the next night. First, you build yourself an igloo like we learned in survival training; then you sleep in it. When I went to sleep that night, the weather was okay, a bit windy, but the storm was supposed to be a couple of days out. There was so much wind that I didn't hear anything, and when I woke up I had to dig myself out of all the new snow. It was already over when I got inside, and whoever did it was gone."

The young man was silent for at least half a minute, and Morgan was glad the face mask and goggles gave him some privacy.

"All because of some bad luck at cards," Jeffrey said.

"Based on the circumstances, I'm not sure your luck was all bad," Morgan replied.

"Still, I just don't know why I was the—"

"I told you. Don't do that. You survived because you survived. And because you did, that young woman is still alive," Morgan said. "And because you're still here, your aunt won't be . . . disappointed. I'll be honest with you, though I will deny it if you repeat this to her, but I don't like to disappoint Diana."

Jeffrey nodded and said, "Olga showed up just as I set up the room you found us in. She even helped me with the generators. I don't know what she did at the Russian station, but she knows something about engines. We ran them for a full hour with the fuel we found at the bottom of a few cans, but the diesel ran out. I think she survived by hiding in a cabinet in the station kitchen. At least that's what I think she was trying to say."

"What were the Russians doing at their station?" Morgan asked. This was an important question and would determine how much he would trust this woman.

"Same as us, ice core samples. I've been there a few times, and some of them have come here. They rotate staff, so I'd never met her before she showed up after her own base suffered the same kind of attack."

When they opened the door to the outside, Morgan saw that, if possible, the weather had gotten worse. Certainly the visibility was nearly full whiteout.

Following Morgan's guidelines, they found his Snowcat and drove it to the wing with the generator. Those outer doors were closed, so they had an easy time bringing the fuel inside. After topping off the Snowcat, they made sure they had two five-gallon jugs in reserve.

All told, they put fifty gallons into the generator tank. That should give them two days of full power at the station. By then, the storm would be over, and they would be able to leave safely.

They spent the rest of the day digging out the two snowed-in vestibules and closed the exterior doors. Morgan worked on one while Jeffrey dug out the other. Olga visited frequently; she seemed reluctant to leave Jeffrey's side and would check on him constantly.

She also cleaned up the kitchen, which was the scene of the death of the man who Morgan learned was Jeffrey's closest friend on the staff.

Clearing the snow took a few hours and Morgan was impressed by how hard Jeffrey worked. By the time they were finished, the entire base had reached normal temperature, except for the temporary morgue Jeffrey had set up before Morgan came.

Morgan went into that room and did a quick examination of the bodies, turning down the heat as low as he could.

Whoever attacked the station were professionals. Each person was killed by no more than two bullets, either center mass or head shots. That was true for everyone except for Jeffrey's friend McMurtry.

Jeffrey and Olga wanted to stay in the room Morgan had found them in, so they simply moved actual beds in there. It was some sort of lounge and was comfortable enough. Olga had come up with a meat stew, and once Morgan had spent some time with her, he realized that she seemed familiar somehow.

The fact was that she reminded him of Natasha Orlov. Of course, Morgan hadn't seen Natasha since just before she'd died almost five years ago. But Olga reminded Morgan of Natasha when she and Morgan had been young.

The reason was obvious. She was Russian, and blond, and had similar high cheekbones and an almost model-like beauty. And, of course, the last time Morgan had been in Antarctica, he had been thinking about a future with Natasha.

Other than his memory, Morgan realized that he had no pictures of Natasha Orlov at that age. He'd never had any, so there were none to keep.

It must have been this place and the fact that she was Russian. And once again, Morgan wished he'd learned a bit more Russian language from Natasha, but of course that was impossible since they had had so little time together.

As it got closer to midnight, Morgan realized he was exhausted. The trio went to sleep, Morgan on one side of the room, with Jeffrey and Olga on the other.

A few hours later, something woke Morgan. There was a sound. . . . No, not a sound. He realized that it was silence that woke him.

The generator was off.

Morgan snapped awake, suddenly sure they weren't alone in the station. Looking over, he saw that Olga's bed was empty.

As soon as that registered, she stepped inside the room and closed the door hurriedly behind her.

"I heard something," she said.

Jeffrey woke with a start when the door closed. He said, "What's happening?"

"The generator is off," Morgan said.

A shaken Olga said, "I think there's someone in here with us."

Chapter 30

Morgan drew his gun and said, "I'll check it out."

Jeffrey picked up a large wrench and said, "I'll go with you." The young man wasn't afraid, Morgan noted. Instead, he seemed angry.

Morgan understood that. Jeffrey had just lost friends and coworkers to people who had invaded his base. It might do him some good to get a little payback, but Morgan didn't want to leave Olga alone.

"Listen, if I find someone, I'll bring them back here, but why don't you stay and keep Olga safe."

That got through to Jeffrey. He was obviously protective of the woman, and not unreasonably. This part of Antarctica had recently shown itself to be very dangerous.

And even if there was nothing wrong but a malfunction of the generator, that was still a serious threat. They would have to either fix it or take their chances in the Snowcat in the morning, no matter the weather.

Morgan didn't like that idea. The ride here was no picnic. As long as they had power, they could hold out indefinitely at Daystrom Base. Eventually, the weather would clear and they could move on.

Once again, he kept his flashlight beam dim and low to the ground, not wanting to announce his presence to anyone waiting to finish the job they had started at the base.

He worked his way down the corridor methodically, checking each room. The last thing he wanted was for someone to get by him and get to Jeffrey and Olga.

Finally, he reached the end of the corridor and the generator room. He searched the room carefully, working his way counterclockwise around the generator. Satisfied that there was no one there, he turned his flashlight to full and headed to the generator control panel. Holstering his gun, he opened the panel.

Propping the flashlight up against the panel door, Morgan pulled the lever to prime the generator and hit the start button. The generator cranked but didn't turn over. He checked the fuel and saw that it was fine; then he tried to start it again.

The generator caught and was soon humming normally. To Morgan it looked like someone had just turned it off. That, of course, raised questions. For one, where were they now?

He flipped on the base power circuits one at a time, careful not to overload the generator. When the lights came on in the generator room, Morgan heard a sound behind him.

Automatically, he reached for the Walther in his shoulder holster, but before he could touch the metal, a voice said, "Just put your hands in the air."

The voice was female and spoke very good English with a Russian accent. Morgan raised his arms.

"Turn around," the voice said.

Morgan turned and saw Olga pointing a gun at him.

"Olga," he said. "I see you found a gun, a Russian Makarov, and you a Russian, what are the odds?"

Very slowly, Morgan started to lower his hands. If he could keep her talking . . .

"Keep them up, Dan Morgan," Olga said.

"I see you've also learned English. You have had a busy night."

She flashed a very cold smile and said, "I have had more than enough time to do what I came to do."

"Where is Jeffrey Bloch?" Morgan asked.

"He is safe," she replied. "He's locked away. By the time he finds his way out of that storeroom, we will have concluded our business and I will have left in your Snowcat."

"And what business is that?"

"I'm here to kill you, Dan Morgan," she said, flashing the cold smile again. The look in her eyes . . . Repeating his name . . .

Whatever this was, it was personal.

"I have to be honest with you. This doesn't come as a big surprise. I haven't had a lot of luck with Russian women."

"Maybe that is because you murder them," Olga said.

"I really never have, but if that story is going around, it would explain a lot of the last twenty-five years of my life."

She sneered at that.

"Olga, let's have a real conversation. I'm going to, very slowly, pull my weapon out of the holster and put it on the ground, okay?"

She nodded and Morgan carefully did what he had proposed. It was a relief to have his arms at his side. If nothing else, it had bought him another minute.

He sensed that she had something to say to him. It was time to get on with it.

"Tell me why you are here, other than killing me," Morgan said.

"I'm here for Natasha Orlov," she said. "My name is Jenya Orlov."

"Orlov? Pasha had a daughter?"

"No, not Pasha. He was my uncle, before you murdered him. *Natasha* had a daughter."

It took a second for that to sink in. The problem was that it was impossible.

"Tell me, Dan Morgan, have you spoken to Alex lately?" she said.

"Not in a few months. I've been away," he replied.

"Yes, so you forget you have a daughter when you are on your trip around the world with your precious Jenny," Jenya said.

Morgan didn't like his wife's name being dropped so casually by someone who clearly hated him. He had to push down his anger.

"How do you know Alex?" he asked, not liking the expression on her face. This time, the anger came without warning. "Did you hurt her?" he said, leaning in to Jenya, despite the gun on him.

She shook her head slowly and said, "Why would I hurt her? Why would I hurt *my sister*? Why would I hurt my family? I would never do those things because I am not a monster, a monster like my father."

Sister . . . the word seemed to echo in his head.

And then he understood. It was impossible, but he realized it was also true. Certainly, Jenya believed it, and based on her age, it not only made sense but it was likely.

"You're mine . . ." he said, the words choking out of him.

"To my great shame," Jenya replied.

Morgan took a deep breath.

"I didn't know. Your mother never told me. All that time, she never told me," Morgan said.

"Would it have mattered? You murdered her only brother, her only family. Then you betrayed her. And because all of that wasn't enough, more than two decades later you killed her."

The hatred in her eyes was almost a living thing. He realized that it made her appear even more like her mother, who had worn the same expression four years ago when Natasha Orlov had had Dan Morgan bound to a chair with barbed wire.

Natasha had believed then that Morgan had betrayed her and murdered her brother.

It was true that Morgan had been forced to kill Pasha Orlov, and he'd done it with his bare hands. However, he had only killed Pasha to protect Natasha. After Pasha had learned about his sister's plans to defect to the United States, he had betrayed her to her Russian spymasters.

When Natasha and Morgan met again a few years ago, Morgan had tried to explain it to her, but she had spent more than twenty years believing he was a monster, like Jenya did now. The only difference was that Jenya now believed Morgan had also murdered Natasha.

He didn't know how to explain, how to make her understand. In the end, he said the simplest, truest thing he could.

"I didn't kill Natasha. I loved her. I did kill for her, and I would have died for her," Morgan said.

"You are about to," Jenya said.

Natasha's daughter . . . he marveled.

His daughter. Suddenly, everything he had lost when he had lost Natasha became clear. Jenya was the future he and Natasha had imagined together.

Before the betrayal, the lies, and the death.

Jenya may have represented the lost future with Natasha, but that future had been twisted.

Morgan regretted everything that had happened with Natasha at the end, but he didn't, he couldn't, regret the path his life had taken. He didn't regret Jenny, and he didn't regret Alex.

"You are right about one thing," Morgan said in the end. "I failed your mother. I had met her brother, and I didn't see he would betray her. She didn't see it, but she couldn't because he was her brother. I should have seen what was coming in his eyes. I didn't. Aside from how I already felt about her, it was my job to protect her, and there I definitely failed her."

"All lies," Jenya said.

"Five years ago, Natasha picked the wrong business partners and they killed her. I couldn't save her then, either."

"I am not my mother, I don't love you, so your lies will do you no good here," Jenya said.

"I'm not asking you to believe me, but before you do what you have to do, I'll ask you to listen. I'm sorry that I couldn't be a father to you. I'm sorry that I couldn't give you anything when it might have mattered. You will still have Alex. Get to know her. Just don't tell her what you did here today. She wouldn't understand."

"No, she would not," Jenya said. "She is not like me, or you."

"Let her help you. Let her in your life since I won't be."

"You are trying to trick me, to pretend . . ." Jenya said, only the smallest sliver of doubt creeping into her expression.

"Believe whatever you have to. Take your revenge. I hope it gives you something I never could. I hope it gives you peace."

While he waited for what was about to come, Morgan realized that he had completed his last mission. Jeffrey Bloch was safe and Diana would see him again. Yes, the mission was a success, and it was for family. Maybe not his, but someone's family, and Dan Morgan was all right with that.

When it came, the sound wasn't a loud crack, it was more of a thump.

A thump *followed* by a loud crack.

A bullet whizzed past his ear and embedded itself in the metal behind him.

As Jenya fell to the ground, Jeffrey said, "I'm sorry. I got here as soon as I could."

The young man was holding his wrench.

Morgan kneeled down and took Jenya's pistol, which was still clutched in her hand. He checked her pulse; it was strong.

Grabbing his own gun, he said, "Thank you."

Morgan realized that the last time he was in Antarctica, Peter Conley had also saved him from a Russian with a gun.

Behind him, he heard a snap and a pop, and then the lights went out. Turning on his flashlight, he pointed it at the generator's control panel, which shot sparks for a few seconds and then went quiet.

"Jeffrey, I'm going to take this as a sign. I think it's time for us to get out of here."

Whatever happened on the ice in the Snowcat, Morgan didn't think it could be any more dangerous than Daystrom Base.

Chapter 31

"Shepard, what do you have for me?" Alex asked.

"Alex, are you okay?" Shepard said, his concern clear, even through the static of the connection.

"We're fine, what do I do?" she said.

"How is your power holding out?" Shepard said.

Alex felt her impatience growing, along with the feeling that they were running out of time.

"We have plenty of power," Alex said, very far from certain that was true. They had much more power than they should have, and Alex would do everything she could to squeeze more out of the batteries, but the fact was the faster they acted, the better. "Tell Nathaniel that his new power management system is going to make his day but I need to know what to do," Alex said.

"We've got access to the sensor data on the *Galene*, which in turn has access to your sonar and radar. We've also re-tasked a satellite to give us radiological data. I'm watching you closely, and I have a plan, but first I want you to understand that our analysis is that this is not a threat or a ploy. Ares means to get that bomb to the bottom of the Challenger Deep and detonate."

"Oh my God," Alex said. "How does that make sense?"

"It's a long story that I will tell you when you get back," Shepard said. "The good news is that for them to achieve the damage they want to cause, the device has to reach the bottom of the Deep. The trench is basically a fault line between two large tectonic plates. They've dropped it above the center of the fault and it will fall like a stone. From what I can tell, the bomb is an automated sub, built to withstand the pressure of the trench, but with a very basic drive system. The first step will be to get your sub close to the device and take out the two propellers with the sub's robot arms."

Alex let that sink in. "Hang on, you've got mountains of sensor data, a satellite looking down on us, and your expert analysis is that I should smash the thing's propellers?"

Shepard actually laughed at that. "Yes."

"Okay, once I've smashed it up a bit, what then? Tell me you've got a way to disable it?"

"No, Alex," Shepard said. "I don't see that happening. I think the best we can hope for is that once its drive is properly smashed, you can drag it off course enough so it hits the ocean floor but does not enter the trench. You're at ten thousand feet now and rapidly approaching the device. Once you reach it, you'll have ten thousand more feet to push it so it doesn't enter the Challenger Deep. Once you've got it safely over the ocean floor you can let go and it should fall straight down."

"And still detonate?" Alex said.

"Yes," Shepard replied. "But at that depth, there will be no tidal waves or geological upheavals. Just make sure you get to the surface before that happens. As long as you are not nearby, you and the *Galene* will be fine with that much ocean between you and the device."

Alex noticed that Shepard didn't ever call the Tsar Bomba what it was, a nuclear bomb.

But Alex wouldn't kid herself about what they were facing and what was likely to happen. She said, "Shepard, hang on, we've got to do some power management."

Cutting the connection, Alex looked at Devan and said, "What can you turn off?"

"The heat, for one, also the fans that move the air. It will get cold, but the power will hold out a little longer. Do you think it will be enough to get to the bomb?"

"No question. And if we're very careful and I pull every watt out of these batteries, we may be able to get that monstrosity away from the trench and over the ocean floor," Alex said.

"After that?" Devan asked.

"I've always wanted to see a giant thermonuclear explosion up close," Alex said.

"Really? Must be an American thing," Devan said. "But for me, I hate to leave a job half-finished. Let's go get it, Alex."

They shared a grim smile and Alex turned the radio back on. "Okay, Shepard, we're ready over here."

"I've got it on the scope," Devan said.

"You're within five hundred feet," Shepard replied.

"Closing," Devan said.

Alex scanned the water in front of her porthole. There was plenty of light, but no . . . wait, there was a cylinder, tapered on the top and bottom.

"I have visual," Alex said.

"I see it too," Devan said. "I'll get you close, Alex."

"The robot arms are ready," she said.

Devan was a good pilot, she realized, as he gently brought them to one end of the bomb. She could see a propeller spinning sporadically.

"Keep it steady," Alex said.

She waited until the propeller was still and brought the right robot arm down as hard as she could on the blade, snapping it cleanly off.

"That's one," she said.

"I'll bring us around," Devan replied.

He really was good, matching the speed of the bomb and maneuvering with finesse.

She repeated the operation on the second propeller and then the bomb was just a falling object.

The *Ometz Lev* followed it, and Alex searched for a good place to grab hold of the bomb. Near the top of the device, there were four rings that she assumed were used to grab and move the bomb by crane.

After a little back and forth, Devan got them in position and Alex grabbed two of the rings with the robot arms.

"I've got a good hold," Alex said.

"How is our position?" Devan asked.

"You're at fifteen thousand feet. You have five thousand more before the ocean floor, but you need to move it one thousand feet west to get past the edge of the trench. I'd like to see you get it a full five hundred feet over the ocean floor before you let go, so there is no chance of it drifting into the Deep."

Devan was quiet as he concentrated on piloting the combination of the *Ometz Lev* and the Tsar Bomba.

The problem was that the sub had a propulsion system designed for movement of just the sub itself. The builders hadn't counted on the need to move a giant, multi-ton nuclear bomb as it fell to the bottom of the ocean.

Alex watched the power on their second-to-last battery get to near zero. She waited until the final second to hot-swap it with the last of the viable batteries.

When the new cell was in place, the lights flickered, and then the battery read zero. Then the LEDs on the battery flickered and it showed 12 percent.

"Full speed, Mr. Martin," Alex said. "That was the last one."

Devan slowly increased their speed.

"You've passed the mouth of the trench. You're now over the ocean floor," Shepard announced a few minutes later.

Then, after what seemed like an eternity, he said, "That's five hundred feet. You can release the device."

Alex manipulated the controls to open the hands of the robot arms. She was glad to be done with it. She didn't like the idea of this beautiful machine attached to that monstrosity.

"Great, Alex," Shepard said, the excitement clear in his voice. "You really—"

Shepard's voice cut out as the lights went off.

There was a moment of silence and then Devan said, "I think we did very well, all things considered."

"I agree. We can call this mission a success. Now, I guess we just wait for the fireworks," Alex replied.

Alex thought about turning on the flashlight on her phone but decided against it. The darkness seemed appropriate.

She felt movement beside her. It was Devan's hand. She took it in her own and they waited.

* * * *

Renard scanned the reports. A huge percentage of the Renard Tech servers were processing the data that Zeta was collecting from the sensors in the Indian Ocean, Renard Tech's satellites, and a surprising number of United States government satellites.

Whatever they were searching for in the Indian Ocean, they would find it. Renard could have called Diana Bloch to get briefed personally, but he had already committed all of the resources he could muster to support Zeta's effort.

Zeta was obviously looking for an Ares facility, and it was just a matter of time before they found it. He had his own reasons to want Ares to pay for what they had done recently but even that could wait.

He had much more personal business to attend to and only one last day to do it. His team had completed all of the work installing the anti-missile system, and he had already had to find reasons to extend the project with further testing.

He needed the extra time to make his plans for today possible. His biggest concern was slipping past his own security. Lily's security protocols required that Renard Tech book the suites on either side of his, as well as the ones above and below.

To accomplish what he needed to do, Renard had to book the suite two stories below his own. Those rooms had also been empty the entire trip but were about to get used for the first time.

The climb from his balcony to the one below was nerve-racking the first time, but he had practiced with his improvised rope made of belts a few times since he'd arrived.

He used the improvised rope again to get to the suite below that one on the third floor. Once there, he put on his mirrored sunglasses and baseball cap and simply walked out the door. It was easy enough to avoid giving the hotel security cameras a good look at him, and then he slipped out onto the street.

The conference center where Hyo was having the last meeting of his trip was close by.

He'd hacked the building's security system weeks ago and his key card gave him easy access to a utility door on the underground parking level. After that, he took the stairs two stories up to the temporary office where Hyo was waiting for his next event.

There were two guards at Hyo's office door, but a message from Renard's phone gave them the order to report immediately to their superiors at the temporary security office that had been set up in Hyo's hotel.

Renard estimated he had twenty minutes before they returned.

As soon as they were gone, Renard opened the door and stepped inside.

The general looked up from his desk as Renard took off his hat and glasses. Hyo was reaching for his phone when Renard said, "That won't work. I've disabled it because I wanted to make sure we weren't disturbed."

Hyo was instantly angry at the intrusion. "What do you want?" he barked.

"Do you know who I am?" Renard asked.

Hyo looked him over. "You are that computer man," he said with some contempt in his voice.

His English was very good. That pleased Renard. He didn't want there to be any confusion about what was about to occur or why it was happening.

"I'm Scott Renard. I'm the fiancé of Lily Randall," Renard said. "Do you remember her?"

For the first time, Hyo appeared uncertain, and then there was the light of recognition in his eyes. *Then* came the touch of fear.

"My men will be back shortly," he said. The general stood up behind his desk, as if by standing he could take control of the situation.

"Not soon enough to help you," Renard said. "By the time they arrive, we will be finished with our talk. Do you remember your talk with Lily? This one will be different. You won't be tied up, and you will be free to defend yourself."

As Scott circled the general's desk, the man backed up. The look in his eyes had graduated from fearful to desperate.

As soon as Hyo's back touched the wall, Renard's fist made contact with the man's jaw. His first cry was mostly one of surprise. The second one was a cry of pain.

In the end, their talk lasted less than ten minutes. When it was over, Scott put his cap and glasses on and opened the door to find the hallway empty.

It took him just a few minutes to get back to the empty suite on the third floor of his hotel. He climbed up to the two balconies easily with the adrenaline from his encounter with Hyo still pumping through his system.

Renard had to remove his bloody clothes and shower quickly. The two hours he had blocked out on his schedule for programming work would end in about an hour, and he was still tweaking a pattern-recognition algorithm for the missile defense system.

Because Lily respected his programming time, she waited until the two hours were up before entering the suite.

"Did you finish?" she asked.

"Yes, and that was the last thing on my list," Renard said. "If there is any other housekeeping on the system, the staff can take care of it."

"Then we can leave tomorrow?" she asked.

"Yes, back home, and I'll run the investigation on the launchpad explosion from headquarters," he said.

Lily was clearly relieved. "Did you hear that the general was recalled early? He missed his last conference."

"No," Renard said, not trusting himself to say any more.

"We can both relax. We don't have to breathe the same air as him. He can rot in what they've made of the North."

Scott sighed heavily. "Still too good for him."

Lily wrapped him in a hug and said, "That was a long time ago. I've moved on, and you and I are starting a new life. Don't give him any power over us."

Renard returned the hug. "Okay, we never have to mention him again."

He would keep his focus on spending time with Lily and making their last night special. He ordered an extravagant dinner made in the hotel kitchen by one of the best chefs in the city.

Renard found that he didn't think much about Hyo other than idly wondering about how the North Korean regime would handle his death. They wouldn't admit he was killed while visiting the South. Most likely, in a few weeks there would be an announcement that he died after a vague and undisclosed illness. Another military henchman would be promoted in his place, and Hyo would be forgotten by his masters.

It was still better than the man deserved, but Renard was satisfied, and as he had thought, he had no regrets.

* * * *

Shepard came rushing into Bloch's office and said, "Director, the device is clear of the trench and is now on the ocean floor."

The news was good. They had somehow managed to avoid a disaster that would have caused devastation on a global scale, but she wouldn't have known that from Shepard's face.

"Where's Alex now?" Bloch asked.

The young man's face fell even further. "We've lost contact."

"Did the bomb detonate?" she asked.

"No, nothing yet. We don't know how they have planned to trigger the detonation. Could be by remote, could be by depth, or even a simple timer. All we know is that it didn't detonate . . . yet." Shepard took a deep breath and said, "My best guess is that Alex's sub has run out of power."

"Which means they are dead in the water, right on top of the largest nuclear bomb ever built," Bloch said.

"I'm about to confer with Nathaniel Drake," he said, looking stricken. "But . . ."

He didn't need to finish that sentence. Even if there was another sub that could go get Alex, she and the MI6 agent wouldn't last long enough without power for rescue to come.

And if the bomb was on a timer . . .

Bloch realized that she might well have to tell Dan Morgan that his daughter was gone. But, of course, that would have to wait until he returned from Antarctica on his mission to rescue her nephew.

Would Jeffrey be with Morgan when she gave him the news?

"Director," Shepard said, "there is one more thing."

Bloch steeled herself.

"We may have found Ares," he said.

"Excuse me?" she said.

"The team has been running down every shipping, warehousing, and manufacturing lead. We have traced many of those leads back to a single nexus point. There's an office tower in Chicago."

For that second, Bloch was grateful—not for the good news—but for something else to focus on.

"Thank you, Shepard. Talk to Blake on the *Galene,* and let me know if there is anything you need to help Alex. And forward what you have on Ares's possible headquarters. I'll talk to Spartan. It's time to put an assault team together."

Chapter 32

Everything that Morgan did as he prepared for their departure felt like a dream, a dream that kept getting interrupted by two thoughts: *Natasha had a daughter* and *I have another daughter*.

Those facts would have been shocking by themselves, but the next two left him feeling hollowed out inside: *She was raised to hate me. She has spent years planning to kill me.*

When he had seen that look in Natasha's eyes, it had hurt him more than the actual blows or the barbed wire digging into his legs.

And had Alex met Jenya? Were they now connected somehow?

It was all too much, so Morgan went through the motions necessary to get them out of there. He used zip ties on Jenya to make sure she didn't cause any more trouble and loaded her into the back of the Snowcat.

Jeffrey offered to drive and Morgan agreed. This would allow him to sit in the back with Jenya—with his daughter—to watch her.

She was still unconscious, but he had no doubt that she would wake before they reached McMurdo. He would have to deal with her soon enough.

Going was slow and they traveled in silence. The weather worsened as they continued, and Morgan felt the vehicle slide to one side and then right itself.

"What was that? Morgan asked.

"I'm not sure. It's a lot of new snow, traction can be tricky," Jeffrey said.

Morgan moved carefully to the front. He was not comfortable taking his eyes off of Jenya for too long.

When the Snowcat slid again he had to grab the seat to steady himself. "Cut the speed," he said. "The scope is having trouble seeing through the snow."

Even as Morgan said it, he felt the back of the Snowcat shifting again, this time sharply. Morgan grabbed the dash, and when the sideways movement stopped, he had the feeling that the Snowcat was tilted backward.

It was hard to tell for sure because of the near whiteout in front of them. With no horizon or visible landscape, there was no way for him to orient himself.

The next movement removed all doubt; the large vehicle pitched backward at what had to be at least a forty-five-degree angle.

There was the brief sensation of falling back, and then they stopped suddenly as the rear of the Snowcat hit something.

The side of a crevasse, Morgan realized. And they were wedged above it.

He had no idea how deep it was. They could be suspended over a ten-foot depression, or they could be hanging over a five-hundred-foot chasm.

Jeffrey turned to Morgan and said, "Should I see if we can just drive out?"

Morgan wasn't sure that was a good idea. Any movement of the treads could shift their position and could drop them into a dark and cold place from which they would never come out.

On the other hand, staying where they were wasn't a much better option. The end might take a little longer, but it would come soon enough. Better to go out trying something.

"Get us out of here," Morgan said.

Jeffrey applied the gas, and the treads turned slowly. For a very few seconds, Morgan felt forward motion, then the Snowcat slid back so roughly that he thought that was it. But their movement stopped again when they hit the wall of ice behind them. However, this time he heard the crunch of metal.

He hoped it was nothing essential, and then he heard the engine die.

The exhaust pipe, Morgan realized. *Damn.* Without the engine, there would be no heat.

"I don't suppose you brought any of your hand sanitizer?" Morgan asked.

"Sorry, no," Jeffrey said.

Morgan pulled out the handheld radio. It didn't have enough range to reach McMurdo, but maybe there was someone close enough to pick up their signal.

"Mayday. This is Dan Morgan. I'm with two other people and we're trapped in a disabled Snowcat about two miles due south of Daystrom Base. The engine is out, so we don't have long."

Turning off the radio, Morgan said, "Sorry about the rescue. They usually go smoother than this."

"Thanks for coming to get me," Jeffrey said. "And I'm sorry about the trouble with your daughter."

"I'll try the message every few minutes. Believe it or not, I've been lucky in Antarctica so far."

The fourth time he repeated the Mayday message, he realized that it was getting pretty cold in the Snowcat. He also realized that he not only felt tired but wrung out.

He looked at Jenya behind them. She was as beautiful as her mother and looked like she was sleeping peacefully.

Turning to Jeffrey, he saw the young man had also fallen asleep. That wasn't a good thing, he remembered. It could be dangerous, especially in the extreme cold.

There was one more thing he could do, he realized. If he broke the windshield, he could push through the couple of feet of snow and then pull Jeffrey out. Together, they could drag Jenya out of the vehicle.

They'd be on foot with an unconscious woman in some of the worst weather Antarctica had to offer, but it was something to try.

Morgan knew that if he kept moving, they would have a chance. The problem was that his eyelids were getting very heavy and simply keeping them open required a massive effort.

* * * *

They had only been in the dark for a few minutes when Alex heard the clang of metal outside the sub.

"What was that?" Alex asked.

"I have no idea," Devan replied.

At nearly the same time, they turned on their phones to give them a little light.

It didn't help; there was nothing to see but each other and the interior of the sub.

Something shifted around her. "Are we moving?" she asked.

"It feels like it," Devan replied.

"How can that be?" she said.

"I don't know. We have no power and there aren't any currents down here."

There it was again, another clang. The ship seemed to rock and Alex had a stronger feeling that they were moving.

With nothing but darkness outside and no reference points, it was hard to be sure, but Alex couldn't shake the feeling that the sub was not only in motion but was accelerating.

"I actually don't know that much about the *Lev*. Nathaniel took me down twice, showed me the basic systems and how to pilot it, but nothing that would explain whatever is happening."

Alex checked the time on her phone. "Assuming the bomb was designed to detonate by timer," she said, "we've got about forty-five minutes."

There was a third clang, another shift in the sub, and more of that feeling of movement.

The forty-five minutes passed quickly and Alex realized that she had been holding Devan's hand the whole time.

"That's about it . . ." Devan said. "This is the point it would have reached the bottom of the Challenger Deep."

"Maybe it won't detonate if it's not at 36,000 feet. Maybe it will never—"

This time, the sub didn't rock, it shook. Hard.

The *Ometz Lev* was tossed firmly for a full three or four seconds and then it was over.

"Was that it? Was that the detonation?" Devan asked.

"Wasn't so bad," Alex said, smiling broadly.

She heard the smile in Devan's voice. "And people make such a big deal about nuclear weapons."

"I guess we're close enough to the surface that the shockwave mostly dissipated," Devan said. "I think that definitely means there won't be any giant earthquakes or tsunamis."

Alex felt a surge of relief. "We can check our primary mission objective off our list."

The sub shifted again.

This time they didn't just feel it. They heard something. "Alex, I think we just broke the surface."

There was another clang, but this was one Alex recognized. It was the clamps on the *Galene* grabbing the sub.

It seemed impossible but Alex wasn't going to complain.

She realized they could cross one more mission objective off their list: *Come back alive.*

She felt the sub getting lifted a few feet up and then steady itself against the loading platform. Devan opened the hatch, and then she heard Nathaniel's voice. "Good to see you, Devan. How is Alex?"

"Fine!" she called out.

Alex climbed out behind Devan and saw a smiling Nathaniel standing on the platform with two of his crew.

"Very good to see you both," he said. Then he dismissed the crew and said, "It got a bit choppy up here for a minute. Was that a detonation?"

"We think so, but not in the trench because the *Lev* performed beautifully," Devan said.

"I suspect that was mostly the two of you who caught the bloody thing and pushed our sub well past its limits."

"Speaking of which, how did we get to the surface?" Alex asked. "When we ran out of power, we thought that was it."

"A fail-safe. If the *Lev* loses power, it releases weights based on depth. Buoyancy does most of the work. It's a simple system, mostly mechanical with independent power. We never expected to need it. One of the many surprises today."

"Was anyone hurt on the *Galene*?"

"No, thankfully," Nathaniel said. "They had no interest in harming anyone. They really seemed to simply want us to know what they were doing and relay that to Zeta."

"I'm happy that we were able to give them a surprise," Alex said. As she and Devan followed Nathaniel onto the deck, she pulled out her phone.

She needed to make her report to Director Bloch.

Chapter 33

Dan felt movement, but he wasn't moving, it was the Snowcat. Was it falling? No, that wasn't it. It was moving too slowly and there was mechanical noise. Finally, both the noise and the movement stopped.

He struggled to open his eyes, and when he did, someone was over him. "Dan, Dan Morgan?" the man said.

"Yes," he replied. Morgan realized he knew this man.

"Walter?" he said, except this man looked like Walter all grown up. Or rather, he looked like Walter's father.

"Yes, it's good to see you," Walter's father said.

"Jeffrey?" Morgan said, sitting up to see someone helping Bloch's nephew out of the Snowcat.

"Come on, let's get you out of here. We'll get you both warm inside our Snowcat."

You both . . . Morgan thought.

"Jenya?" he asked, scanning the interior. "The woman?"

"There was no one else inside when we pulled you out of the crevasse. You were lucky. Should we search for anyone?"

Morgan shook his head. She had gotten to Daystrom Base on foot. And she had slipped out of the Snowcat somehow. Morgan didn't think they would find her if they wanted to, and at the moment he wasn't sure he wanted to.

He needed to talk to Jenny before he did anything. And he also needed to talk to Alex to see what she knew.

"What are you doing here?" Morgan asked when they were in Walter's vehicle.

"I run a microwave telescope not far from Daystrom, biggest in the world. We heard your message. I got here as soon as I could."

Morgan was too stunned to speak for a minute. More than a quarter century had passed and time seemed to be folding in on itself. He was here with Walter again, except the man was saving *his* life.

And somehow, Morgan had been followed to the ice by a daughter he didn't know existed.

"Thank you," Morgan said.

Walter grinned. "My pleasure, Dan."

"Dan?" another voice called out. It was Jeffrey. He was waking up, his voice dragging Morgan back into the present.

"You okay?" Morgan asked.

"I'm not going to lie. I'm a little chilly," Jeffrey said, and in the young man's voice Morgan heard an echo of Peter Conley.

"Must be a draft," Morgan said.

By the time they got to Walter's base, Morgan felt like himself and was satisfied that neither he nor Jeffrey had serious frostbite.

"Walter, I need to get Jeffrey here in touch with someone in the States," Morgan said.

"No problem," Walter said, giving instructions to one of his people, who led Jeffrey away.

"Jeffrey," Morgan said, "tell your aunt I said hello." Turning to Walter, he said, "Thank you. That call is going to mean a lot to someone."

"Anything I can do, Dan, but if you are up to it, I need to talk to you in private," Walter said.

Morgan didn't like the sound of that or the look on Walter's face. The man took Morgan into his office.

"It has to do with the nuclear waste site we visited the last time I saw you," Walter said. There it was again, that feeling that the past was bleeding into the present.

"What's wrong?"

"There's something happening that I can't quite explain."

"Is the waste spilling, getting out?" Morgan said. It didn't seem likely. He and Conley had practically dropped a mountain on top of it.

"No, whatever is happening isn't an accident, and it's much worse than some leaked material," Walter said.

Morgan's stomach started to turn. "Is there any danger of an . . . explosion?"

Walter's face set. "No, frankly, it's worse than that, and if I hadn't come to get you, I would have been trying to get the Pentagon on the phone. What's happening in that mountain is a low-level, continuous nuclear reaction. When they tested the early nuclear bombs, they would sometimes get an incomplete reaction. It's called a fizzle. This is like that, but much slower. It's continuous, and it's generating heat—a lot of heat. It's also putting out minimal gamma radiation and a lot of heavy alpha and beta particles, which usually aren't dangerous but, again, generate heat."

"How much heat?" Morgan asked.

"Not much, right now, but based on how much material we saw down there, once the reaction spreads through all of the waste, it will be enough to melt a lot of the ice in the area. And that's where the problems really start. The waste is sitting just above a potentially active volcano, which is part of a system of volcanoes. The Antarctic ice is part of a delicate system that keeps pressure on one of the most volcanically active areas in the world. Melt too much of it too quickly and we have a problem, a chain reaction of what they call super-volcanic eruptions."

"How bad would it be?"

"I'm a physicist, not a geologist, but we've all heard the stories. It would be catastrophic, the kind of thing they make big-budget movies about just to show you how bad it would be. Now that you're here, I thought that given who you work for, maybe you could make a call."

"Let's go find Jeffrey. He's already talking to the person we need to talk to," Morgan said.

They found Jeffrey, and Morgan asked for a few minutes with Bloch. When they were alone, the director said, "Dan, I can't tell you what this means to me. You know if there is anything you ever need . . ."

"You're welcome, but the fact is that there's something I could use help with right now. I need you to listen to someone I met on my last mission here."

Walter repeated his analysis. Bloch listened solemnly and said, "What would it take to stop it?"

"I honestly don't know. A nuclear detonation would be too dangerous, and I don't think any traditional explosive would be large enough to do what needs to be done."

"What exactly needs to be done?" Bloch asked.

"We need to blow it all so far into the ground that it's swallowed up by the system of magma that runs under us. And it needs to happen before the reaction goes any further."

Bloch nodded and said, "I think we can do that."

"Really?" both men said together.

"Yes," Bloch said. "I'll take a page from your book, Morgan. Last time you blew it to hell. And I think I know just the thing to do it again. Mr. O'Reilly, would you please get Mr. Morgan and my nephew to McMurdo as soon as possible. I'd like to bring them home."

"Yes, ma'am," Walter said.

"About that," Morgan said to Bloch. "Is my daughter in the States?"

"She's in the Pacific. She just completed a mission that I will brief you on when you return. She is going to need to spend some time debriefing Naval Intelligence in Hawaii and should be home in a week or two."

That would have to be soon enough to talk to Alex about Jenya. Morgan had hoped to talk to his daughter before he spoke to Jenny, but that wouldn't be possible.

"What about Peter Conley?" Morgan said.

"He's on an active mission in the Indian Ocean," Bloch said. "You've done all you can do in Antarctica, and Alex and an MI6 agent have taken care of a problem we were facing in the Pacific. Conley is trying to track down something related to our third and last major threat. It couldn't hurt to have you out there if you're up to it."

"I am," Morgan said. He guessed that meant he was on active duty again. Antarctica had brought back a few things, and he'd be happy to give Conley some backup.

"I do want to get Jeffrey back to the States as soon as possible, but I can arrange to have you dropped on the ship with Conley and Dani Guo. You're actually closer to them than you are to us. I can have you there in a day or two."

Chapter 34

Mr. Smith's handsome, sixty-something features appeared on Bloch's computer screen. It did not surprise her that behind him was the image of a wall and a monitor that clearly placed him in the White House situation room.

"Hello, Diana," he said.

"Sir," she replied.

There was movement and then the president of the United States sat down next to Smith. Unlike Mr. Smith's placid exterior, the president appeared exhausted, his eyes sunken. He had seemed young and robust less than two years ago when he was elected. Now he looked ten years older than his fifty years.

"Mr. President," Bloch said.

"Director Bloch," the president replied. Not "Ms. Bloch," which was what he had called her the last time they spoke. Using her unofficial title showed how much had changed. Zeta was now a recognized intelligence agency that was an ally of the United States.

It was no longer a rogue or secret organization that operated completely outside of government channels. Though Bloch had resisted the shift, it had been necessary for Zeta to seek the help and cooperation of various governments and agencies.

And that cooperation was absolutely necessary for what Bloch was about to ask.

"It's good to talk to you again," the president said. "I want you to know that I and the United States still remember what Zeta and its agents did for us in Nevada a few months ago."

Bloch was glad to hear that from the president. That mission had almost cost Alex Morgan her life. She had been the subject of a nationwide manhunt but had still managed to prevent a massive loss of life at the nuclear waste repository in Nevada. One of the lives she had saved was that of the vice president.

"And Mr. Smith has personally briefed me on the recent . . . incident in the Pacific. NSA confirms the massive nuclear detonation that was dangerously close to the mouth of the Marianas Trench. It seems that the United States and much of the world owes you our thanks again."

"Thank you for that, Mr. President. We believe that the organization we call Ares initiated the Tsar Bomba plan as part of a series of dangerous operations that have the potential for regional, if not global, destruction. They have initiated another one in Antarctica, and we need your help to stop it."

Bloch laid out the problem under the ice and the implications if it wasn't stopped quickly. He asked a few intelligent questions for a politician and Bloch was reminded that he had an undergraduate degree in engineering of some kind.

"What do you need?" the president asked.

"I'm asking you to deploy the remaining two assets in the Project Thor program, targeted to precise coordinates of the site in Antarctica. Our belief is that the penetration of the weapon and resulting seismic destruction will stop the reaction and drop the dangerous waste into the magma system under the ice, where it will quickly dissipate."

"Director Bloch, by Project Thor, I assume you are referring to the planned but never deployed Air Force kinetic energy weapons program," the president said.

"Yes, Mr. President, I was working at Naval Intelligence when one of the assets that had never been deployed was suffering from a decaying orbit and needed to be brought down in the Atlantic."

The project had been very simple. Three tungsten tubes about twenty feet in length and a foot wide were placed in orbit. They were tapered and had a basic propulsion system. As a result, they didn't violate any of the nuclear or biological treaties about weapons in space.

They were, however, extremely effective weapons. Once directed at a ground target, they would deorbit and hit the surface at speeds far exceeding Mach 10, allowing them to penetrate hundreds of feet into the ground. They would also strike with the power of a tactical nuclear device but with none of the fallout.

And all of that energy would be directed at a single point on the surface. Project Thor was designed as the ultimate bunker buster, from which no underground facility would be safe.

However, with cuts to the space program and the enormous cost of launching the heavy tungsten rods into orbit, Thor never got past the initial testing phase and the three deployed rods, which were smaller proof-of-concept assets.

However, the test that Bloch had witnessed in the Navy had shown that the decades-old technology had pinpoint accuracy and great destructive power.

"Sir, I'm forwarding our analysis to you. We don't have much time to stop the reaction now that it has begun."

"I understand. You will be hearing from me very soon," the president said and Bloch's screen went blank.

She hoped he was as good as his word. Once targeted, the rods would be on-site in less than ninety minutes, and possibly much less depending on where they were in their orbit.

Bloch got up from her desk and headed for the conference room that acted as Zeta's situation room. Shepard was waiting for her, and the main and smaller screens were showing various angles on an office building in Chicago.

If Zeta were truly part of the intelligence community, she would have briefed the president on this operation, but they didn't have time to engage in interagency cooperation, let alone rivalry.

They had a chance to strike at Ares's worldwide headquarters. This was a shot that they had to take.

Spartan was leading the TACH team herself. For her, this was partly personal. She had been the only survivor besides Alex Morgan of the firefight with Ares operatives in Chicago. She had lost a number of friends, and she had barely survived.

Now there was a real chance that Spartan and her twenty agents could put an end to Ares once and for all.

The intelligence that Conley had gathered in the Indian Ocean allowed Shepard and O'Neal's team to finally trace Ares to its source.

However, the Ares organization was still dangerous, and Bloch braced herself for potential casualties among the Zeta agents. However, Ares had threatened millions—if not billions—of lives. They had to be stopped.

"Director," Shepard said as Bloch took her seat. He pointed to one of the screens and said, "That is Spartan's body camera. We also have live audio."

"Spartan, good hunting today," Bloch said.

"Thank you, Director," Spartan said as the camera showed a nearly empty parking garage.

Studying the exterior images of the building, Bloch realized that there was no one coming or going. For a ten-story office tower, it was a ghost town.

To Bloch, that suggested that Ares might know they were coming, and she braced herself again for what might follow.

The camera showed a stairwell and then the building's lobby. It was empty as Spartan approached the security desk. Two guards were slumped at their chairs.

Spartan's hand checked the pulse of one of the men and then turned him over. There was white foam on his lips.

"Dead. Looks like cyanide," Spartan said. "We're going to search the lobby before we move upstairs."

One of the other monitors showed the feed from the lobby's security cameras. Bloch saw the twenty black-clad members of the tactical team. They were all wearing body armor and leading four bomb-sniffing dogs on a search of the lobby.

The TACH team split into two groups of ten, each with two bomb-sniffing dogs and each entering emergency stairs on either side of the lobby.

Spartan was the first through the door on the second floor and Bloch could see no movement. There was an outer ring of offices, with cubicles filling the center of the floor.

In the nearest office, Spartan found a woman in a business suit slumped over her desk, foam on her lips. Bloch saw the same process play out again and again, in each of the offices and then the center cubicles.

There was not a single person alive on the floor, which, other than that, looked like a shockingly ordinary office building staffed by businesspeople. The important difference being that these workers were all dead, apparently by suicide.

Bloch saw the same thing on the next floor, and the next. The fourth floor contained labs and some fabrication equipment. There was also a bank of computer stations. On this floor, the dead people were in lab coats, while jeans and T-shirts seemed to be the uniform for the programmers.

When Spartan reached the single large office on the floor, there was a man of maybe thirty slumped at the desk.

Shepard started at the image when Spartan turned the man over, and he said, "That's him. That's Kurt Richter."

The computer on the man's desk flashed a message that read, "Tell Shepard he won't stop all three."

"Spartan," Shepard said. "Show me what's on the desk."

The camera view shifted to an orderly desk with a single file on top. "What does that say?" Shepard asked.

Spartan brought the folder to the camera and repeated what was typed on the cover of the file: "Project Hercules."

Shepard gasped.

The top floor showed more dead businesspeople—though these were in better suits.

When the survey was completed, Bloch said, "Good work, Spartan. Get your team out of there."

It was time to turn the site over to her contact at the FBI.

"Shepard, what's Project Hercules?" Bloch asked.

"It's a NASA project, not one of our Friends of Feynman exercises. The idea was to strap a nuclear rocket engine to an asteroid that was going to hit earth. If you caught the asteroid early enough, you could change the trajectory to miss the Earth."

"You think Ares has this technology but wants to use it to create that kind of disaster?" she asked.

"It would make sense. We know they have nuclear material and have collected important pieces of aerospace tech. But mostly, it fits with the destruction of all other heavy launch systems. I'll have to search their computer network to confirm this, but I suspect they have a rocket somewhere that could put this kind of nuclear device into space."

"But where? They destroyed all the facilities that could do it," she said.

"The Indian Ocean . . ."

"There's nothing there. We've checked all of the platforms large enough to launch anything."

"There's one place we haven't looked. It might be an underwater launch," he said.

"Underwater?" Bloch asked.

"There was a NASA proposal after the Apollo missions. They planned to launch a rocket even larger than the Saturn Five from the ocean, from under the water. The process would solve a lot of problems with launching anything that size, but there were technical challenges they couldn't overcome at the time."

"Do you think there is any chance that Ares, or whatever is left of them, could launch a sizable rocket any other way?" Bloch asked.

"No," Shepard said.

"Is the Indian Ocean the most likely launching point?"

"Yes, based on all of our materials tracking," he said.

"Okay, see if you can optimize our satellite search and Conley's plane's sensors to scan for any underwater facility that could do that, and, of course, any giant underwater rockets," Bloch said.

Shepard nodded solemnly and left.

Zeta had stopped a catastrophic event in the Marianas Trench, and then the organization had identified the situation in Antarctica while providing the president with a solution. And now they had tracked Ares to its apparent headquarters.

That all felt like plenty.

But now it appeared that Ares was poised to make one final strike from the grave. And they had eliminated the capability of launching anything that could stop them.

If they really had a rocket preparing to launch, Bloch could not allow it to get in the air.

For that, she'd need help again. She'd have to call the president back. She would need a naval force with advanced anti-missile capabilities on-site if they hoped to knock the Ares rocket out of the air.

That meant a carrier group, and that would take some time, even if the commander-in-chief gave the order in the next fifteen minutes.

Bloch hoped they still had enough time to make a difference.

Chapter 35

Bloch entered the Zeta War Room, and Shepard was waiting. Only the main monitor was live; it showed a single overhead image of what Bloch recognized as a mountain in Antarctica.

The resolution was surprisingly good for a satellite image. There even would have been color if the colors in the actual location were something other than white snow and gray rock.

"Any second now," Shepard said.

Bloch waited a full minute and then, almost faster than she could follow, there was an orange-and-red flash on the screen that disappeared into the mountain.

The mountain shook and Bloch could see a new hole through the snow that wasn't there before. As soon as that image registered, Bloch saw another flash and then the mountain seemed to sway. It shuddered visibly and then started to recede into the Earth as it literally fell away from the camera.

If they had been viewing the mountain from the ground, Bloch knew that it would look like it had been flattened—as if by Thor's hammer.

Shepard checked something on his computer. "We'll have to wait for seismic readings taken locally and a thorough radiological survey, but that looks like success to me."

"Good," Bloch said.

"I doubt the event will even turn up on any nation's warning systems. If it does, it will appear like a meteor. Of course, the strikes will show on seismometers there, reading as a minor and localized earthquake. And

Antarctica will likely be more seismically active for a week or so, but nothing that will cause any damage or raise any alarms."

"Very good," Bloch said. "Thank you, Mr. Shepard."

Bloch got up and headed for the elevator that would take her to the main entrance. The president had a carrier group en route to the Indian Ocean, though Dan Morgan would beat them there by a full two full days.

Morgan would find a pleasant surprise on board the ship when he arrived, and Bloch took some pleasure in that.

Bloch quickly banished all thoughts of the remaining operation from her mind. All the elements were in place. She and Zeta had done everything they could to protect the world from the madness that Ares had inflicted on it for years now. Events would play out now without further input from her. That was a relief and allowed her to focus on something that didn't involve a global crisis.

Once she was in her car, she pulled out of Zeta's underground parking lot and headed for Logan airport.

It was a surprisingly normal activity for something that seemed so important. She was simply an aunt picking up her nephew from the airport, an ordinary, civilian airport. Yet it also was a miracle, and Bloch did not take those for granted.

Miracles, she had found, were in short supply these days.

* * * *

After the helicopter dropped Morgan on the deck, he scanned the area for Conley but didn't see anyone.

Then a door opened and a man that Morgan didn't recognize appeared from inside . . . followed by Jenny Morgan.

Morgan would have been less surprised if it had been John Wayne himself.

"Hello, Dan," Jenny said, greeting him with a quick hug and a kiss.

The man with her extended his hand and said, "Captain Taylor. Good to meet you."

"Dan Morgan," he said, shaking the captain's hand.

"Conley wanted to be here when you arrived, but he's on patrol right now," the captain said, pointing up at a jet Morgan could see flying close by.

Taylor handed Morgan a headset and said, "This will patch you into the flight communications system if you want to say hello. I'll let Ms. Guo know you are here and leave you both to it."

The man disappeared into the ship, and Morgan looked at his wife, raising one eyebrow.

"Dani asked me to come. She wanted to talk to all of us together, and then she wants us to do something after the mission. So I called Diana and, well, I don't think she would say no to any request that came from you or your family. Her nephew should be landing at Logan shortly. I can't believe what you did for her, and for him. She actually got choked up when she spoke to me."

"He's a good kid, and I wouldn't have made it back if it wasn't for him," Morgan said truthfully.

There was a lot more he needed to say to Jenny, but that would have to wait until they were alone in their quarters later. For now, he put on the headset and turned it on.

"Peter, looks like they gave you a fancy plane," Morgan said.

"You have no idea," Conley replied. "Flies like a dream. I wish you could be up here with me. There's a second seat in this model, but they filled the space with sensors and equipment."

"Next time," Morgan said. "Did you know Jenny is here?"

"Yes, I saw her before I went out," Conley said. "Dani has something planned for the four of us when this one is over."

"Sure," Morgan said.

Shepard cut in. "Conley, we were right to focus on this area. Something is lighting up the satellites about five miles west of the *Demeter*. I'll send you the coordinates."

"On my way," Conley said. "I'm east of them now." There was a moment of silence and Conley said, "Shep, could you give us a minute?"

"Okay, I'll sign back in when you are over the location," Shepard said.

"Dan, there's something going on with Dani. She hasn't told me yet but she's pregnant. Can you believe it? I'm going to be a father."

"For twenty-five years I would have said no, but lately, with you and Dani it makes perfect sense."

"Yeah, for me too," Conley replied. "When the mission's over we'll celebrate, maybe at that barbecue place you showed us in Austin. It's her favorite."

"Absolutely, but first let's deal with the bad guys."

A minute later, there was a beep on the line and Shepard said, "Shepard here."

"What have you got?"

"You're close and your sensors are lighting up as well," Shepard said. "Keep on your heading. There's a structure under that water . . . and we're getting hits on the radiological sensors. I think you found it. I'm sending you new coordinates. Keep circling them and I'll alert the carrier."

"We may get that barbecue early," Morgan said. "Jenny is going to be very excited for you both."

"There's something happening in the water," Conley said. "I'll come around."

There was thirty seconds of silence, and then Conley said, "I'm seeing something. Looks like a ship, there's white water now."

"Whatever it is, it's lighting up everything," Shepard said. "Give me a second to make sense of the data."

"I think I can help you with that. Looks like there's a giant rocket slowly lifting out of the ocean," Conley said.

"You can actually see it?" Shepard said.

"Hold on, I'll come around. Check the feed from my wing cameras. I'm seeing some kind of exhaust shooting out of the sides now."

"Oh my God," Shepard said. "That's it. It's lifting off *now*."

"You've got the location?" Conley said.

"Yes," Shepard replied.

"Can you call it in?" Conley said.

"Yes, but the carrier task force is two hundred miles out of range."

There was a silence that followed that Morgan didn't like. At that Dani appeared. She waved to Dan and huddled with Jenny.

There was a very bad feeling growing in the pit of Morgan's stomach.

"How hard can it be to shoot down a giant, fully fueled rocket?" Morgan asked.

"I could do it with machine guns, but this plane doesn't have weapons of any kind, Dan," Conley said.

There was a flat calmness in his partner's voice that Morgan didn't care for at all.

"Shep, what have you got for us?" Morgan asked.

"I'm sorry. I don't have anything . . ." Shepard said. Morgan decided that he didn't like the resigned tone of Shepard's voice either.

"We can't let that rocket get out of the atmosphere, can we?" Conley said.

"No. If it gets into space, there's nothing anyone can launch that can stop it," Shepard said.

Both Jenny and Dani were looking at Morgan, reading something in his expression.

"Shep?" Morgan said.

"It's okay, Dan. I've got something," Conley said. "It's a Dan Morgan solution."

"I don't like the sound of that, Peter," Morgan said.

"Now you know how the rest of us feel around you most of the time," Conley said.

"Whatever you are thinking of doing, don't. I just got here. We'll find another way."

"I think we've run out of time on this one. It's a shame. I'm sure Bloch had to move heaven and earth to get a carrier group out this way."

"Don't do it . . ." Morgan said, not liking the croak in his own voice.

"Listen, Dan, Dani is going to need you now, both you and Jenny. You'll take care of her . . . and the baby."

Morgan found that he could barely get words out. "You know we will. Peter, do you want to talk to Dani?"

"I can't," Conley said, his voice losing some of its calm, businesslike tone. "I won't be able to do what I need to do if I hear her voice."

Morgan could see the rocket in the distance. He could also see Conley's plane circling.

"Best to hit it before it gets to ten thousand feet, it will be picking up speed by then," Shepard said. His voice was flat, almost sounding like it was automated.

"I'm coming around now," Conley said. "I'll be able to get it well before that."

Jenny moved closer to him and grabbed his arm. "Dan," she said.

Dani clutched Jenny and said, "Dan, what is he doing?"

Morgan found that he couldn't speak.

"Dan, you have to stop him," Dani said, strain in her voice.

The rocket seemed huge, even at that distance. Morgan could see Conley's plane on a direct path toward it.

Morgan had lost count of the times that Conley had stepped in and saved him from certain death. More often than not, the Morgan luck, he realized, came down to one thing and it had nothing to do with good fortune. It was Peter Conley.

And now Morgan was watching his partner use up his own last bit of luck.

"Peter . . ." Morgan said.

"It really is a beautiful plane," Conley replied.

There was a terrible, long moment of silence on the radio and then the plane disappeared into the rocket and then both were swallowed up by a flash of orange light.

He heard Dani's anguished cry as they watched the fire in the sky.

Morgan felt Jenny's hand squeeze his arm. In all the years they had been together, Morgan had leaned on Jenny in more ways than he could count and more than she ever knew. However, in that instant, she was literally holding him up, and if she let go of him, he would fall to the deck.

Epilogue

By the time Dan Morgan fired up the grill, almost everyone was settled. Shepard was engrossed in a discussion with O'Neal and Maryam Nasiri, an award-winning mathematician that Alex had rescued from Iran and who now consulted with Zeta. The woman had come with Spartan. They were an unlikely pair. Spartan was the best tactical agent Morgan knew and Nasiri was a Fields Medal–winning mathematician, but they had gotten close.

Morgan knew that when Spartan had been shot in the Chicago incident last year, Nasiri had never left Spartan's bedside, so he wasn't completely surprised.

Spartan herself was engaged in an animated conversation with Valery Dobrynin, something about Russian- versus American-made weapons.

The biggest surprise was Diana Bloch.

In shorts.

In his backyard.

Jenny had insisted she come, and as his wife had predicted, Bloch could not say no to the Morgans these days.

Bloch had arrived with a nice British man she introduced as Peter. Of course, Morgan had been out of government-run espionage for many years now, but he definitely recognized the head of MI6 when he saw the man.

One of the most pleasant surprises was that his daughter Alex and Bloch's nephew, Jeffrey, had become as thick as thieves. They had met for the first time today and had soon disappeared on a walk with Nikkita, the Morgan family German shepherd. Now they were in a corner of the backyard, deep in conversation.

Though she was in her dignified middle age, Nikki had jumped and wagged her tail like a puppy when Alex arrived. Now, the dog had adopted Karen O'Neal and was lying by the young woman's side while she spoke to Shepard and Nasiri.

Jenny and Dani were fussing over the baby, who was crawling around the portable crib. At six months, little Danny was growing fast. He could also move very quickly for a child that age.

Jenny had wanted Scott Renard and Lily to come, but they were on what seemed like a never-ending honeymoon.

Morgan had been worried about telling his wife about Jenya's existence. Like him, she'd been shocked, but she was Jenny, after all, and she'd been more concerned about him and his reaction to the knowledge that the daughter he didn't know existed had tried to kill him.

They had both gotten a surprise when Alex came home and had some stories to tell about Jenya.

Morgan was sure that he had not seen the last of his and Natasha's daughter, but he refused to worry about that now. The future would have to take care of itself.

If nothing else, he had the Morgan luck to fall back on.

The grill had just gotten up to temperature when Peter Conley burst through the back gate with a cooler over his shoulder.

Conley had insisted on bringing the steaks, claiming that he had a guy.

"Just in time," Morgan said as his friend approached.

Morgan had still not adjusted to the eye patch that Conley wore over his left eye.

The scar on his forehead and the injury to the eye were the only permanent reminders of Conley's last-second ejection from the jet over the Indian Ocean. The superficial burns from proximity to the blast had healed in a few weeks.

Conley's survival had been, in Morgan's mind, a miracle, but his friend had brushed it off as good piloting and a bit of the Morgan luck rubbing off on him.

Either way, Morgan was glad to have his friend back.

"It must be healed by now," Morgan said. "Aren't you milking it a bit with the patch?"

Conley grinned and said, "Just a little longer . . . Dani likes it, a lot. And with the baby . . ."

There was a fuss at the playpen, and someone muttered something about changing the baby.

"I'll get it," Conley said, striding over.

Coming to it late, Conley had embraced fatherhood like he was born to it. The enthusiasm amused Morgan, and he put it on the growing list of things he had never seen coming.

About the Author

Photo by Carolle Photography

Leo J. Maloney is the author of the acclaimed Dan Morgan thriller series and its new spin-off series featuring Alex Morgan. He was born in Massachusetts, where he spent his childhood, and graduated from Northeastern University. He spent over thirty years in black ops, accepting highly secretive missions that would put him in the most dangerous hot spots in the world. Since leaving that career, he has acted in independent films and television commercials. He has seven movies to his credit, both as an actor and behind the camera as a producer, technical adviser, and assistant director. He is an avid collector of classic and muscle cars and has won numerous awards in tenpin bowling. Visit him at www.leojmaloney. com or on Facebook or Twitter.

TERMINATION ORDERS

LEO J. MALONEY

SILENT ASSASSIN

LEO J. MALONEY

BLACK SKIES

LEO J. MALONEY

TWELVE HOURS

LEO J. MALONEY

ARCH ENEMY

LEO J. MALONEY

FOR DUTY AND HONOR

LEO J. MALONEY

ROGUE COMMANDER

LEO J. MALONEY

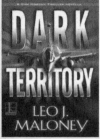

DARK TERRITORY

LEO J. MALONEY

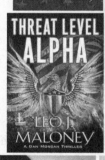

THREAT LEVEL ALPHA

LEO J. MALONEY

WAR OF SHADOWS

LEO J. MALONEY

DEEP COVER

LEO J. MALONEY

THE MORGAN FILES

LEO J. MALONEY

A LE TACK

LEO J. MALONEY

HARD TARGET

LEO J. MALONEY

STORM FRONT

LEO J. MALONEY

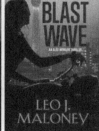

BLAST WAVE

LEO J. MALONEY